MIRRORED HEARTS
Sealed By Fire

Encounters of the Heart Series – Book 2

I0556454

BESTSELLING AUTHOR
Ann Marie Bryan

Victorious By Design
Tallahassee, FL

To order copies of this book, please contact:
Victorious By Design, LLC
P.O. Box 6141
Tallahassee, FL 32314
Lighting the path to your next level

Visit our website at: www.victoriousbydesign.com
Email us at: orders@victoriousbydesign.com

Cover photo courtesy of bigstockphoto.com
Cover creation by Global Multi Media Enterprises (GMME)

ISBN-13: 978-0985146863
ISBN-10: 0985146869

ENCOUNTERS OF THE HEART SERIES
Praise for Book 1: Shades of the Heart
#1 Amazon Best Seller (African American Christian Fiction)

"This book in one word: POWERFUL! As a married woman, this book ministered to my soul. I loved how the author took us through every emotion of dealing with the extreme lows in crisis to the extreme highs. The personal battle to move towards forgiveness, restoring, rebuilding and ultimately the true meaning of love were all brought in full circle showcasing that love truly endures all things. This is an excellent display of how our faith and relationship with God can develop and the importance of having strong and true supporters in your corner. I loved Blake and Gabby together but what I loved most was their individual story of growth. Excellent job and excellent read!" *Author Untamed*

"I loved this fabulously written Christian romance novel centered on a married couple dealing with infidelity by the wife. Although it contained prayers, Scriptures, and a few short sermons, it wasn't preachy but right on time for me. I loved reading about the trials and tribulations of Christian marriages and this one covered all of the emotional basis to draw me in and keep me turning the pages. I couldn't wait to read the beautiful ending. Just a fabulous story that pulled on all the heartstrings!" *Barbara Joe Williams, Author of Love Never Felt So Good*

"This story was an absolute joy to read. The characters were honest and flawed, the way we are in real life. I truly enjoyed going through the process with the characters and experiencing every emotion they went through. Often times we focus on the end result, but never appreciate the journey

3

for what it brings to our lives. This was my first novel by Ann Marie, but I would definitely recommend her work." *Melinda Michelle, Author of Color Me Blind: A Divine Love Story*

DEDICATION

To all husbands and wives who are moving toward more
perfect unions through Jesus Christ.

CONTENTS

ACKNOWLEDGEMENTS

Many persons contributed to the completion of this book. Thank you so much. It was a blessing to work alongside each of you.

My Heavenly Father, I cannot imagine my life without You. Lord, I love you. I stand in awe of your greatness.

Extra special thanks to Orville, my husband, my beloved. Thanks for letting me into your heart. I love you always and forever.

I am grateful for my mother, Mrs. Estrina Johnson and my ten siblings - six sisters and four brothers. Your support means everything to me. Thanks for your love, friendship, and encouragement. You are all wonderful, and I am grateful that God gave you to me. I love you.

A big thank you to my sister and second mom, Mrs. Icylin Morgan, for listening to me talk about the characters in this book. You are the best.

Thank you to my pastor, Bishop John E. Baker and his beautiful, anointed wife, First Lady, Elder Ann-Marie Baker, for continuing to impart God's word in my life. Thanks also to my church family, New Hope International Outreach Ministries.

Heartfelt thanks to my literary sisters, Authors J.L. Campbell and Barbara Joe Williams for their encouragement and invaluable help with completing this book.

Thanking God for Mrs. Palmyra Williams and her son, Mr. True Holt. I am still marveling at the mighty hand of God. Thank you for walking in purpose.

Members of Tallahassee Authors Network Christian Sub-Group, under the extraordinary leadership of Authors Angela Hodge and Melinda Michelle, you are all amazing. Thanking God for each of you.

I love my sisters who make up my editorial team - Millicent Battick, Melissa Mallory, Yamecike McMillan, Paula Owen, and Julianne Veira. Thanks for your prayers, critiques, words of encouragement, wisdom, and your attention to detail. Thank you for helping me to get life-changing Christian Fiction out to readers. You are all awesome women of God and my life is so much better because of the friendships that we share. You are living examples that God is moving in the lives of believers. I am smiling at each of you - You rock!

ABOUT LOVE

"Love suffers long and is kind; love does not envy; love does not parade itself, is not puffed up; does not behave rudely, does not seek its own, is not provoked, thinks no evil; does not rejoice in iniquity, but rejoices in the truth;" (1 Corinthians 13:4-6)

CHAPTER 1

A vision of loveliness! Larry stood at the side of the bed, carelessly looping his tie around his neck as he gazed at her, nestled by myriads of soft, white, fluffy cushions. His eyes traced every curve of her body and he drew in a deep, shuddering breath as she purred, stretching her arms above her head and smiling. Whatever she was dreaming about clearly stirred her because the smile remained on her lips.

He couldn't help but smile too. His heart beat blissfully only for Rozene. Delighting in the way his body responded to her, he bent to kiss her then drew back as her fevered eyes met his, then frosted over before she rolled away from him.

"Good morning, honey. Did you need something?" she asked, with extra warmth in her voice.

"Doing your wifely duties would be a start," he growled, irritated by her pretentious behavior.

She sat up, ready for battle, then decided to change tactics. She'd always received a more positive response when she added 'sugar' rather than 'lemons.' "Honey, my fast will be over soon."

"Great. Fast all you want, but did you have to include fasting from sex?" His bow-shaped lips tightened with displeasure.

"You only have to wait two more days," she pleaded softly, tossing her curly, light-brown hair over her shoulders.

"Two more days! I have been waiting for over a month," he hissed, glaring at her. "Plus, this is the third time in five months you're doing this kind of fast."

"But, honey, I satisfied you -"

"You call that lovemaking, two weeks ago when you pitied me? On my birthday, of all days?" Shaking his

11

head, he walked to the dressing table and adjusted his tie in the mirror.

Rozene swung her legs over the edge of the bed, grabbed her robe from where it hung off the bedpost, and followed him. "I thought we had fun," she encouraged, slipping on her robe.

His nostrils flared. "Fun. You accommodated me." His blood boiled when he recalled that up to fall last year, they couldn't keep their hands off each other. Back then, he didn't have to beg his own wife to make love with him.

"How can you say that?" Rozene asked, knitting her brows.

"You did." His dark brown eyes pinned her in place before he turned away to pick up his watch from the dressing table. His eyes narrowed when he looked at her again. "Why are you wearing new lingerie when …?"

"I'm preparing for you," she said cheerfully. He watched as she modeled flirtatiously. "Saturday is game on." She smiled lovingly at him, a smile that always made his heart pitter-patter.

He gazed at her full lips and straight nose, perfectly placed on her oval shaped face, but it was her vivid hazel-colored eyes that usually held him captive, many times stealing words from his lips. But not this morning. He turned away and clasped his watch on his wrist.

Rozene came up behind him and lovingly caressed his back before brushing imaginary lint from his navy jacket. "I'll try to be a better wife. I just wanted to seek the Lord while I write." Her gaze slid down his long muscular, slightly bowed legs, before she gently rubbed his back.

He closed his eyes momentarily, enjoying the warmth of her touch, then opened them and faced her. "I told you, you can slow down with writing your books. You should do one a year." He knitted his brows. "Plus, with doing writers' conferences, book tours, and TV programs," he sighed, "you're always tired."

She pursed her lips, taking in his handsome face and confident eyes. He was self-assured but not cocky, certain of his God-given ability and authority, and the correctness of his path. "Just two more days, please," she urged.

Larry felt like a child screaming for attention. He turned abruptly from her and walked to the nightstand to retrieve his laptop. His legs felt heavy and he was getting more and more 'ticked off' by the second. He leveled her with a stern glare. "What am I to do in the meantime?"

"We can do other things or you can play golf with your friends."

His mouth dropped open, and he quickly snapped it shut. "Are you serious? What happened to you, Roz?"

Without waiting for an answer, he grabbed his car keys from the nightstand and marched out of their bedroom.

She ran after him. "Aren't we going to pray before you leave?"

"Will pray by myself," he roared, without a backward glance. "And don't forget to add my appointment to sleep with you, to your calendar."

He heard her gasp but continued walking.

A few minutes later, he glanced at their fleet of cars, and wondered which one to drive. *Need something to cheer me up.* He slid behind the steering wheel of the red Audi S5 coupe, then dropped his laptop on the back seat and closed the door. A deep sigh he didn't know he was holding left his body, and he leaned forward to rest his head on the steering wheel. *Where did my ever loving wife go? How can a woman who is so spiritually sensitive, be so insensitive to my needs?*

He was not as fervent a Christian as she was, but he knew the Bible encouraged husbands and wives to "...not

13

deprive one another, except perhaps by agreement for a limited time..." He and Rozene had fasted together a few times but never from sex. Still, he didn't know if he could, even if she'd asked him.

"Help me, Lord," was all the prayer he could offer up before pulling out of the garage.

After nineteen years of marriage, he and Rozene were well adapted to each other. The twins, Mason and Madison, came along during the second year of their marriage, right after they had both completed their Master of Business Administration degrees. It was a tearful experience when the twins left for MIT last fall, but after he and Rozene got over the initial shock of a soundless home, they began making plans to enjoy the 'empty nest.' That was before Rozene started to behave differently towards him. He wondered if she was going through hormonal changes. She'd become emotionally unavailable. *Is she no longer attracted to me?* He chided himself each time the thought came. She had been wearing new lingerie, and that gave him hope.

Pulling into his parking space at Pallecia Worldwide All Suite Hotel, he switched off the ignition then exhaled loudly before saying a prayer.

> *"Lord, please help me. I need your peace and patience to deal with Rozene. I don't know how to fix whatever is happening in our marriage. On the surface, we are okay but in my heart, I know something is wrong. I need your guidance and direction, Father. Amen."*

After centering himself with prayer, Larry stepped out of his car. It was a slightly chilly January morning, and the cold air seeped right through his tailored suit. *Just what*

14

I need to cool me down. Grabbing his laptop from the back seat, he closed the car door and put on his "professional face." He was not in the mood for work but these days going to work was a better option than staying at home. His eyes brightened. Gabrielle would help to jump start his day.

Seven years her senior, he and Gabrielle had hit it off from the day she started working at Pallecia Hotel, a luxurious golf and spa resort, with the head office located on the outskirts of Orlando, Florida. He was Vice President of Human Resources for the past eight years and she came in as a Human Resources Manager just over a year ago. She was brilliant at her job so when the Human Resources Director resigned five months ago, he immediately promoted her to that position.

Entering the foyer, Larry greeted his co-workers before taking the elevator up to the fourteenth floor. He decided to pop into Gabrielle's office before heading to his office, four doors down. Her door was slightly open and he pushed it in, only to be greeted by her smooth derriere covered in a navy pencil skirt. She was retrieving something from a bag on the ground.

Not quite the jump start I was expecting. Warmth spread through his body as he watched her. Sensing a dangerous shift in his mood, he pulled himself together. *No self-respecting, God-fearing man should look at a woman that way.* Still, he liked looking at Gabrielle Montgomery, her smooth, honey-brown complexion and slender yet curvy frame. He hastily reminded himself that she was a woman of God who always treated him professionally, so the last thing he wanted was to get caught gawking at her derriere. "Good morning," he announced loudly as he moved towards her desk.

She spun to face him. "Larry, how's it going?" A gentle smile lit her face.

Just the smile he needed. He felt like lying on the small red plush sofa near her desk and telling her all his troubles. "Good. How are you doing?"

"Good." Then she looked sheepishly at him as she arranged herself behind the large cherry wood desk. "We can't do the mock presentation today. I'm behind with my part of the presentation, but asking God for extra strength to finish by tomorrow."

He smiled encouragingly at her. "Don't worry. We have another day before the board meeting. We can wrap it up today, even if we have to work late. We'll do the mock presentation tomorrow."

"Thanks." She flashed him a grateful smile while adjusting strands of her dark brown hair behind her ears. "Nice tie. Bet Rozene selected it for you."

Strangely, Gabrielle found herself wondering what he was like at home. She stared at Larry, and perhaps, for the first time, noticed he was a fine looking forty-two-year-old man. His naturally sun-kissed complexion glowed with vitality. He was all male - physically appealing, tall, and lean with toned legs. His clean shaven face, highlighted by miniature dimples from a drop dead gorgeous smile, reflected his bold personality and freedom of spirit. He always seemed indomitable and comfortable in any environment. It was fascinating to watch him navigate the political arena at work.

"You're welcome. Yep. Birthday present," Larry responded, his heart fluttering under her scrutiny. He was no Mr. Universe, but he thought she'd looked a little longer than she should have. These days, he seemed to have the ability to reach every woman on the planet except his wife. "Any questions for me?" He had often provided answers to her work related questions.

"Nope. Focusing on the presentation."

He wished she had several questions as he didn't feel like being alone. He racked his brain wondering what else he could ask her, then he remembered her husband was going out of town. "Did Blake leave?"

"Yes."

Gabrielle smiled, but Larry saw that the smile didn't reach her eyes. He hoped all was well between her and Blake. He'd noticed how her eyes would twinkle whenever she called his name.

"Great," he responded, watching her keenly. He had been so busy, thinking about his own troubles that he didn't realize she was submerged in a cloak of sadness. He did not know her well enough to ask questions but he wished he did. Then, maybe, they could share their marital woes. Lord knows, he needed to talk with someone. "Okay. I'll be in my office," he told her.

She nodded.

He walked into his office and sat in the swivel chair behind his oversized mahogany desk. *At least, Gabrielle is not shunning me ... like Rozene.* He was happy when Rozene took early retirement from her executive marketing position and decided to pursue her passion for writing. In less than three years, she became an international bestselling author. She had written four books – *Letters to God, Letters to My Daughter, Letters to My Son, Letters to Husbands*, and was now writing, *Letters to Wives*, which seemed to be taking forever.

He loved watching her at book signings; she enjoyed being a 'celebrity' and he enjoyed being the husband of one. A smile he couldn't help, curled his lips. He literally had to remind himself to breathe when she spoke with that delightful look on her face about how God inspired her writings. She would have her audience spellbound. Her last book signing occurred last fall - *Letters to Husbands*, he recalled. It seemed so long ago.

Now, she was busy traveling to present at writers' conferences. He wished she would slow down so they could spend more time together.

The ringing of his cell phone interrupted Larry's thoughts. "Hello, Pastor Fotola," he answered.

"Larry, how's it going?"

"Great. How is it going with you, Pastor?"

"Going great on this side too. Still trusting in Jesus." Pastor Fotola laughed in his usual jovial manner. "Just thinking, we need to go over the plans for our upcoming leadership retreat. Wanted to take another look at the agenda and the organizational chart you prepared."

"Okay. Which day did you have in mind?" Larry served as the church's Operations Director, so he was heavily involved in the planning of the annual leadership retreat which was scheduled for next Saturday.

"Next Wednesday evening, before Bible Study," Pastor Fotola replied. "Say, six o'clock."

"That time would work for me," Larry responded. He and Rozene usually attended Pastor Robert Fotola's interactive Bible Studies. It was a blessing to have a spiritually sensitive Pastor and he had benefited from the healthy relationship they shared as Pastor Fotola willingly gave him advice on personal matters.

"See you then. Have a blessed day," Pastor Fotola said.

"You too, Pastor," Larry responded cheerfully before hanging up. Staring at the wall ahead of him, Larry wondered whether or not to seek Pastor Fotola's advice on his marital woes.

******

Later that evening, Larry sat across from Gabrielle, working on a part of the presentation on his laptop while she sat at her desk, working on her desktop. His body temperature climbed as she got up and walked towards the white board that was hanging on the wall in her office. She radiated grace and femininity that appealed to his masculine nature. *Get it together,* he cautioned himself as the words of his pastor's sermon hit him forcefully, *'The lust of the eye can ruin your life.'* He swallowed hard, shifting his focus to his laptop.

"I'm seeing where we can cut a bit more cost," Gabrielle told him, looking at the organizational chart for the newly reorganized advertising division. "Let's merge the positions of Deputy Vice President of Advertising and Manager of Advertising, and call the new position Senior Manager of Advertising."

Larry drummed his fingers on the arm of his chair and then moved to the white board to inspect the organizational chart. "Love it."

"That should give us another checkmark with the Board," she said, while massaging her aching temples with her fingers.

He smiled at her, taking in her tired eyes. "You need to relax, Gabrielle," he said, touching her shoulder. "You should take off your shoes."

"My shoes ... why?"

He looked at her and had to hold back the urge to kiss her confusion away. "Get comfy. We have another hour or so before we leave."

She sighed. "That may be a good idea." She placed a hand on the white board and almost fell over trying to get out of her pumps.

Larry steadied her. "Here, let me help you." Dropping to his knees, he held on to one of her ankles.

"Oh, okay," she muttered, grabbing his shoulders and wiggling one foot and then the next to help him remove her shoes.

Enjoying the feeling of her smooth skin under his fingers, he took his time to help her out of her shoes before standing. "There, that should help, Shorty."

She grinned at him. "Thanks. Feeling better already. Did you call me, Shorty?"

He chuckled as he moved back to his seat. "I sure did."

Her eyes sparkled as she smiled at him. "I'm going to forgive you." She stood at five-feet-six inches, but he towered above her at over six feet.

His mouth curled in a smile as he removed his tie and threw it on his jacket, which was resting on the chair beside him. "Please …" His eyes fastened on her body as she removed her jacket, exposing her silky, red inner blouse neatly tucked in her skirt. "Forgive me," he continued, his eyes now resting on his laptop screen.

Smiling, Gabrielle slid in her chair and was quiet for a moment, clicking away on her desktop. Fifteen minutes later, she stretched her hands above her head and announced, "I'm finished with this part."

"Great." Larry pinned her with his gaze, then his eyes became fixated on her chest. "You have a nice cleavage," he stated matter-of-factly, as if he had complimented her about her hair.

Blushing, Gabrielle lowered her arms. She had hoped that it was only her imagination when she saw him staring at her chest. "We're tired. Let's finish up tomorrow."

Larry knitted his brows. "Come on, Gabrielle. You're married, so am I, but that doesn't mean I can't admire a nice body when I see one."

She nibbled on her lips as she always did when she was pondering. He could see that she was feeling bad for making him feel bad. "Thanks," she said quietly.

"We need a break," he said, sliding out of his chair and opening the small refrigerator in the corner of her office. He motioned for her to join him at the small conference table nearby. "All work and no play makes Gabby a dull girl."

Smiling, she took her seat before him and sipped on a can of Mountain Dew he had placed on the table. "Just what I needed. Thanks."

He flashed her a triumphant smile, deepening his dimples. "You're welcome."

Gabrielle fought the urge to hold his lingering gaze, but failed. He looked great. *A fine specimen of a man.* Her eyes roamed him up and down taking in his raw masculinity. *Why am I admiring Larry Kanate?* Gabrielle shook her head slightly then took another sip of her drink. *I must be tired,* she rationalized.

"Can't wait for Blake to get back, huh?" Larry drawled teasingly.

The warmth in his voice shot enjoyable tingles down her spine and she lowered her gaze, her confused senses threatening to derail her composure. "Yep. He'll be back in two weeks."

Larry eyed her. "Are you okay? You haven't been yourself all day."

She sighed, her eyes brimming with tears. "I'm okay. I just miss my Aunt Jean. I could talk with her about anything."

She must have had a fight with Blake. "Life happens," he told her. "But we know God is good. He's working everything out for your good." He knew that Aunt Jean was laid to rest two months ago and she was like a mother to Gabrielle. Whatever was bothering her, he was sure she would have talked to Aunt Jean about it.

"Yes. God is good," she agreed, dabbing her eyes with her finger tips.

"Do you want to talk about it?"

"Not really. But thanks for asking."

"I know exactly what you need," Larry said, feeling an overwhelming need to comfort her. He slid out of his chair and stood behind her. "A massage."

Her brows shot up. "A massage?"

"I'm good at this," he countered, kneading her shoulders with both hands.

Out of reflex, she jumped, grabbing his hands.

"Just relax. Think nice thoughts about Blake," he offered and she relaxed. He continued to gently massage her shoulders and moved to her neck. "You have a tight knot at the base of your neck," he mentioned, keeping his voice impersonal.

She let out a long sigh, closing her eyes as his hands traveled the length of her neck, applying deep pressure. His hands moved to her back and she tensed slightly. "Relax," he said softly, and she did.

Gosh! I miss Blake. I hope we can get past this 'bump in the road' quickly. Why wasn't I honest with him before he found out so callously that I wasn't ready to have a child? Then, before he left for Atlanta, we would have made love and all would be well. Hmmm, passionate love!

Larry gazed at Gabrielle's slightly parted lips, and heat seared through his body. Whatever she was thinking about was causing her to breathe a little heavier. Feeling as if he was committing emotional adultery, he closed his eyes, trying to recall a Scripture to clear his mind. An inner voice cautioned him, *Stop flirting with temptation.*

He opened his eyes, and then bit his lips to steady himself when he realized his hands had taken on a mind of their own and was gently massaging her sides.

"Hmmm," she sighed, arching her chest.

He watched her respond to his touch, and he liked that. She made him feel ... needed. When his fingers caressed the base of her breasts with exceeding tenderness, deliberately teasing, she shivered. Emboldened by her reaction, he cupped her breasts, and then moaned loudly as his hands melted into their softness.

"Larry!" She flew off the chair, hugging her chest with her hands.

He followed her closely, then stepped back as she leaned against the wall. For a moment, he gazed at her, and the only thing he could think about was his thirst for her ... all of her. An inner voice begged him to desist, but his flesh craved her, needed her. He had no doubt that he would have her. "You feel so good," he drawled huskily, his eyes glistening with desire.

She placed her hands on his chest as he leaned towards her. "We ... shouldn't."

Larry gazed at her for a second before brushing his lips against hers. "We both need this," he said without hesitation, his mouth temptingly close.

On their own volition, her lips parted invitingly and he eagerly captured her mouth with his, trembling at the velvety smoothness of her lips. Her eyes fluttered shut and she shivered, wrapping her arms around his shoulders as his lips traveled the length of her neck, dropping soft kisses along the way. Just when she could take no more, he lifted his head, his lips hovering above hers. "Absolutely love your lips," he gushed.

She could feel the heat of his breath on her face as she surveyed his lush mouth, his lips beckoning seductively to her. "We ... shouldn't," she offered weakly, mesmerized by the aura of his charisma.

Struggling to restrain himself, he silenced her objection by kissing her again, passionately, urgently, and with the confidence of a man who knew what he wanted. Clutching his shoulders for strength, she returned his kiss with more fire than he imagined she would, and his body

23

melted against hers. When he was finally able to pull back, they were both breathing heavily.

"I need you," he whispered, barely able to contain himself.

Their bodies inches apart, he looked into her yearning eyes, then brought her hand to his mouth and lightly kissed her knuckles, his warm breath stroking her skin. He released her hand and they stood there, drinking in each other.

She swallowed hard, mumbling, "We need to stop."

He wanted to stop. If only he could tear his eyes away from her lips. "Maybe, just this once?" he asked, his chest heaving in breathless anticipation.

The seconds dragged by as Larry waited for her response. When none came, he turned away from her.

Gabrielle pushed out a gagged breath. Despite all that just occurred between them, she had to let him know that they should not ever go down that path again. "Lar-Larry," she called out, her voice faint. She was still reeling from the surge of warm, delightful sensations in her body.

In a flash, Larry swept her into his arms, his body crushing hers. "Your body feels amazing," he said, smiling slightly.

Mercy! I need to fix this quickly. "Thanks," she said softly, nibbling on her lips.

He admired the beautiful pout of her mouth, then watched fascinatingly as her lips parted, and she began to speak.

"Larry, we can't-"

Before she could catch her next breath, Larry eagerly and hungrily covered her lips with his. As desire welled up in him, he paused, unsure whether he had her permission to proceed.

She arched closer to him, mumbling, "Let's talk … about this," as a wave of heat enveloped their bodies. Then,

24

she froze, her mind screaming, *No. No. Please don't*, as he lifted her skirt. *This is not happening ... not again.*

Larry was glad she did not protest when he lifted her skirt. He needed her. She was like a drug and he desperately needed a fix. He heard her whimper, "Let's ... not ..." But he couldn't stop. He had to possess her, to get rid of the insatiable desire he'd been carrying around. "I won't hurt you," he whispered.

A few minutes later, he buried his head in her neck, muttering, "Thank you. Thank you."

He felt drops of water stoning his face and pulled away from her. She was crying. Self-loathing crept up his spine and he moved further away from her. Without looking at her, he mumbled, "Are you alright?"

She didn't utter a word.

When he looked up, he saw her walking hastily towards her office door. "Gabrielle, don't ..."

But she kept moving, literally sprinting through the door.

He crumbled to his knees, his face twisted with agony. "Oh, God," he muttered over and over again.

CHAPTER 2

Work should fill up the void. A diversion from this loneliness, he was feeling. *Will the pain in my heart ever subside?* A sigh escaped Larry's tortured soul and a teardrop fell from his exhausted eyes and landed on the portfolio that he was reading. He quickly reached for a napkin on his desk and mopped it up before dabbing his eyes. Guilt was wreaking havoc across his mind as he grappled with his incomprehensible heat-of-the-moment behavior. He'd never done anything like that in all of his nineteen years of marriage. What if Rozene found out? Surely, she would leave him. His shoulders slumped in self-pity, just as the intercom on his office phone buzzed. He leaned forward to press the flashing button. "Yes?"

"It's going to be an amazing Monday, Mr. Kanate." His executive assistant's cheerful voice filled the room. "I've managed to reschedule all your appointments."

"Thank you, Marjorie."

"You're welcome, sir. On another note, did you see Mrs. Montgomery's email?"

Immediately, Larry felt a headache coming on. "No. Haven't checked my email account yet."

"She's on indefinite sick leave."

Suddenly, air was sucked out of his lungs and he couldn't breathe. In the distance, he heard Marjorie saying something, then silence. "What were you …?"

"I was asking if you wanted me to respond to Mrs. Montgomery's email."

"Yes, please," then he cut off the call. He exhaled loudly, trying to destress.

The day after the incident, Gabrielle had emailed to say that she was out sick. He had tried several times that day to call her, but she would not answer her phone. When there was no sign of her on Friday, he did the board presentation. That evening, on his way home, he also called her phone but it went to voicemail.

"I have ruined her. God, help her," Larry muttered.

He hadn't prayed since the incident ... couldn't pray. How could he go before God? He prided himself on being the sort of man that didn't ogle other women, much less to commit ... He couldn't even bring himself to say the word. *Did I suffer temporary insanity?* A helpless sigh escaped his parched lips and tears rolled down his cheeks.

The shrill beeping of his cell phone brought him out of his misery. He dabbed his eyes, then cleared his throat. "Hello," he answered.

"May I speak with Mr. Kanate?" a pleasant voice asked.

"Speaking."

"This is Gloria Rogers from Dr. John Cerdon's office. We have managed to squeeze in your appointment for twelve noon."

"Thanks, Gloria. I'll be there." He had called his doctor's office on the way to work because since Friday, he had been experiencing a burning sensation during urination and his testicles were slightly swollen. He had spent the whole weekend avoiding Rozene's sexual advances.

The call ended and Larry stared blindly at his cell phone on the desk. *What a mess my life has turned into.* It then occurred to him that he'd been calling Gabrielle from his work cell phone. Picking up his personal cell phone, he dialed her number, and almost bit off his tongue when she answered.

"Gabrielle, please don't hang up." He heard her inhale and knew he had but a minute.

"What do you want?" she asked firmly, her annoyance evident.

He cut to the chase. "I know what happened between us was unexpected. Are you okay?"

27

She didn't respond.

"Gabrielle?"

"Is that it?" He could almost see the dead look in her eyes.

Before he could think, he blurted out, "Please don't tell Rozene." This was one secret, he was determined to keep close to his heart.

He heard her sharp intake of breath and could have kicked himself. "No. I will NOT tell your wife that you take advantage of unsuspecting females," Gabrielle said through clenched teeth. With that, she disconnected the call.

Is that what I did? A painful cry left Larry's mouth and he slumped over his desk, sobbing.

******

Later that day, Larry had all but driven his car into the house, braking just before he hit the steps leading to the front door.

"Roz!" he bellowed, slamming the front door, then running through the oval entryway. When no response came, he raced across the handcrafted, vintage French oak flooring in the formal living room, shouting her name. When she still did not answer, he veered right and entered the foyer with the grand double staircase leading to their private quarters. Taking the steps two at a time, he continued to yell her name.

"In the bedroom, honey," Rozene called out, seemingly unperturbed.

Gritting his teeth, Larry moved swiftly across the elegantly decorated circular landing, and entered a softly lit passageway to access their bedroom. The door was slightly open and he kicked it, banging it against the wall.

"What on earth is …?" Rozene lifted her head from the book she was reading to lay eyes on a steaming Larry. The degree of anger on his face had her shrinking back into the pillows on the bed. She couldn't recall ever seeing him so furious. "What is the …?"

"Is that how you treat me after nineteen years of marriage?" Larry clenched his fists in rage.

Rozene refused to let his outburst unsettle her. "Are we talking about sex, again? I tried all weekend to -"

"You gave me Chlamydia," he hissed at her. "Who are you sleeping with?" He saw the look of guilt in her eyes and knew he was right. In a mad dash, he crossed the room, grabbed her by her shoulders, and brought her closer to him. "Who are you sleeping with, Roz?"

Dread descending, Rozene lifted her chin. "No one."

Anger flared in Larry's eyes, and his hands bit into her shoulders. "Stop lying to me." He pushed her roughly against the pillows and stood looking down at her. "Fasting from sex, huh?" A hollow laugh left him. "Right?"

Tears streamed down Rozene's face. "Larry, please. I … I'm not sleeping with him anymore."

Larry's features turned to stone. "Anymore?" Confused voices screamed in his head. *How did this happen? Who is this man? Where did she meet him?*

"His name is Chandler," Rozene filled in. "I met him last fall at the book tour for, *Letters to Husbands.*"

Words failed Larry as he sank into the bedroom chair. Something had cut off his air supply and he couldn't breathe. Even though he knew it, hearing her confess it placed him in an emotional tailspin. In the distance, he heard her droning on through tears but he covered his ears to shut out the humming sound of her voice. Leaning forward, he attempted to find his equilibrium.

He vividly recalled how he almost fell off the chair when Dr. Cerdon gave him the news that he had Chlamydia. He grabbed his head, muttering, "No! No! No!" His heart sank further when he remembered that Rozene was still on her 'revive our sex life drive.' Now, he would have to avoid sexual contact with her, for God knows how long. His secret would be out, and she would leave him. But, as Dr. Cerdon supplied information about Chlamydia, a light shone in the darkness.

"Did you say, 'signs and symptoms could appear between one and three weeks after having unprotected sex with an infected person'?" Larry asked.

"Yes," Dr. Cerdon replied.

Larry's entire body shook as Dr. Cerdon's response sprinted through his brain. *My incident with Gabrielle was five days ago. Why then* ... He paused as the voices in his head settled on ... *Rozene.* Revelations flooded his spiraling mind - Her smiling face as she whispered on her cell phone. Her refusal to sleep with him. New lingerie ... for the new man. And the reason that she was taking so long to finish, *Letters to Wives.* "Noooo!" he shouted, covering his face with both hands.

Dr. Cerdon offered words of comfort but he just needed to go. The traffic would be heavy but he had to get home 'quick, fast, and in a hurry.' His body was still shaking when Dr. Cerdon asked for the name of the pharmacy where he would like to pick up his prescription.

"Larry! Larry, I'm ..." Rozene cried out, transporting him back to the present.

He flinched, pushing her hands away from his knees and got up. He hadn't even realized that she was kneeling before him. He glared at her. "You brought someone else into our marriage. Why?" he asked in a pained whisper. "Why, Roz?" He could hardly look at her. She had taken what was sacred in their marriage, and given it away.

She clutched his arm and he snatched it away. "Don't touch me!" he roared. "Is this how it's going be, you sleeping with random people?"

His words came out with such fury that she cringed. "Please forgive me," she sobbed. "I found out that I have Chlamydia and started on medication. But the week after I found out, you insisted on having sex so I just gave in."

Larry's face etched into tight lines as he looked at her. "You should have resisted."

She eyed him sorrowfully. "You know how you get when I say no. You have sex with me anyway."

Tears crowded Larry's eyes as Rozene's words pierced his heart. He gulped, attempting to get more air as nausea blocked his throat. *Am I that narcissistic?* The fury drained from his body as the unsolicited memory of the incident with Gabrielle assailed him. He stood there, rooted to the spot, feeling immensely overwhelmed at what he had just discovered about himself.

CHAPTER 3

Larry woke with a start to an incessant ringing. Rolling on his back, he realized he'd spent the night on the floor in the study, where he was penitent before the Lord. He was still trying to wrap his head around how he could have committed adultery. *Let go of the buzzer,* he willed whosoever was squeezing it. He crawled on his knees to get to the intercom on the desk, then reached over and pressed the flashing button for the entrance gate. "Yes?"

"Larry, it's Pastor Fotola. I've come to see you."

Larry pressed his hands to his temples. The last thing he wanted to do was see anyone. Guilt was enough company. Guilt from what he had done to Gabrielle. Guilt for not telling Rozene what he had done. Guilt for treating Rozene like a leper when she had mirrored his sinful behavior.

"Come on, Larry, open the gate," Pastor Fotola pressed him gently. "Just want to sit with you."

Larry shook his head as images of Gabrielle's dejected face ran through his mind. *Maybe, company would be good.* "Give ... give me a few minutes, please." He pressed the button to open the gate, and then slipped on his sandals.

A few minutes later, he stumbled through the formal living room, and entered the oval entryway leading to the front door. He paused as his eyes caught sight of a photo of Rozene and himself, that was standing in a frame on the console table. His eyes brimmed with tears. Clearly, he'd lost her.

The day after their big blow-up, Rozene told him that she still loved him and wanted their marriage, but he'd glared at her in disdain. "You should have thought about that before you cheated," he told her angrily. "Why would you risk everything for an affair with that ... man? Were you flattered by the attention he was giving you?"

Rozene hung her head in shame, and with tears streaming down her face, she ran out of their bedroom. Their relationship had become unbearably strained to the point where they spoke to each other only out of necessity. Over the weekend, she'd packed some of her things and told him she was moving in with her parents.

He was glad when she left. It was just easier. He definitely did not need the constant reminder that she'd mirrored his improper behavior ... mirrored his imperfection.

Larry shook his head.

Who would have known it would come to this?

When did their gaze shift from each other?

What could have gone so horribly wrong in their marriage, that they both committed adultery?

Strangely, it wasn't money, sickness, or even when they had different priorities, that derailed their marriage. They had survived all of that.

The doorbell chimed and he pulled the front door open without looking out.

Pastor Fotola stepped in. "Good to see you, man." He shook Larry's hand, ignoring his haggard and defeated appearance. Larry was almost a shadow of himself - cheeks sunken, beard unshaven, hair overgrown, just looking way older than his years.

"Morning. Afternoon, Pastor. Don't know what time it is." *Or, what day of the week it is, for that matter.* He stood there, feeling weak and emotionless.

"It's afternoon. Let's sit on the back patio."

Larry dragged himself through the living room, down the passageway near the kitchen area and out the door leading to the huge back patio. He squinted against the assault of the afternoon sun, and then slumped on the sofa near the door.

Pastor Fotola placed a cup of coffee on the table in front of them. "Here's something to jump start your day."

Larry looked sharply at him. The last time he thought he needed a jump start he'd coerced Gabrielle. "Thanks."

Pastor Fotola watched Larry for a moment. When he had not turned up for their Wednesday meeting and leadership retreat, he sensed something was wrong. Further, Larry did not respond to any of his calls. He tried to reach Larry at work and was told that he was on leave. Surprised by that bit of information, Pastor Fotola had taken it upon himself to call Rozene. Although she didn't divulge anything, she'd told him that Larry was home, and probably could do with a friend. After church, he decided to swing by their home and was glad when he saw Larry's car parked on the circular driveway in front of their luxurious French-style mansion.

"Larry," Pastor Fotola spoke quietly, "What's going on? Whatever happened, it's not beyond repair."

"My life is … ruined," Larry muttered, his expression impassive. "I just hurt people who I care about and they return the favor."

"Sometimes, we hurt the ones we love the most," Pastor Fotola offered, "but we will grow from it. What the enemy meant for evil, we know that God will turn it around for our good."

Larry got up abruptly and walked to the patio door. Leaning against it, he stared at the lush vegetation in the back yard. "They say, 'Hurting people often hurt other people.' Now I can safely associate myself with that quote. I never ever thought that I would …" His voice caught and he wiped his eyes, his emotions quickly turning from sadness to fierce anger. "How could I perpetuate what my

34

father did?" Growing up, Larry had vowed never to abuse anyone. He had seen abuse first hand, when his father verbally and physically abused his mother. Although his mother never admitted it, Larry always felt that his father had also sexually abused her.

"Let's talk about it," Pastor Fotola said quietly behind him. "I want to help you get through this."

Larry briefly looked at Pastor Fotola, and then cleared his throat. His vision blurred with unshed tears. "How? I don't know where to start."

Pastor Fotola's heart broke when he saw the vulnerability in Larry's eyes. He touched Larry's shoulders. "Come, my friend, start anywhere. Free yourself of the anger and judgment. Let God's perfect peace dwell in you and the richness of His forgiving power."

Larry hesitated, then decided to return to the sofa. He had good reasons not to talk about what was troubling him.

Guilt.

Shame.

Embarrassment.

Self-preservation.

Regret.

All good reasons ... but all faded in comparison to the revelation that hit and illuminated his heart when Rozene uttered, 'You know how you get when I say no. You have sex with me, anyway.' He eyed Pastor Fotola, and drew in a deep breath, then slowly released it. *It stops here.*

It was time for change.

No excuses.

Under the guidance of the Holy Spirit, it was time to resolve what he had seen in the mirror. For he realized that in order to understand his heat-of-the-moment behavior, he would have to delve deeper and reveal more of himself than he had ever disclosed to anyone.

"I committed adultery," Larry began.

CHAPTER 4

Knock! Knock! Knock!

Rozene scrunched her face and squeezed the pillows tighter in her arms, determined to play deaf.

Not deterred by the lack of response, Elizabeth Bennady entered her daughter's bedroom, and pulled back the curtains. It was 11:30 AM and her sole intention was to get Rozene out of bed.

Her gaze fell on Rozene, her first born, curled around two pillows, and sympathy permeated her heart. *God is able*, she reminded herself as she bent to pick up several pieces of crumpled tissue at the bedside and toss them into the bin nearby. She knew Rozene was hoping she would go away, and some days she actually did. But not today. It was time to do a bit of "mothering" because Rozene had been operating on empty for the past two days.

Elizabeth perched on the side of the bed and stroked Rozene's hair which streamed behind her on the pillow. "I love you," she told Rozene quietly.

Rozene stirred and rolled to face her mother, but she did not open her eyes. "Thanks, Mom. I love you too."

"I made you Cheese Soufflé. Thought you would like that."

"Um ..."

"You better stop it," her mother chuckled. "You know you absolutely love my Soufflés.

Rozene opened her swollen eyes to look at her mother, and a tiny smile curved her lips. *Beautiful*, was the only word that entered her thought.

Elizabeth was equally as gorgeous as her daughter. Her stunning hazel-colored eyes were as enthralling as Rozene's. The years had only made her more attractive in mind, body, soul and spirit. Naturally affectionate, her joyful laughter was a part of her aura - she would tip her head back and laugh delightfully. Thanks to her morning exercise rituals, this sixty-two-year-old was in great shape.

"A smile, albeit a tiny one, but I'll take it." Elizabeth patted her daughter's shoulder. "I'll set up brunch on the patio, if you like."

"I'll eat later, Mom."

"You haven't eaten all morning, baby. You need to eat something."

But eating was the last thing on Rozene's mind. "Stupid! Stupid, mindless behavior!" she lamented, tears escaping. Her mind failed to brighten on any memories from the past three months, even with the sunny day that surrounded the Bennady Estate. It had been over three months since she ran away from her own home but still, that wasn't enough time for pity parties, plus, she couldn't run away from herself.

"Rozie, the Lord will fix it. You can't," her mother encouraged. "You have to find a way to get your mind off your situation."

Rozene gazed past her mother. *Rozie.* A glimmer of hope rose in her heart. Very few people called her that, mostly her parents, her brother, and other close relatives. It reminded her that she was loved.

Her body shook as she held back from sobbing. "No, it wasn't a mindless act. I deliberately did that. I broke the vows I'd sworn to keep."

Inwardly sighing, Elizabeth watched her daughter's stubborn expression. She had the same expression her father would hold for days when he had done something that shocked his system. "It already happened, Rozie. You must find it in your heart to forgive yourself."

Rozene couldn't bear to look at her mother. Had she raised an adulterer?

"How can I, Mom? My-my life is ruined … my marriage," she gulped, "I've destroyed my marriage. And if word ever gets out, my ministry is over."

Her mother squeezed her shoulder reassuringly. "God will fix it. I know He will."

Why don't you scream at me, mother? Rozene frowned, looking away to hide her shame.

Her mom caught the look. "I love you. I need you to take care of yourself."

Rozene wiped her eyes with the bedcovers. "Thanks, Mom."

"Now, get dressed and let's eat. How much time do you need?"

"About twenty minutes. I'll need to freshen up."

Her mother smiled at her, knowing she meant an hour. That's how long it had been taking Rozene to climb out of bed these days. Elizabeth moved towards the door. "I'll come knocking if I don't see you."

"No need, Mom. I'll be there."

"Okay, baby," her mother responded before closing the door behind her.

Rozene pressed rigid fingers to her temple. *Some things in life will always be a mystery.* For this inexplicable occurrence in her life was just that … a mystery. Well, to her anyway.

Truth be told, she was in trouble from the get-go. Nothing she did or said would turn him off. Chandler had simply refused to back down or take no for an answer. Back then, although she wouldn't admit it, his obsession sparked a flame in her.

Indeed, their first encounter felt like playing with fire.

Of all the things she'd imagined dealing with that day, a bizarre emotional warfare was nowhere on the radar. His words were shifting her senses, and worst, he knew it.

Armed with a microphone in hand, she waited to speak - poised and controlled. Her expression neutral under his laser beam gaze, while he made his point.

The conference room had become remarkably quiet and she was struck with the uncanny feeling that the audience was eagerly awaiting her response. The stillness was unsettling and making it worse was the fact that he was gazing at her like she was his for the taking.

Still, little fazed her.

Little.

Taking a deep breath, she stilled herself, thinking, *I need rest. There could be no other explanation. What else could be causing my rollercoaster emotions, this Jekyll and Hyde behavior?*

As if sensing her mental deliberations, he shot a laugh in the air, before telling her, "From what I've read of your life story, you should understand what I'm talking about." His husky, distinct laughter floated through the air, and tingled her eardrums. She would have laughed out too, if the situation was not so serious.

Forcing a faint smile, she briefly observed him, standing at a table in front of the platform. She was conscious he had been watching all her movements and absorbing every word she'd spoken. While she'd gotten accustomed to men checking her out with open curiosity and undisguised admiration during her presentations, his gaze was different. It held the audacity of hope which was sending anxious shivers down her spine. Supposedly, the good kind, but unwelcomed and unwanted, nonetheless. Then, at one stage, he had the gall to send a silent request - the real question he wanted to ask. Was there a possibility?

NEVER, she almost yelled.

Moving to stand behind the podium, she lifted the microphone to her mouth, while praying her smile came off less fixed and awkward than it felt.

"Sir," she began, "as I already stated, I do not believe in love at first sight."

She looked into the audience, realizing she'd let the volume of her voice rise. "Any two persons can experience an instant attraction towards each other - an attraction that is intense and overpowering ... even an intimate connection. Your eyes meet across the room, your hearts begin to pound in sync, and," she covered her heart with her hand, "suddenly you know, you've found the one." Her eyes widened, before she playfully added, "So in essence, you are saying, Cupid, for it had to be Cupid, aimed for your heart and stole it."

Pockets of snickering broke out in the audience.

She eyed the man who asked the question and instantly regretted looking at him. Ignoring his incredulous expression, she decided to fix him with a question. "Seriously," she said, stifling a laugh, "can you decide in a few minutes that you're in love?"

He blinked in surprise before moving the microphone to his mouth. "Yes, I can," he responded charmingly, flashing even white teeth that drew female interest.

Rozene's desire to laugh vanished.

His eyes raked her frame. "And, I simply refuse to believe that you don't. It has happened to me," he said in all seriousness, smiling at the other participants with an air of confidence as they purred under the influence of his powerful, authoritative voice.

That smug grin rode her last nerve, and Rozene fought to keep the hostility out of her gaze.

His lips blossomed into a full eat-your-heart-out smile. "I couldn't break the intensity, the intensity," he emphasized, "that I felt in this first interaction between me and this wonderful lady. Didn't want to anyway. It was surreal. My heartbeat quickened at the thought of speaking with her. It was not just an attraction. It was … a mystical experience. An undeniable magnetic pull. I knew she felt it too." He held Rozene's gaze, daring her to respond in anything but the affirmative before taking his seat.

I knew she felt it too. His words swam towards her, just as a shiver stole through her. She pressed her lips together and plastered a smile on her face. "I can agree that two people can be attracted to each other and that, of course, is an important aspect of love, the emotional component of love. But I have learned that love is what is stated in 1 Corinthians 13:4-6, "Love suffers long and is kind; love does not envy; love does not parade itself, is not puffed up; does not behave rudely, does not seek its own, is not provoked, thinks no evil; does not rejoice in iniquity, but rejoices in the truth;""

She looked at the audience, emotions whirling on her inside. "It takes but a moment to be attracted to someone, to get a crush on someone, but I dare say it takes dedication, passion, perseverance, and leaning on the Word of God and the Holy Spirit to create a love for all times."

Perfectly pitched with passion, experience, and insight.

Spellbound, the audience cheered, and the man stood and bowed deeply, mouthing to her, "Let's agree to disagree."

She attempted to return a gracious smile before announcing, "You have fifteen minutes to complete your prologues. After that, we will listen to a few."

She could barely think straight as she gathered her documents from the podium and returned to her seat at the table nearby. Usually, she would move about the conference room to talk with participants and offer help but not this time, in case he attempted to share personal space with her again.

Her mind flashed back to the first time she spotted him across the room during the lunch break. It was an automatic double take. Then her mind went straight to the gutter. This blast of unexpected desire was the craziest experience she'd had in a long while. She could only hope that her mouth wasn't hanging open. She came out of her senselessness just in time to witness his cocky grin. Like a lion on the prowl, he had found his prey and was moving in for the kill. When he started walking towards her, she all but ran to the podium to announce fifteen minutes to the end of lunch break. As if anyone needed a reminder.

Shaking off her mental hopscotch, Rozene decided to browse the prologue handout while giving herself a much needed pep talk to get through the rest of the session. This was the last session of her three-day writers' conference and book tour in Washington, D.C. and it couldn't be over sooner.

Feeling eyes on her, she looked towards where he was sitting and was startled to see him staring at her while chatting in a small group. If he was surprised to see her looking at him, he didn't show it. But her gaze must have given him an invitation of sorts because in the next minute, he hauled his tall frame away from the group, and began strolling towards the platform.

Her heartbeat frantically pounded her eardrums.

Trapped by his intoxicating allure, she couldn't bring herself to move, couldn't stop staring, and couldn't even blink.

After what seemed like an eternity, he paused on the step leading to the platform to answer his cell phone. His mouth began to move but she couldn't hear what he was saying. In the next minute, he walked swiftly back to his seat, and took up his bag. With that, he left the room.

Immediately, tension left her body, reminding her that she had placed herself in a vulnerable position.

Silently, she thanked God for making a way of escape. She was grateful too, that no one knew her little secret.

A gentle knock on her bedroom door drew Rozene out of her musing, and she stumbled out of bed. "Ten minutes, Mom," she called out.

"Ten minutes it is," her mother responded.

Rozene dragged herself to the bathroom, thankful for her mother who refused to let grief consume her. Her mom had become her therapist, her prayer partner, and her security blanket.

She had always admired her mom, not only for being an exemplary woman of God, but for her determined spirit and the passion she exerted in every task she undertook. Her mother helped to manage the fifty-year-old family business, Bennady International Citrus Company with her father, Benjamin. When she was not busy working, Elizabeth was out and about doing charity work and ministering to women in the various organizations she'd established.

Elizabeth Bennady was the ideal wife too, and Rozene had always hoped to follow in her footsteps. *So much for that.* Tears filled Rozene's eyes as she stared at her ghostly reflection in the bathroom mirror. *This is not my life.*

CHAPTER 5

Elizabeth popped her head out the door leading to the huge back patio, and watched Rozene staring at nothing in particular. Dark clouds of uncertainty and sorrow were still lingering over her.

Offering up a silent prayer, Elizabeth stepped out the door to drink in the warmth of the day and soak in the energy. *I'm going to need it*, she thought.

"You should be writing," Elizabeth called out to Rozene. "It's such a beautiful day."

Startled, Rozene gave her a tight smile before placing her laptop on the table before her. "That was the idea." She pushed back in the chair as her mother arrived by her side. "Well, I can now spend my days writing about divorce."

"Stop punishing yourself, Rozie. Larry said nothing about a divorce." Her mother eyed her. "I prepared Soupe a L'oignon. Would you like some?"

"I'll be in shortly, Mom."

A sigh of relief escaped Rozene as her mother kissed the top of her head and left.

Back in the day, sitting on the patio would have calmed her nerves, and it would have been a time to reflect on God's continued blessings. Plus, the panoramic view of the land that had been in the family for over a hundred years was simply awe-inspiring. Their home, Bennady mansion and private estate, was framed by beautiful landscape and gardens as far as the eyes could see. Although renovated a few times to include modern amenities, the twelve-bedroom, ten-bathroom mansion retained its original elegance and charm.

During her teenage years, Rozene would sit at this same spot, in her favorite rocking chair, and dream about all the books she would write. It was in that same spot that her mother and father would also find her fast asleep with the book she was reading in her lap.

Now she felt like dozing off into oblivion. There was a draft in her soul. Her infidelity would destroy everything she'd worked hard to achieve.

She wiped her eyes thinking how nice it would be if things were different, and she never had that crazy season.

After her silent encounter with Chandler in Washington, D.C., she'd hoped ... well kinda-sorta, never to see him again since he hadn't returned to her writers' conference and book tour.

But three weeks later, he was back again, staring at her during her, *Letters to Husbands* book tour in Chicago. All week, she had seen him at the events, and he did the same thing - just stared at her in a way that continued to disturb her senses and caused goosebumps to attack her arms.

After lunch on the last day of the book tour, he sat at the end of the second row, disregarded her steely determination to ignore him, and simply gazed at her ... a slow, intense appraisal of her body especially when she stood beside the podium. When his eyes finally returned to her face, she could anticipate his smile of total appreciation. By the close of the book tour, he'd launched into full-scale flirtation. His expression dared her to stand under the heat of his gaze. Again, his eyes asked, if there was a possibility.

Possibility?
Of course, there was no possibility.
I've made vows I intend to keep.
Are you insane?

Her lungs thrashed about for oxygen as she briefly scrutinized his striking, beguiling features, before looking away.

Gripping the podium, she steadied herself, and looked at the audience. "Again, thanks so much for coming out. This is the final day of my book tour for, *Letters to Husbands* and I hope," she said and flashed her winning smile to the more than two thousand in the audience, "it was as great for you as it was for me."

A chorus of "yes" rose from the audience.

"Hope you plan to hang around," someone shouted. "We love you."

The participants cheered and her smile widened. "I love you all too. It has been an awesome experience. Thanking God for you. And yes, my husband and I do plan to enjoy a little more of the windy city before heading back home."

More cheers came from the audience, and she let out a grateful sigh. It was a pleasure to use her talent to serve and bless others.

"On another note, ladies," Rozene smiled at the audience, "please don't feel left out. As promised, I will have, *Letters to Wives* ready for you by next year. Have a great evening, everybody! Stay victorious."

The audience cheered and shouted their thank yous as she bowed in reverence before walking towards an area of the platform designated for signing her books.

What on earth? She could barely process what was going on. She found herself eyeballing the mystery man. He had moved to stand near the desk stacked with her books. His deep-set eyes locked on hers long enough to let her know he was intensely fascinated by everything about her.

Even his navy blazer couldn't hide the fact that he was fine - well-built and all together wonderful. Not counting Larry, Rozene couldn't recall the last time a man captured her attention in such a blatant way.

This is crazy! Irritation washed through her. She was annoyed at the mounting desire in his eyes but most of all, she was bothered by her own abnormal behavior. Ignoring him, she took her seat behind the desk and smiled at a loving, young couple who was eagerly waiting in line.

"Hello! Thanks for coming out," she greeted them with a smile as she reached for the copy of her book from the woman.

"Hi, Mrs. Kanate! I'm Sophia. I'm thrilled to meet you at last."

Rozene smiled at her and shook her hand. "Great to meet you too, Sophia. Please call me Rozene."

"Okay, I will. I read all your books," she gushed.

"Thank you," Rozene beamed. "Hope you were blessed by what you read."

"I sure was." Sophia tugged the arm of the young man beside her. "This is Chris. We're engaged. Getting married in December."

It was Rozene's turn to gush. "Wow! Congratulations!" She smiled at them, and then with an eyebrow lift, told them, "You know what the Word says, 'Whoso findeth a wife findeth a good thing, and obtaineth favor of the Lord.'"

"Amen," Sophia and Chris responded in unison, high-fiving each other.

Rozene grinned at them. "You are ready for married life, aren't you?"

"Can't wait," Sophia said ecstatically.

"Me too," Chris agreed, hugging her waist.

Smiling, Rozene handed Sophia the autographed copy of her book. "Great. Enjoy each other."

"Thanks, Mrs. Kanate," Chris responded. "We will. Have a -"

"Can we take a picture with you?" Sophia asked.

"Sure." Rozene pushed back her chair and walked towards them.

The mystery man eagerly volunteered to snap the photo and after that, Sophia and Chris bid her goodbye.

Rozene prepared herself with a tight smile to meet the mystery man, but when she turned to do so, he was walking away.

Almost three hours later, Rozene massaged her hands after hugging, and then waving goodbye to the last attendee. It was finally over, now she needed to kick back until Larry arrived in the morning. Frankly, she couldn't wait to fall in bed.

She glanced around and a smile lit her face, her efficient book tour team had started to pack up the exhibits. She was gathering her belongings when the familiar sensation ricocheted through her body. It was then that she saw him talking to Donovan Peynard, her book tour manager. She had almost forgotten he was there. Almost.

Oh God! She shook her head as they began walking towards her. *For God's sake, pull yourself together. You are a globe-trotting, bestselling author. You can handle this.* She placed her purse on her shoulder and twiddled with her cell phone, hoping to get her nerves under control by the time the two men arrived by her side. As they got closer, she turned away and started to stack the pens she'd used in the container on the table.

"Rozene," Donovan called out.

"Hey, Don." She threw him a glance and continued stacking the pens.

"No need to do that," Don said. "The team will take care of it. Let's get you back to the hotel so you can relax."

"Okay." She hugged him. "Thanks so much."

"The pleasure was all ours. As usual, we enjoyed touring with you." Don's razor sharp eyes latched on to hers and he smiled pleasantly. He was a tall, lean man with wavy black hair with a tinge of gray that shot off at the edges. An air of expectation surrounded him and he always seemed like he was not only in control of his emotions but of the situation … whatever the situation may be.

Rozene had met Don through Larry almost two year ago. Don had done a seamless job of promoting, marketing and handling all matters pertaining to her books, and ministry. After collaborating on ideas, she would turn up at an event, knowing it would be organized as discussed.

Rozene smiled at Don. "Please tell the team thanks too. We will get together as usual to debrief when we get back home."

All this time, her eyes were focused on Don. She was determined that whosoever this alluring man was, he was not about to get the better of her.

"Today was exceptional though," Don said. "You were excellent, but then you always are." He looked at the mystery man. "This is Chandler Peynard, my half-brother on my father's side of the family. I may have mentioned him but I don't believe you've been formally introduced. Meet my little brother."

Don was a mere five years older but he took pleasure in pointing out that Chandler was his little brother.

Rozene had no choice but to look in Chandler's direction. "Yes, I remember his name. I also remember him trying to stir up controversy at my book tour in D.C. Nice to meet you, Mr. Peynard." She gave him a tight smile, extending her hand and found herself looking into the softest pair of light-brown eyes she'd ever seen on a man. With some amount of certainty, she knew for all his life he must have stirred the hearts of females, whether young or old, single or married.

"The pleasure is mine, Mrs. Kanate." His voice was sincere and smooth. Way too smooth. "No controversy. I am a fan." His touch was more like a caress and for the brief moment their eyes met, she knew she had to guard herself.

She withdrew her hand and faced Don. "Thanking God everything went well. Now for some down time."

"Praise God," Don said smiling. "Just to let you know, Chandler has been a great help to us on this book tour. He's on leave from his job so he volunteered to help with logistics and communication."

Oh, that explains it. Rozene attempted a polite smile. "Thanks, Mr. Peynard. We appreciate your help, and of course, you will be rewarded."

Chandler's lips slanted in an amused smile.

"No payment necessary," Donovan jumped in. "He was only helping out."

"Well, thanks again," Rozene said to Chandler before turning to Donovan. "I'm going to sit near the door. Please let me know when you're ready."

"No need. Chandler has volunteered to take you back to the hotel."

No! "Mr. Peynard has done enough, I wouldn't want-"

"Please call me Chandler. It's not a problem, Mrs. Kanate. I'm staying at the same hotel."

"O-Okay. Let me get my portfolio."

She turned, fully aware that in return she should have told him to refer to her as Rozene. But she wouldn't do that, mostly because she needed the reminder she was a married woman.

"Don." She faced him. "Have a safe trip back. Tell Marianne thanks for lending you to me. I'm sure she can't wait to have you home."

"I sure will. Have fun this weekend."

"You know I will. Can't wait for Larry to get here," Rozene said loudly, before looking at Chandler.

The speck of amusement in his eyes told her he knew exactly what she was doing. "Ready?" he asked.

"Give me a minute, please." She slipped into her coat and made sure to button it from head to toe. It made her feel protected from the chilly fall weather she was anticipating on the outside … and safe from this man, whose eyes had not left her body since he'd arrived before her.

"I'm ready now," she told him.

His lips shifted in a lazy smile. "Let's go."

"Bye, everyone. Thank you. Have a safe trip back." She waved at the members of her book tour team. Some waved back, while others shouted their goodbyes.

Together, she and Chandler moved across the room towards the exit door.

"Rozie! …Rozie!"

The sound of her mother's voice brought Rozene out of her reflection. "On my way, Mom," she answered. The rumbling in her stomach reminded her she needed to eat. *Now that's a more positive direction for* my *thoughts.* With that, she lifted herself out of the chair.

CHAPTER 6

For the second time that weekend, Larry drove the two-mile stretch of private road to Chateau de Kanate, beneath the cloud of overhanging pink cherry blossoms trees. For once, he paid no attention to the pale spring light filtering through the trees from above, and the petals fluttering around before dusting the ground.

His expression was pensive as it usually was after his counseling session with Pastor Fotola. After over three month of emotionally draining face-to-face and telephone counseling sessions about his father and his marriage, he was still learning to cope with his new season ... constantly willing the pain in his heart to diminish enough so he could function.

He had decided to spend the weekend at Chateau de Kanate and that was good for him. It had become increasingly difficult to be at home, constantly bombarded with thoughts about his marriage. Of course, he didn't want that. His counseling sessions gave him enough time to grieve over how his life had gone down the drain, beginning with his heat-of-the-moment behavior with Gabrielle.

After Gabrielle resigned, he'd quickly advertised her position, interviewed and selected another human resources director, David Genier. Intense training brought Genier up to speed.

A month later, Larry executed his plan for a month and a half long world travel to meet with all the human resources directors and managers as well as customer service representatives of Pallecia Hotel. He had four regional meetings in the United States within two weeks, and then the rest of his days were spent conducting meetings in Central America, South America, Asia, and Europe.

He had only returned home two weeks ago, and was still having difficulty adjusting to living alone. He would have to hurry and make that adjustment, because coming out to Chateau de Kanate was supposed to be his kick back time. Not a time to take questions about the state of his marriage. No. Not at all. But his mother refused to take the hint.

"Late last year, you'd mentioned Rozene had changed emotionally towards you," Darlene Kanate said yesterday, after returning from an evening walk with Larry. "But I remembered you thought she was having a hard time dealing with the children going off to college."

Larry's mood soured. "Exactly. That's what I thought. Little did I know, she had some other man all over her."

"Something else must have been going on with her,' his mother jumped in. "Rozene is tough … not easily broken."

"Right?" he griped beneath his breath, before politely excusing himself.

In all their nineteen years of marriage, not once had he ever cheated on Rozene. Not that many opportunities hadn't come his way. In his line of work, women were constantly making themselves available. He would even admit he had been tempted a few times but never had he broken his marriage vows.

Anyway, after all his mother had gone through with his father, he'd made a sacred vow to the Lord, to be a great husband. Now, he wasn't perfect and their marriage had seen hard days managing family life and two high-powered jobs, but he had been faithful. He had even gone to great lengths to ramp up their bedroom frolics, keeping it fresh, and Rozene had never once complained.

He recalled her interest in their bedroom activities had dropped way below zero, last fall. Months later, he was still trying every trick in the book to get her to sleep with him.

Every trick.

He was that desperate and all the while, she was handling her business elsewhere. Just thinking about it made him angry all over again.

He had gotten so tired of begging her to make love with him, that he'd carefully laid out a plan to get some action on his birthday in January. She was still a bit resistant but she gave in after a while.

He wished she hadn't. That five minutes, yes five minutes, of pitiful sex gave him Chlamydia. He had never in his life had a venereal disease. *Dear God, why?*

Picking up the prescription was something he was still attempting to wipe from his memory. He could barely look at the pharmacist, although he collected it at the drive-through.

Anger welled up in his chest as he whipped onto the driveway of the magnificent dwelling he once called home. Nestled on a gentle sloping peak in the heart of the fifty-acre property, stood the imposing Chateau de Kanate, with its spectacular view of a pristine lake and flourishing vegetation of all colors, shapes, and sizes.

Larry pushed back the scowl that was threatening to overtake his face as he made his way to the front door. Before he could push the key in the lock, the large oak door flew open and Zalletta welcomed him in. He landed her a dimpled smile before hugging her. "Seriously, Aunt Zal, how do you manage to look younger every day?"

Zalletta had been with the family since Larry's elementary years. Larry had heard from his mother that Zalletta had taken over right out of college after her mother died. Now Zalletta operated as chief of staff at Château de Kanate.

"You need to come up with something new, Larry," Zalletta teased. "You told me that yesterday."

"Oh, is that so? It's the truth. You keep looking younger." He threw his arms open. "Every day!"

Zalletta slapped him playfully on his arm. "You're good, Superman!"

"Yes, I am."

She shook her head and grinned at him before moving to exit the room.

"You know, I'm good like that," he yelled at her back, before stepping further into the interior of the spectacular Chateau de Kanate. Down to the last detail was one for the history books – grand living rooms, libraries, galleries, terraces, and huge bedrooms with ivory shag carpets and enormous canopy beds, draped with sheer white veils. An ivory and gold theme mixed with several shades of blue ran through the general areas of the entire house. But the most unique feature of this magnificent home was the impressive double-helix staircase that gave access to the sleeping quarters.

Larry and his three siblings – thirty-eight years old Alexandria, born after him, followed three years later by his twin brothers, Zane and Zadan - lived at the Chateau, pretty much up to their college years. After college, Zane and Zadan had moved back in, only to move out shortly thereafter. They were unable to live under the same roof with their father. However, they moved back in to live with their mother after their father died.

Larry entered his room, and headed straight for the bathroom. Twenty minutes later, he fidgeted a bit before resting comfortably on his back on the bed. He chucked as he gazed at a picture of Zane and Zadan in football gear on the wall before him. It was a proud moment when their high school won the championship that year.

Larry's lips curled into a lopsided smile, for he remembered his mother saying, God had a sense of humor when he was creating her boys because they were the spitting image of their father, and just like their father, they were all six-feet-three in height.

Where did the years go? Larry thought.

Yesterday after dinner, he'd spent quality time with his brothers. They were good company, as always, even though the two were as different as night and day. The only similarity being that they were both confirmed bachelors in an unusual way.

Zane who served as Chief Operating Officer for the family business, Kanate Management and Realty Corporation, was funny, affectionate, charming, and smart with an air of brilliance. His best trait – his 'off-the-chain' creativity. Nevertheless, his taste in women left a lot to be desired. The tabloids labeled him - Ladies' man, Zillionaire playboy, Devoted womanizer, Lover-lover, and several other titles that thanks to the Internet, he would have difficulty explaining to his children ... should he decide to have any.

Zane's public image was a constant source of stress for the public relations team, and his mother, even though she would never say it aloud. Larry just knew his mother was praying night and day for Zane to commit his life to Jesus Christ. Thankfully, Zane's public image had not affected the profitability of the family business. Then too, the goodwill of the Kanate name helped in this regard.

On the other hand, Zadan was the most random person Larry knew, especially since his wife died, his personality had been most difficult to define. In his own words, 'Life is too short to be consistent. Do what you can, when you can.'

Nevertheless, like all the Kanate males, Zadan was multi-talented. Strange was how he was unable to settle in one particular field of study. At one stage, he was a professional student. After he graduated from MIT's School of Engineering, he moved on to the J.D. Program at Harvard Law School, and then finally, he attended Yale School of Management and completed the MBA program. Currently, Zadan operated as the head of legal affairs for the family business. However, through the family grapevine, Larry was told he was pursuing his masters in divinity, which was what the family thought he should be doing anyway.

Larry smiled to himself thinking, Zadan loved the Lord. Even now, he was waiting for the Lord to provide him with another wife.

He'd noticed that Zane and Zadan stayed away from conversations about his marriage. And he was glad. What else was there to say? His wife committed adultery. Would talking about it help the situation? Plus, she had no reason to commit adultery. None at all. Their sex life was never a struggle … Ever. Not even on their most exhausted day.

He rolled on his side and all but hissed his teeth as unwanted memories rushed in.

He had taken the time to bathe her with love before she'd left for her book tour in Chicago last fall. In fact, that was one lovemaking experience he'd never forget.

He had missed his flight while returning from a three-day business trip, and had come in a few hours before she was scheduled to leave.

And boy, was she ready for him.

He was tired, but what do you know - rest is overrated.

She met him at their bedroom door, her fine body draped in jaw dropping lingerie, and he'd thrown his bag down and surged forward, kissing her hungrily with a sort of desperate passion. All the desires he'd locked away for three days came out in full force. His body wracked with

58

shudder after shudder as he kissed her deeply, hard and fast, eagerly sampling her lips.

Every part of her body was on fire from his touch, a matching yearning came from her, as she met his mouth with hungry kisses.

The wait had seemed forever, but it was all worth it. Intense.

It had always been like that between them - an electrifying passion that burned everything in its pathway, leaving them trembling and glowing with satisfaction.

Breathing heavily, he told her, "Need to take a quick shower."

Unwilling, she released him, murmuring, "Don't be long."

He'd rushed to the bathroom like he was being chased by a pack of hungry wolves. In less than five minutes, after watching him dry all that God had favored him with, she moved closer. Her lips parted softly, seemingly in slow motion as her eyes beckoned to him. The idea that she was seducing him turned him on even more. Shivers chased over his body and a moan gurgled deep within his throat as he pulled her closer to trace the outline of her lips with his own. But she beat him to it, distracting him with a naughty smile, before pecking his lower lip. She caught his surprised gasp in her mouth and giggled.

Her mouth an inch away from his, Larry watched as her lips parted invitingly again. Her full lips were hard to resist, so he didn't try. Growling, he seized her lips in another intense kiss, his hands stroking her with exquisite care and precision.

Suffice to say, they didn't make it to the bedroom.

The warmth rolling around in his core dragged Larry out of his contemplation. He cleared his throat, berating himself, when his cell phone rang. He reached for it on the nightstand, and a flash of irritation hit him. It was Rozene.

CHAPTER 7

Rozene listened until Larry's phone went to voicemail, but she didn't bother to leave a message. She bit her lips to hold back the tears as she allowed the phone to slip out of her hand. It landed with a slight bounce then settled somewhere on the bed. Just then, her phone rang and she pushed out a shaky breath. *At least, he's responding.* She reached for the phone and touched the answer button while using the tips of her thumb and index finger to wipe her eyes. "Larry, I'm glad you-"

"Larry?" Chandler's voice echoed over the phone. "But what else can I expect. I'm the other man."

Rozene grabbed a handful of the bedcovers to steady herself. "Chandler, we agreed not to call each other." She hadn't heard from him in over two months. *Knew I should have changed my number.* She hadn't bothered to because she didn't want him calling her office to track her down. Persistence was his first name.

A little gasp of surprise came from Chandler. His way of saying how hurt he was. "Did I agree to that?"

Rozene did not respond, but that didn't stop her from wishing he would drive himself off the face of the earth.

"Ro, you surprise me." She could picture him knitting his brow. "Is this what we've become? I spend all my waking hours thinking about you. The way we were. Deep down, I sensed you miss me."

Rozene was almost cross-eyed from rolling her eyes. She resisted the urge to hurl the phone into the land of no return. Instead, she fell back on her training. "Please don't call again. Goodbye, Chandler."

"I miss waking up beside you, Ro," he drawled huskily. "Touching you. Holding you. Kissing you softly until you beg me to stop. You remember don't you?"

Rozene closed her eyes, and for the second time that evening, tears burned them. *What have I done?* For a moment, guilt held her hostage. "Bye, Chandler," she whispered unsteadily, before disconnecting the call.

She sank deeply into the bedcovers, tears running down her cheeks and on to the pillow beneath her head. Chandler was bent on forcing himself in her life. That was his intention from day one. Albeit, she'd given him the opportunity.

She rolled on her back thinking, way too many opportunities.

After exiting the conference room in Chicago that afternoon, she'd kept her eyes focused on the elevators but couldn't help but wonder what Chandler did for a living. Gym instructor popped into her head. *P90X extreme workouts?* His firm abdomen and strong thighs could attest to that. She caught a glimpse of his profile, noting that his smooth caramel-colored frame was taller than she thought, well over six feet. She put his age in the late thirties, no more than forty.

She glanced down his frame and almost gasped. He was wearing a wedding band. *Now, that was unexpected.* He didn't look like the type of man who could settle down ... at least not for long. *But what do I care?* She centered her thoughts as the elevator arrived.

Wordlessly, he allowed her to step in before entering and punching the button to the ground floor. He stood beside her, way too close in her estimation but she refused to look at him. She was busy clamping down the frenzy as her mind went into overdrive. Her lips quivered as her stomach knotted with a bout of unexpected desire. Breathing was becoming a chore, at best, for now his eyes were fixed on her chest.

Every muscle in his body taut, Chandler watched her. He loved being in her presence. She was like a breath of fresh air. He had watched her sizing him up outside the elevator without making a comment. Now it was his turn and he intended to feast on her.

He'd heard Don on numerous occasions bragging about her and her achievements. Admitted, he was remotely curious, but he was not into this God thing. However, one night, he was finding it difficult to sleep, so he'd decided to go channel hopping, and that was when he discovered her. The more he listened to her TV program, the more he liked her, and before long, watching her program had become a weekly routine ... his little dirty secret. Her beautiful, hazel-colored eyes consistently beckoned to him from the screen, fueling his passion.

But this week was temptation at its finest. It was sheer agony to see her every day, sharing and interacting with the audience. *Much better than TV.*

Watching her now, he knew she felt his desire for her. But he knew that because of her status as bestselling author, and a Christian author at that, she would never do anything to jeopardize what God was doing in her life. He'd heard enough from her TV programs and at her book tour events to know that.

He let out a ragged sigh.

He was on work assignment in Washington, D.C. about three weeks ago when they had their first heart-thumping encounter. However, an emergency on his job had caused him not to meet her then, but he'd vowed to get close to her. When Don told him about her Chicago book events, he'd taken leave from his job to volunteer for a worthy cause.

"We are almost there," he said, attempting to break the tension between them.

She swallowed tightly then nodded, still not looking at him. She refused to look into his perfectly gorgeous light-brown eyes, set in an equally perfect, square shaped face that was flawlessly proportioned with slightly high cheek bones, chiseled jawlines, full symmetrical lips, and a prominent chin. He sported low, slightly curly jet-black hair, complemented by a neatly trimmed beard, and a thin mustache. Everything about him conveyed vigor, and primal heat radiated from every pore in his body.

She couldn't wait to get out of his presence to examine her own head. She was surprised by her intense and immediate attraction to a complete stranger. His gaze alone was sending jolts of electricity through her body. She righted herself, determined to stop the lunacy.

"We'll go through the front entrance. We have plain clothes security personnel on hand in case of an emergency."

"Thank you," she said quietly, glad for the change of pace. She loved her readers but some had been known to go overboard with their exuberance. That was the one thing she didn't like about being in the spotlight.

"Ready?" he asked, as the elevator reached the ground floor.

"Yes."

As they exited the elevator, she heard someone calling her name and saw a man hastily approaching her. They stopped and Chandler stepped before her, blocking her from the man.

"How can we help?" he asked the man.

The man smiled timidly. "I'm sorry. I wanted Mrs. Kanate to sign a copy of her book for my son."

Rozene stepped beside Chandler. "No problem," she said, smiling widely while taking the book from his hand. "What is your son's name?"

"Joel," the man replied, gratefully. "He's getting married soon."

"Now, that's good news." She smiled at the man, and then proceeded to autograph the book. "And, what is your name?"

"Rohan. This is where I do my day job. I hope I wasn't out of line to ask for an autographed copy. I know this is the end of your tour."

"Not at all. So nice to meet you, Rohan," Rozene said, extending her hand, and smiling, "Added perks of the job, huh?" she teased.

"For that, I'm grateful, ma'am." Rohan shook her hand, giving her a dimpled grin.

"Don't forget to chat and pray with me and my team online," Rozene said, handing the book to him. "You know we are on weekly, right?"

"Yes, I heard about that. I will."

"Thank you. God bless you. Have a great night."

"You too, ma'am!" Rohan said, before walking away.

Chandler gently touched her elbow. "I got the all clear from the security team. We can exit."

She gave him a bemused look before walking beside him towards the front door.

Seeing they were not on the same page, he remarked, "Have you any idea how many incidents we've handled since you've been here? I know you want to be with your readers but you have to admit some are a little fanatical."

She lifted her perfectly plucked eyebrows. "Mr. Peynard, I mean Chandler, my ministry comes with great moments and not-so-great moments. God has provided me with a wonderful team, and I'm grateful."

His eyes narrowed in disbelief, but he said nothing. He allowed her to step into the revolving glass door then stepped in behind her.

After greeting the valet, he collected his car key and made sure she was seated before hopping into the red Lexus GS sports car.

He glanced at her to make sure she was settled before pulling away.

Ten minutes later, Rozene thought the silence in the car was going to destroy her.

As if reading her thoughts, he asked, "Why don't you like me, Mrs. Kanate?"

She glanced at him, but before she could respond, her cell phone rang. "Hey, Don," she answered.

"Rozene, hi. Are you at the hotel yet?"

"No. On the way."

"Glad I caught you. Can you please give Chandler the box of books I'd asked you to hold for me? Zion's book club president wants to pick up the copies later and I don't want to disturb you."

It was on the tip of her tongue to say, it's okay you can disturb me, but she did not want to be difficult. "Okay, I will."

After bidding Don goodbye, she looked at Chandler who had come to a stop at a stoplight. "Don is asking you to collect a box of books that I have for him."

"Not a problem," he said, eyeing her. "I'd asked a question."

"Yes, you did."

"And?"

"I don't know you Chandler, so you are mistaken in saying I don't like you."

"Get to know me then. You may need my services again. Plus, isn't that the Christian thing to do – treat everyone well?"

She almost sighed aloud, glad that they only had a few minutes before the hotel would be in sight. Then, she wouldn't have to see him again. *Lord, forgive me. It is best*

66

to have no contact with this man. She softened. "What do you do for a living, Chandler?"

He took his eyes off the road momentarily to look at her. She knew from the look in his eyes that he did not appreciate her question.

"Is this your getting-to-know-Chandler strategy?"

"Don't be difficult. There's no point in us speaking if you're going to fuss."

Chandler chuckled - one of those you've got to be kidding ones – before deciding to take the high road. "I'm the Chief Aerospace Engineer at Renauto Aeronautical and Design Corporation."

"Nice." She remembered that Renauto was one of the world's largest aerospace companies and leading manufacturer of anything that could fly. "So you are good with your hands."

His sharp intake of breath echoed in the car. "You have no idea how good."

She saw the rousing sensations springing from his eyes, when he glanced at her briefly. She could just imagine what was going through his mind. Strangely, he terrified her and thrilled her all at the same time. Refusing to comment, she turned her head and stared straight ahead, glad that the hotel was finally in sight.

Some fifteen minutes later, her hands trembled as she opened her room door. "Wait here," she told him before stepping into her lavish suite. She turned when she heard the door close behind her.

He held up a hand to stop her before she commented. "I'm coming in to get the box of books. Why do you want me to hang out at the door? Can't handle what you're feeling?"

The eyes staring back at her were determined, to say the least.

"Chandler," she spoke quickly as dread spread through her heart before exploding and settling in her body. "Thanks again for all you did and for taking me here." She pointed to the box of books next to the desk. "Thanks for giving that to Don for me. I do appreciate your kindness."

He gently took her hand in his, and brought it to his lips. His arresting gaze was filled with desire ... all-consuming desire.

Oh God! "Wha-what are ...?" She found herself holding her breath.

Triumph flared in his eyes and he all but took a victory lap.

"You were leaving," she said breathlessly, pulling away her hand.

"It's a matter of timing," he said, ignoring her comment.

Momentarily thrown off guard, she stared wide-eyed at him for a couple of seconds. "More like never."

He smiled wickedly at her. "Never?"

"That's what I said."

His eyes etched in ruthlessness, he moved to retrieve the box of books.

She put on a determined gaze as he walked past her towards the door. He was way too sure of himself. "Thanks. Have a good evening." *And, a great life.*

He turned to look at her before opening the door and she felt the hard thud of her heart. She knew at that moment, he wouldn't hesitate to seduce her if the opportunity presented itself.

"Have a good evening," he drawled before going through the door and closing it behind him.

Thank you, Lord. Rozene released a sigh of relief. She had always picked her battles and this was not a battle she was willing to even acknowledge, much less fight. In the back of her mind, she knew it wasn't over. *I must stay prayed up.*

That memory brought her back to the present, and she reminded herself, *I must stay prayed up.*

CHAPTER 8

"Don't allow the war to cause you to fight dirty, Larry. Don't allow the heat of the battle to cause you to lose your testimony. God will fight your battle, keep trusting Him."

"Mama, trust me, I'm not fighting dirty. I'm not even fighting. I just don't have anything to say to her."

"Well, at least take her calls. What if Rozene was calling about the children?"

Larry fought to hold back the scowl that was creeping over his face. Clearly, his mother had a conversation with Rozene.

"I'll try then," he responded, forcing away dark thoughts about Rozene.

"Thanks, son. I know it's not easy, so thank you."

"You're welcome, Mama. Anything for you."

"Anything?" She sighed. "Not true or you would have fulfilled your father's request. He loved you in his own way you know."

"Mama, we've been through that. Not going to happen."

His mother knew better than to start another war with him. "Okay, son. Are you still heading my way?"

"Yes, Mama. I'll see you in another two hours."

"Later then, son. I love you."

"I love you too, Mama." Larry smiled slightly at his cell phone, after his mother disconnected the call.

It was early Friday morning and his mother had called and prayed with him. He was glad she did. Last night was a long, emotionally exhausting night for him after another deep heart-wrenching conversation about his marriage with Pastor Fotola.

Pastor Fotola wanted him to tell Rozene he'd been unfaithful. He had pretty much lost his cool, blurting out,

"Never!" But Pastor Fotola remained silent, and he felt forced to ask, "And why would I do that?" He had all intention of keeping his infidelity buried. Yes, buried. Anyway, what was the point of telling Rozene? He was not taking her back.

But even as his mind rehashed memories, Pastor Fotola's words kept echoing in his ears. "You committed the same sin that she did. You are being unfair to her. At least give her a chance to explain."

Pastor Fotola even had Bible verses lined up - "And why do you look at the speck in your brother's eye, but do not consider the plank in your own eye? Or how can you say to your brother, 'Let me remove the speck from your eye'; and look, a plank is in your own eye? Hypocrite! First remove the plank from your own eye, and then you will see clearly to remove the speck from your brother's eye."

Larry flinched, pushing out a harsh breath. It was difficult to stop the debate running to and fro in his head.

He'd taken the day off from work, but not to be bombarded by unwelcome thoughts. *What is this? Beat up Larry day.* He then decided to focus on his next move.

After visiting his mother, he would fulfill his once a month motivational speaking engagement at Kanate Educational Learning Center, one of the charities that he'd set up to coach and train, K-12 and college students. Today, he would encourage the college students to write about their goals, pray about them, and pursue their destinies. *Now that's something to smile about.*

He was proud to be associated with the learning center. The center was making a great impact in the lives of the students, opening weekdays and Saturdays.

His mother had instilled in him and his other siblings, the principle of giving back and lending a helping hand to others. 'How fruitful have you been with what God has given you?' she would ask them on a regular basis

71

while they were growing up. Then, she would add, 'Always let the blessings of God flow through you to touch others. Let them know, not only are you thinking about them but that you are doing something to help them.'

Thinking about his mother brought another smile to Larry's face. She was a testament of God's faithfulness. And what did Mama say about Fridays, 'If you've made it to Friday, that's something to shout about.'

Almost two hours later, Larry meandered through the beautiful garden at Chateau de Kanate to find his mother. "Mama," he called out.

No response came.

He stood for a moment, watching the warm rays of sunlight shining through the elegant purity of blossoming garden. *She could be anywhere*, he deliberated as yellow petals danced in the gentle breeze around him.

Then he remembered.

He took another five-minute walk deeper into the garden, and his pride soared when he saw his mother. She was sitting in one of her favorite spots – near a pear tree. She seemed oblivious of the soft white petals floating around her before settling on the grass. Her head was buried in a book and he had no doubt that it was the Bible.

She lifted her head and stared at Larry momentarily, before leaping out of the chair to hug him.

"My son!" she squealed with joy. She had the knack for making him feel like he was her favorite child, actually her only child. Yet, he knew she loved her other children.

"Mama!"

She held him at arm's length, her large, light-brown eyes joyful. "I'm so glad to see you on this beautiful day."

"You too, Mama. Beautiful day, but you know it's going to be pouring later today."

She smiled at him. "Sounds like life. Come sit with me. Have you had breakfast?"

"Yes, but I'll have a glass of apple juice," he told her, walking towards a table that was laden with breakfast goodies.

"Let me get it for you." She smiled at him before reaching for the glass.

"Thanks, Mama." Larry returned her smile before moving to sit near the pear tree.

"What are you up to?" his mother asked, handing him a glass of apple juice.

He was silent for a moment, his brows raised at the sight of his mother's red and white form fitting dress that clung to a surprisingly trim, five-feet-six-inch frame. Her salt-and-pepper, wavy hair was pulled back in a loose ponytail to show off her beautiful heart-shaped face.

"Thanks, Mama," he said, before taking a sip of the juice. "What am I up to?" he repeated her question, his face crumpling. *Is she seeing someone?* Lord knows she deserved happiness after her life of misery with his father, real estate mogul, Peter Kanate. He had passed from a heart attack, some five years ago.

Unaware that his mother was observing him, Larry smiled. He would have some tough questions for the dude if she was dating again.

"Had me worried for a moment with that look on your face," Darlene said as she sat next to Larry.

"Worried?"

"You seemed far away."

He eyed her. "Are you dating? The air around you seemed a bit different."

His mother grinned at him. "Would you have a problem with that?"

"No, Mama," Larry hastened to tell her. "Just curious."

Darlene smiled, for she knew him only too well. *That man would get no peace.* "No, I'm not seeing anyone.

But it's great to know you would not have a problem with it."

Larry chuckled. "I know what you're thinking. That man would get no peace, right?"

"I'm sure he would. Right after you got his background check, fingerprints, and all. Well, that's if he survived the many interrogation sessions." She smiled at him. "Your father was not all bad, you know."

His jaws dropped. He had to hide it by turning to place his drink on the small table next to him. "Mama, not disrespecting you, but really?"

She got up and walked a few paces, before turning to face him, her expression introspective.

"Mama, he was abusive," Larry all but shouted. "You of all people shouldn't forget."

Darlene drew a long breath, preparing for the discussion she knew she couldn't avoid. "Yes, he was abusive, Larry. I'm not denying that."

Frustrated, Larry stood up. "But you're making excuses for him, Mama. Not only was he abusive but he was a womanizer, of the worst sort ... everyone around us knew about his affairs. He never hid them. All up in your face with that mess."

She smiled and calmly reached for his hand. "Come sit with me, son. Don't upset yourself."

Running a hand over his low-cut, black hair, Larry let out a ragged breath before returning to the chair with her. Even so, he stared straight ahead.

"Look at me, Larry," she said quietly, releasing his hand.

But Larry didn't. Instead, he closed his eyes and drew in a tight breath, the kind that steadies you when the hurt is way too deep for you to immediately cry.

"Larry," his mother called out quietly.

"I don't want to look at you right now, Mama," he managed to say.

"Son, I know you love me. You would move heaven and earth for your Mama. I get that."

He glanced at her, tears brimming, but did not speak.

"So let's talk. I know you wished I hadn't stayed with your father, the monster." She grasped his hand that was fidgeting on his leg.

Larry responded in a harsh whisper. "I hated that I couldn't help you and," he paused for a moment to dry his eyes with the back of his hand, "and I hated it even more that you stayed with him. I hated that I had to see the marks he left on your face. I hated that you were always sad."

Darlene let her heart relax. "Son, listen to me. I'm so sorry. You were young and you should never have witnessed the abuse I suffered. Now that you are older, there is no need for you to carry that burden. It is over. It had been over, for a long while." She clutched his shoulder, and moved closer. "I'm sorry too that I disappointed you. I'm not making excuses for your father; what he did was wrong. But he was not always like that. We started off well, but things got real bad after the death of his father and he had to take over the family business. Everything changed between us. A lot happened back then. I'm thankful I survived."

Peter Kanate had inherited the family business from his father, Etalon, a French-American business tycoon whom the press described as having the Midas Touch. In his father's eyes, Peter did not possess the prowess to help carry out the vision he had for Kanate Management and Realty Corporation, so after Peter inherited the business, he spent many of his waking hours at the office trying to prove just that.

Later in life, since he didn't get along with Larry, he'd taken Zane and Zadan under his wings and schooled them in the running of his empire. Still, he'd secretly hoped Larry would come on board, so he stated in his will that Larry should be the Chief Operating Officer. Larry, of course, never took up that position. Not for lack of trying on his mother's part, because her husband had always begged her to convince Larry to run the corporation. Still, Larry was not interested, telling her, 'Sorry, Mama. Not my calling.'

Darlene clasped her hands to her chest. "Yes. I'm grateful too that I didn't die on the journey and that I lived to testify of God's faithfulness. There are a lot of things that I know now that I didn't know then. That's why I share my story and minister to women. That's why I set up over forty Victorious Women's Shelter in so many states. I'm helping to empower women and at the same time give some of them a second chance at life.

"I'm sorry, Mama." A pensive expression shrouded Larry's face. "I shouldn't have said what I said."

"You're fine, son." His mother squeezed his hand. "Please let it go. It happened already, and no amount of sorry or words can fix it. I have to pay it forward. Don't-don't you ..." She choked up. "Don't you dare think, I don't ask myself why I didn't leave. I'm sorry, son."

Larry got down on his knees and hugged her. "Sorry, Mama."

"It's okay, son," she said, stroking his hair. "Every day, I walk in victory. Every moment God's grace is with me. Every time I lay my head down and rise again, it's a great accomplishment." She kissed the top of his head, and then smiled. "We're going to make it. We are trusting in Jesus, so we're going to make it. One hundred percent guaranteed."

CHAPTER 9

A crash of thunder reminded Rozene of the bleak night and provided the perfect ambiance for what she was experiencing - total defeat. Surrendering to her feeling, she threw herself atop the bedspread and curled up near the edge of the bed. The digital clock on the nightstand indicated 10:30 PM, yet sleep was nowhere in sight. She'd even tried writing again but nothing flowed from her usually sharp, creative mind. Not even after mentally gluing herself to the chair.

Shifting her body, she pulled back the bedspread and then moved beneath it. She studied the ceiling considering the memories she and Larry had made in that very room ... sharing their dreams, their joys, and their sorrows. Some days, they would talk until sunrise. She remembered how sometimes he would fall asleep during their conversation and she would listen to him breathe on the other line before attempting to wake him up.

She wondered if she should call him to see how he was doing. At least, they were communicating, even if only in monosyllables. They were careful not to let Mason and Madison know that they were separated. At least, she'd pressured Larry into that agreement. She hadn't decided how and when they would drop that bit of news on the children since their classes were still in session. It had to be soon though because summer was approaching.

Mason and Madison had come home last Christmas, when all was seemingly well between her and Larry. When they did come home for a few days in the spring semester, Larry was traveling on work related activities. Thankfully, the children were accustomed to calling their cell phones so they had no inkling of their separation.

Rozene picked up her cell phone, noting she had an unknown caller. She wondered if it was Chandler. She

77

hadn't heard from him since that mess of a call he made to her a few weeks ago.

She dialed Larry's number.

"Yes."

Her heart welled up with sheer joy that he'd answered, but it didn't translate in her response. "It's me." She wondered where that weak, needy voice came from.

"I know. Is there something that you need?" he asked, pacing his tone.

She could hear his emphasis on the word need. "I was just seeing how you're doing."

"I'm good," he responded coolly.

She waited for him to ask her likewise. When he didn't, she blurted out, "Larry, you could have asked how I am doing."

He gripped the phone. "You know I'm not a hypocrite." *I am not interested in another empty, eye-rolling conversation with you.*

"Okay," she said, her frustration obvious, "have a good -"

"Can't sleep?"

"Yes."

He couldn't sleep either. They had been married for so long that neither of them knew how to sleep without the other. Even with months of separation, it had not gotten any easier. He'd taken to putting a king-size pillow in her spot and hugging it.

"Have you tried praying?" Larry asked. "That usually works for me."

"Yes, I have."

"Well, maybe you need to call your special friend."

Rozene gasped as a sharp pain hit her heart and then intensified. "Wha-what? I told you I'm not seeing-"

"That's what you said, Rozene. Who knows?"

"Larry, stop it. Why are you saying that? I love you … always have."

"You sure have a strange way of showing it."

She could hardly get the words out. "I do love … you. I -"

"Only, you love yourself more," he interjected.

"Larry, please -"

"Like I said, you have a strange way of showing it. I hope sleep comes soon. I have a project to work on early morning so I have to go."

"Bye," she said quickly, hanging up.

Tears slid down her face, and her sobs came out louder and faster. She flipped on her stomach and buried her head in her pillow, hoping her parents did not hear her.

Fifteen minutes later, she curled up, still sobbing. Thinking about her future, she shuddered even more, the enormity of her past failure once again catching up with her.

That evening in Chicago, after Chandler had left her room with the box of books, she'd taken a bath and crept into bed but sleep was nowhere in sight. When 9:00 PM came, she got dressed and decided to relax in the lounge at the hotel.

It was a quiet evening and several guests were hanging out, but the area was not crowded when she ordered a glass of non-alcoholic wine. The lounge had comfortable couches and chairs but she selected a table in the corner where she could watch television while she sipped her wine.

Almost an hour later, she caught herself yawning and covered her mouth. *Time to hit the sack*, she thought glancing around. Her eyes widened as they landed on Chandler, who was sitting on a bar stool. *How did I miss him?* Her body temperature rose with his gaze as his dreamy eyes traveled her body, and then locked on hers.

Oh God! She could actually feel the blood rushing through her veins and her heart was thudding out of control.

He flashed a hello-beautiful smile, moving in her direction.

Watching his every step, she wished she was not so drawn to his fit anatomy. By the time he arrived before her, she was swooning like a teenage girl over the cutest boy in school.

"I-I was just leaving," she told him, gathering her purse.

A stirring sensation stemmed from his eyes, and he flashed her a disarming smile, offering his arm. "Me too."

She was about to refuse but did not want to make a scene. She tucked her hand in his arm, murmuring, "You don't have to."

"I want to," he told her as they moved off.

They walked out of the lounge, then across the foyer to the bank of elevators. She withdrew her hand as he pressed the up arrow.

While they waited, she happened to glance at his hand and noticed he wasn't wearing his wedding band. "What happened to your wedding band?"

He appeared surprised at her question. "I didn't know you were observing me so keenly, Mrs. Kanate." He smiled at her. "I hope you like what you saw."

Her brows crashed together. "Why did you have to go there?" *Don't know why I even asked. It's none of my business.*

The elevator came and he allowed her to step in before joining her. "I am not married," he said, pressing the number to her floor on the side panel of the elevator. "I like to wear a wedding band to hopefully scare off the ladies."

She looked at him, trying to see if he was being pompous, but his expression was one of frustration. "Well, sorry on behalf of my specie."

He chuckled, displaying immaculate white teeth as the elevator came to a stop. "Don't be."

His hand scorched the small of her back where it rested as they walked in silence to her room door. She swiped her key. "Thanks for the company," she said, entering her room. "Have a good night." She turned to close the door and bumped into him. "Ouch!" she gasped, gazing at his solid chest.

He closed the door, and scooped her into his arms. "Did I hurt you?"

Her stomach flipped. Warning bells turned to clanging cymbals as desire welled up in her belly. Her mind was yelling, "Nooooooo!" but her body was certain this was where it needed to be. She murmured something unintelligible, and his fingers tipped her chin and forced her gaze towards him.

"Tell me you want me as much as I want you," he said, running his hands down her back.

All her thoughts ceased. All of them, as a surge of heat washed up her body. Her breath was exploding out of her lungs. She closed her eyes tight to avoid speaking, yet struggling with her primitive response to him.

"Hmmm," he purred, enjoying the deliciousness of the warmth emanating from their bodies. "Don't be afraid, sweetheart."

His voice sent butterflies through her stomach, and when their eyes met, she sucked in her breath as she witnessed the flames of desire in his eyes, eyes that held one intention … consuming her.

The phenomenon sent waves of desire to her core, and her body shuddered against his. "Chandler, I-I-"

"You won't regret it," he told her softly, his hands tightened against the soft skin at her waist.

Unexpectedly, he gently swayed her in a slow intimate dance that wreaked havoc on her sensibilities. He brushed his lips along the curve of her jaw, slowly making his way to her lips.

Oh God! She was terrified he would find her lips, and then would be horribly disappointed if he didn't. She would definitely question her sanity later.

A satisfied "yes" issued from the back of her throat when his lips finally found hers. He parted her lips and began delivering slow, long kisses designed to drug her. It was as if he was sampling his favorite meal, and couldn't get enough. Her moans of delight only served to fuel his hunger. He lifted his lips from hers, feeling elated. No … more like ecstatic. Had he died and gone to heaven? Maybe he had, her languid expression indicated pure bliss.

But in a matter of seconds, her expression changed … to one of wide-eyed astonishment.

Stop it! Stop it! Echoed so loudly in Rozene's ears that she thought someone was yelling at her.

Chandler dotted her lips with butterfly kisses, but noticed her lips were tense against his. "It's okay, sweetheart," he said softly between kisses, "it's okay."

But, Rozene couldn't relax. All she kept doing was shutting down warning messages that were springing up behind each other in her brain. Images of Larry, her children, her ministry, and her relationship with God.

"N-nooo." She tore her lips away from his and dropped her forehead on his chest. "I can't."

He slipped a hand up the small of her back while the other hugged her waist. "Hey. Hey. It's going to be all right," he said, kissing the top of her head.

He lifted her chin with his hand and she looked at him. In that instant, in the dim light, her heart leaped at the

82

sweetness of the desire in his eyes. She watched his eyes dilate as he dipped his head towards her lips again. "Let's have a little fun," he begged softly. "You can tell me when to stop."

The vibrations in his husky voice stirred her senses. And against everything she knew to be prudent, she nodded.

He wasted no time. His mouth found hers again, teasing her with desire.

She moaned softly clenching his shirt and pressing her body against his as he cupped the back of her head and kissed her deeply, thirstily. When he scooped her up in his arms, she curled up against him like her life depended on him.

His eyes lit up and a slow smile spread across his face as he headed for her bedroom.

******

Early the next morning, Chandler smiled lovingly at her as he got dressed. "I've fallen in love with you."

She returned his smile, tying the belt on her robe around her waist. "But you don't know me, Chandler."

"Oh, yes, I do. You bet I do." His knowing smile put his teeth on display.

"Behave. I'm not talking about that … way."

He chuckled and then stopped abruptly as if he wanted to say something but changed his mind.

She couldn't read his thoughts. "You okay?"

"Nothing will wipe this smile from my face," he told her softly. "Absolutely nothing!"

She gave him a brilliant smile of her own. "Glad I can make you smile."

In silence, they walked towards the door with his hand draped around her shoulder.

He turned her to face him as they arrived at the door. "I'm in love with you," he told her quietly, running his fingers through her rumpled, curly hair then smoothing it down. Satisfied with his handiwork, he placed his back against the door.

She could feel the passion he had for her. Frankly, it kindled her desire for him. But love? That was not what this was. She was a mental mess but she had all intentions of keeping the vows she'd made to Larry Randolph Kanate. "Chandler, I-I can't-"

"Come away with me," he said.

As he awaited her reply, his eyes lowered to her mouth and he ran his fingertips lightly over her full lips. She closed her eyes, unable to bear the shivers that were churning through her body. He kissed her deeply then released her, deciding he should leave before it was too late.

"If you ever need anything, please don't hesitate to call me."

Still gasping for breath, she nodded unable to speak.

With that, he blew her a final kiss, opened the door and closed it behind him.

The rolling of thunder forced Rozene out of her reverie. Tears spilled as dark thoughts gathered like a storm in the horizon. "Why, oh why, did I have to go there? Lord, help me," she groaned in the pillow.

"And, He will," she thought she heard someone say.

She became still, clutching the pillow and wondering if she was hearing things.

"It's not over, not yet. You'll have to reach for what you want."

She took the pillow from her face and looked into her mother's smiling face.

All choked up, she couldn't return her mother's smile.

"I was knocking," her mother told her, perching on the side of the bed. "With all this thundering, I came to check on my baby."

Someone cares. Rozene's eyes watered.

"Now, don't start that again." Her mother touched her hand. "It's going to be okay."

"I don't know, Mom. Larry is not really speaking to me. The children will be home sooner rather than later. I'm the bad person in all of this. And for what?"

"Do you love him? This Chandler."

"What? No, Mom! I -"

"Think about it. Do you love him?"

Rozene squeezed her fingers into the palms of her hands. "Mom, I have thought about it. I don't love Chandler. What we did had nothing to do with love. I was attracted to him. Not just attracted, violently attracted to him, I will say that. But I don't love him. I don't care if I ever see him again. I love Larry. Always have and always will."

Elizabeth Bennady looked at her daughter whom she had been praying for daily. She hated to see her sitting around moping, every single chance she got, and literally wasting her life away when she was so gifted. Tonight, she intended to give her tough love. She could handle it. She was a Bennady woman, a woman with a great sense of self. It was time for Rozene to rise from the ashes she had created.

"Rozie, you are not stupid. You teach women to honor their husbands. There is a reason why you committed adultery. You are the most rational woman I know. Does that mean every time you're attracted to a man, you intend to sleep with him?"

Rozene's head jerked up as if her mother had struck her. "Mom, no!" She pulled herself up to lean against the headboard. It was painful to face the reality of the mess

85

she'd created in her life. She looked at her hands as she spoke. "I was afraid of the change that was about to come my way with the children leaving home. It would be me and Larry at home and somehow, I just never felt I was going to be enough for him."

Her mother watched her. "I have known Larry since you've both been in high school and his only desire was to marry you. He was only seventeen when he told me and your father that. We begged him to wait until you finished your first degree. And he did. You've both done well for yourselves and with the kids gone, it would have been a great time to reconnect. At least, that's what Larry told me and your father. He couldn't wait to have you to himself again."

Rozene's eyes widened. "Really. I didn't get that feeling and it's not because he didn't tell me that he loved me." A quiet sob escaped her. "Oh, God, please help me. I want my husband back."

Her mother eyed her. "I am suggesting that you pray and ask God to reveal to you, the real reason you brought that man into your marriage. Come now, give your mother a hug."

Rozene hugged her mother tightly, and her mother cradled her. "Rozie, it's going to be all right. God is on the case. In this tough season, He'll make everything smooth."

Rozene sighed contentedly. She trusted God even though He seemed to have disappeared in her storms. *Certainly felt like it.*

"All you need to get through this season is in you."

"Thanks, Mom," she murmured tearfully. "I'm so sorry for what I did. I am so-so ashamed. How will I explain to the children? They're going to hate me."

"Shhh." Her mother comforted her, stroking her hair. "It's going to be all right. You're just in between blessings."

Rozene snuggled closer. In her mother's arms was exactly where she needed to be.

Her mother was quiet for a moment before she began to make declarations over Rozene's life.

"You are God's masterpiece, a treasure in an earthen vessel. Your covering is the righteousness of Christ. You are like a tree planted by rivers of water that will bring forth fruit in season; your leaf shall not wither; and whatsoever you do will prosper. Length of days is in your right hand and in your left are riches and honor.

I declare blessings over your life – Blessings shall come on you, and overtake you. Blessed shall you be in the city, and blessed shall you be in the field. Blessed shall you be when you come in, and blessed shall you be when you go out."

The favor and anointing of God are forever on your life. Fear will not, will not capture you and paralyze your strengths. You will keep on hoping, you will keep on praying, and you will keep on believing that God will make every crooked path in your life straight. He is God and He will do it. The Lord bless and keep you, in the name of Jesus Christ I pray, amen."

CHAPTER 10

Larry descended the double-helix stairs at Chateau de Kanate, wondering if he was spending too much time by himself, which was making him self-absorbed. For what else could have brought on that episode with his mother concerning his father.

He paused to roll his eyes to the sky before moving on. *What was I thinking?* His mother had been through enough. Yet, he had to admit he was glad to get it all off his chest, even if he had suddenly become a small boy during the process. He was glad too that his mother took it so graciously. But what else was she to do when her eldest child flipped out on her.

Still, he liked being at the Chateau, for only then could he stock up on his sleep without the malignant nightmares about his marriage that kept nibbling away his heart.

A few minutes later, Larry veered left of the kitchen and entered the sunroom. After greeting his mother with a kiss on her cheek, he took a seat across from her at the table. He prayed and they placed generous portions of food on their plate and began to eat lunch.

Since conversation was flowing between them, Larry decided to mention his infidelity, hoping to get another perspective. Pastor Fotola was still adamant that he should have that conversation with Rozene. *Again, for the record, Pastor Fotola, I have no intention of taking her back.*

Yet, Larry had to "fess" up to someone else that he trusted because he was tired of being miserable. Tired of pretending he was happy. Tired of wearing the, I'm-good smile. He didn't like being home alone. No, sirree. Rozene was a fixture, a constant in his life and he felt unbalanced without her.

Oh, God! As soon as he presented the situation to his mother, he regretted it. Apparently, he'd uttered the unforgivable. Perhaps, this would go down as the saddest Saturday morning in his life.

He'd witnessed his mother's transformation from shock to annoyance then anger and finally, disappointment. Even now her eyes accused him.

He felt like a small boy all over again. Like the time when he'd beaten up Zadan and she'd told him, 'Shame on you. You should be protecting him.' He'd never forgotten the look of disappointment in his mother's eyes. He was the oldest of the flock and she had always expected him to be the guardian.

Larry gave up a shamefaced expression as his mother continued to glare at him. Trying to explain the purpose of his existence on earth occurred to him, but when he opened his mouth no words came from his lips. Only her love and respect for him was keeping her this quiet.

He wondered if he was expecting too much from her. "Mama, I'll see you later," he told her, struggling to mask his disappointment.

Finally, she spoke. "Son, sit with me for a few minutes. I know you have the time."

"Mama, I know what I did to Gabrielle was wrong," he choked out. "I tried talking with her but she still refuses to take my calls. I cannot undo the past but I would like her to know that I'm sorry, from the bottom of my heart. It doesn't matter whether I tell Rozene or not. It's over between us."

Darlene frowned. "Are you seeing anyone now?"

Surprised, he looked at her for a moment, before responding. "No, I'm not. I have never cheated before. Never. I love …"

"I know you love Rozene," his mother filled in. "I remembered the glow on your face the morning after our

89

Thanksgiving charity ball where you laid eyes on her. You told me you had met a "gorgeous flower" but after breakfast, you said, 'Mama, she was an amazing experience. I'm going to marry her.'"

Larry remained silent.

"Son, I know what she did to you was wrong. But look at how you are treating her, when you did the same-"

"I did not ..." He stopped, realizing that he'd raised his voice at his mother for the first time. But he was red hot. "It's two different situations. She was in a relationship with that man."

"Larry, you don't know that. You didn't hear her side of the story."

"What's there to tell, Mama? She played me like a fool."

"So your feelings are hurt."

"I gave her everything. Everything. I can't believe she of all people - Holy Ghost filled, water baptized, Jesus on her mind - did that. If anyone told me she did anything remotely like that, I would have called him or her a liar. Without a thought. Flat out - a liar. But what can I say?"

"Son, I want you to leave Rozene out of this for a moment. Think about yourself, your life. This is not good. The way you are denying that you mirrored her sin." She held up her hand as he began to protest. "You did, son. You know Mama loves you. It would be wrong of me not to point this out to you. I mean you no harm. You need to check yourself. And you need to find it in your heart to forgive her, for your sake."

Agitated, he stared beyond her out the window.

"Son, I know she did you wrong. Sure, she did. But you did her wrong too. How do you think she will feel if she ever found out what you did? You practically threw her out of the house." She paused, seeing he had morphed into some kind of stature. "Son," she said gently, "please, let the Lord lead you."

"Okay, Mama." He rose stiffly from his seat. "I'll talk with you later."

"Okay, love. Later then. God bless you."

"You too, Mama," he said, lightly kissing her cheek, before leaving the room.

Fifteen minutes later, Larry drove away from Chateau de Kanate, still miffed. He was at least hoping for a little compassion from his mother, even if she did not understand his situation. *Mirrored sin, huh?* The thought made him angrier.

But he had been raised right...

He was raised to be a gentleman, so after conducting the seminar at the Learning Center, he would call and apologize to his mother. Her intentions were honorable, but she was mistaken.

CHAPTER 11

Shivers of anxiety hit Don's stomach as he stood waiting for Rozene in her parent's living room. It seemed like Rozene was now permanently at her parents' home. He feared the worst. This was not good. He hoped his predictions were incorrect.

"Don," Rozene called out to him, disrupting his thoughts.

"Praise the Lord, dear lady. Good to see you."

"Praise the Lord. Good to see you, too." She hugged him warmly before releasing him.

He smiled fondly at her. "The pleasure is all mine. Absolutely wonderful to see you. It's been a while you know." He shuddered playfully. "I almost called the FBI. You had me running scared for you." Seriously, I am worried about you, he wanted to say. Her spirit was different so he knew she was going through something. He was thankful her winning smile remained even though her eyes lacked the usual vibrancy.

Smiling, she patted his back. "No need. Here, I am. Would you like something to drink?"

"No, but thank you. I want to get down to business. Time for us to hit the road again, right?"

She gave him a tight smile. "We'll see." Then, leading the way, she told him. "Let's use Dad's office."

A few minutes later, they entered the office and sat on two huge, brown leather sofas that gave them a great view of the backyard.

"Hope you've been looking at the reports," Don remarked, smiling. "The ministry is growing just as we've been praying. God has been super goooood. And I must tell you, my wife is really enjoying filling in for you. She has become mini you."

"Way to go, Marianne." Rozene couldn't help but laugh. "She and I have been chatting. Glad she's loving her new role in the ministry." Rozene became still, looking down at her hands where her fingers were locked in a tight ball in her lap. "Thank God for," her voice broke with gratitude, "you and her."

Don touched her shoulder. "And we thank God for you too. We love being a part of your ministry.

"Thanks, Don." She gave him a taut smile.

He smiled back at her. "Now, let's get down to business."

She nodded.

As customary, he prayed, then he opened his black portfolio and filled her in on what was happening in her Ministry. Things were going great as he had mentioned but as he droned on about the increase in book sales and her growing viewership and readership, her heart sank. *How can I in all honesty teach about love? About faithfulness? Family life? Marriage?*

"I responded to an email from a lady," Don told her. "Her name is Delly, I believe. She said she heard your session about loving your husband and you were so profound, she got the courage to return to her marriage." He clapped his hands, elated. "Isn't God great and -"

"I can't do this anymore, Don," she blurted.

"Roz, don't say that. You've been on a break for over four months. You can't hide away forever," he said gently. "It's called Rozene Kanate Ministry, you know. Remember, we're publishing, *Letters to Wives* so I've been busy planning your book tour for the fall. I have a few press releases for you to go over and I'm renegotiating your contract with TBC Television Station. The station wants you desperately."

Her shoulders slumped. "As you know, I'm having family issues. I don't know when they will be resolved."

That much he'd gathered. He'd even tried several times to reach out to Larry, but he'd been away for a while, and 'couldn't talk'. He knew Larry was just making up excuses. The last two times he'd called, Larry told him he was at Chateau de Kanate.

Rozene flashed Don a woebegone look, hanging her head in shame. "I'm not-not … I have no right to be doing this."

Don was silent for a moment before asking, "Are you staying with your parents … permanently?"

"Yes." She decided to be honest with him. He and Marianne had been nothing but devoted, kind, and trustworthy. After all, he could be affected if all of this went south. Tears brimming, she continued, "I know you always wanted me to write about the other side of love … unfaithfulness, lust of the eyes … now I might be able to do all that and more, perhaps divorce."

Don listened, hardly believing his ears. That was the last thing he expected to hear from her. He jumped from his seat and looked out the window, trying to contain his anger. He swung around to face her. "Ugh! I want to hurt him for doing this to you. Rozene, I'm so sorry. I have known Larry for years. All he talks about is you. I can't imagine how he could have done this to you."

She shook her head at him, opening her mouth to speak as he moved towards her. "Don …" She paused as he knelt before her and held both her hands in his.

"So sorry, Rozene," he said. "I never expected this from him."

She wished she had the heart to blame it on Larry so she wouldn't see the disappointment in Don's eyes when she made her confession. But, alas. She knew a part of the healing process was acceptance of the sin she'd committed.

"It's not Larry's fault, Don."

He eyed her puzzled. Then, shock and disbelief covered his face as the truth dawned on him.

"Yes, I am the one who committed adultery," she confessed, staring above his head. "But I'm not in the situation anymore."

He released her hands, and moved to sit on the sofa; and then he too began to stare ahead.

Rozene glanced at his stoic frame. She would understand if he decided to leave her ministry. He was a man who upheld Godly principles. *God help us all, when the others from the ministry find out.* She couldn't help the tears that spilled down her cheeks.

Don pulled tissue from the box on the small table next to him, and handed a wad to her.

She took the tissue and wiped her eyes.

Don watched her and his heart broke. *I need to pray for her daily.*

"I'm so sorry, Don. Please forgive me," she pleaded.

The kindness in his eyes brought fresh tears to hers. She was glad he did not pry further. For he probably would have passed out if he'd found out it was Chandler. Not that she would ever tell him.

"There is nothing to forgive. I want you to focus on taking care of yourself and your family. Are you getting help to heal?"

"Yes. I-I have had counseling sessions with Dr. William Thayer for about two months. Not sure if you know the name. He's a world-renowned marriage and family therapist. Now, Mom has taken over. She has been praying me through."

"Great. Glad your mother is taking care of you. Glad too that you choose a faith-based therapist. Dr. Thayer is very good."

Her head swung in his direction and her eyes held a surprised look.

He smiled encouragingly at her. "Hey, we all have issues that need to be resolved. What about..." He stopped short, unsure whether to ask.

"Truthfully, Larry is pretty much hating me right now. Rightly so." She let out a defeated sigh and Don could see her withdrawing into the comfort of her protective shell. "He has done nothing to deserve this."

"Rozene, you are a mature believer. This situation will not destroy you. You are on the path to being whole. Stay with God's plan and let Him work it out. I know you are praying for His guidance and direction, and I will definitely continue to pray for you and Larry. You are going to make it through this."

She eyed him gratefully. "Thanks, Don."

He stood. "We are going to keep things afloat as long as we can, so take all the time you need to sort yourself out."

She rose and hugged him. "Thanks for everything."

"You are welcome. Always."

She walked with him to the front door, and was looking at him descending the steps when he turned to face her. "Don't go," he said, "Chandler gave me an envelope to give to ..." He watched the color drain from her face.

"Are you okay?" he asked, rushing to her side.

"I'm okay," she told him trying to regain her composure but not meeting his eyes.

"Are you sure? You look like you were about to faint. It's just an envel ..." The word died on his lips, and he turned away from her. "Let me get it for you."

Don legs felt as heavy as logs, but somehow they managed to take him to his car. He opened the door trying to regain a normal breathing pattern. *Rozene and Chandler? No. Error. Delete now*, he commanded his brain, feeling sick in his stomach. *What on God's green earth?* But he couldn't shake the feeling as he rummaged through the glove compartment and found the envelope. He wondered what was inside. *Is Chandler forcing or threatening to expose her? No.* That was not Chandler's modus operandi. He had more of a love-them-and-blow-them-off style. His ego was too big to go there. Plus, what would he gain from that. He would not only ruin her, but himself.

Don quickly closed the glove compartment and walked back to Rozene who had now regained her mask. He dared not probe her, especially since she had not divulged that pertinent bit of information when she was spilling a while ago. Just as well. He didn't think he could handle it anyway.

He handed her the envelope and she gave him a brief smile. "Thanks."

Her hands were shaking as she took the envelope but he pretended not to see. "Chandler has been out of state," he told her. "The job, you know."

No. I don't know. "Okay." She tried to keep her voice light, hoping she sound more like - *That does not concern me.*

"Take care, Rozene," he told her in a voice he thought was too firm, before turning and heading to his car.

"I will," she said quietly. "Bye."

Soon afterwards, Rozene marched into her bedroom and flung the envelope into the small garbage bin next to the desk. She hissed her teeth when she missed and the envelope landed on the floor near the bin. She glared at the envelope wishing it was Chandler so she could wring his neck.

Annoyed, she stomped off towards her bed and fell face down on the bedspread with a loud groan. She could only hope Don didn't pick up anything. *Jesus, fix it. Lord, please fix it.*

She rolled on her back, staring blindly at the oval shaped ceiling. *I must keep focus. Too much to do.* With that she reached for her cell phone on the nightstand to call her children. For in this season, it was critical that she continue to build an even stronger, more secure relationship with them.

CHAPTER 12

Larry spread out in the chair around the desk in the study, and gave himself a much needed stretch. Then, yawning widely, he powered down his laptop. He would definitely be ready for leadership meeting tomorrow at work.

He was about to lift himself to full height when his cell phone rang. He retrieved it from the desk and let out a loud groan when he looked at the screen. It was Rozene. He watched it ring, and ring some more, and then he remembered his mother's words - 'What if Rozene was calling about the children?'

This had better be good. He sank deeply on the chair and answered, "Hello."

Rozene was overjoyed he'd answered. Better still, he'd moved on from answering with that dry 'Yes'.

"Larry, hi. How's it going?"

"Good. You?"

Well! Well! Even if he didn't mean it, he was trying to be civil. "Good. I'm not sure if the children called you, they got internships for the summer." She rushed on breathlessly, "So they are both doing summer classes and then the internships after." She paused to get his response.

"Yes. I spoke with them."

"Oh, great. Wasn't sure you did. So, how was your day?"

Larry forehead furrowed. He absolutely hated when she did that – pretended like they could have a regular conversation. "Good. It has been a long day. I'm going to call it quits. Have a good night."

Rozene's heart sank but she managed to maintain her cool. "Okay, great. Have a good night too. Bye."

"K."

Larry stared at his phone briefly before dropping it into his shirt pocket. He knew she wanted to talk longer but he was not accommodating her, and he was tired.

Shortly thereafter, he headed to the bathroom, grabbed a quick shower, and slipped between the sheets. He stretched himself fully, murmuring, "Yes. Yes. Just what the doctor ordered," before he launched into prayer.

The prayer energized his mind, for now he was staring at the ceiling. Frustrated, he rolled on his side, and his eyes landed on the wall that had a huge photo of him and Rozene on their wedding day.

Happy day. His mouth twitched into a tight smile, before turning down. He was morphing into sadness when he reached across the nightstand and turned off the light. But he refused to cry. *Why cry over someone who has already let you go?*

Although, his mind resisted, his traitorous heart went back in time.

The first time he laid eyes on Rozene was in the high school's cafeteria. One look at her and his life was changed forever. 'Completely derailed,' according to Benson, his cousin.

He was jesting with his crew at the lunch table, when her curly, light-brown hair came into his view. Unfamiliar desire stirred in his loins. He remained fixated … watching her, deep in discussion with her three friends, two tables behind his table.

She must have felt his eyes for she looked up. He was sure his eyes bulged, as he gazed into her stunning hazel-colored eyes. Their eyes held, and at that moment, he became perfectly still, his imagination roaming into forbidden territory. He was brought out of his stupor by the deafening silence from his buddies, who had begun to look for what he was staring at.

"You okay, man?" Benson asked. "You look like you'd seen a ghost."

Laughter followed, and he shifted his gaze to Benson. "Yes. I'm looking at one."

As soon as he could, he excused himself to walk to the buffet line. Of course, he deliberately took the path to pass by the table where the "gorgeous flower" was sitting.

A gorgeous flower. Yes, she is, he decided as he slowly walked by her table.

She glanced at him, and if she noticed his fixation, she didn't respond to it.

He was trying to decide which drink to pick up, while strategizing how to meet the gorgeous flower, when a melodious voice said, "Hi there."

He almost suffered a whiplash when his seventeen-year-old head whipped to his right where the voice originated. And there she was. Standing a few feet from him. Smiling and exposing her perfect white teeth.

Eyes glistening, he drank in the sight before him.

Soft, full lips

Perfectly positioned straight nose.

Beautiful oval-shaped face.

Tall and well-proportioned body.

Her caramel complexion was flawless, and he almost reached out a hand to pull on her long curly, light-brown hair.

Coming out of his stupor, his gaze slid back to her eyes, and he was certain his heart stopped for a few hot seconds, for he found himself with a death grip on the counter before him as electrical vibrations saturated his body.

She smiled boldly at him and he opened his mouth, but his voice refused to come forth. He gave her what should have been a charming smile, but instead the smile felt more like a grimace. He then tried to speak again, but

101

his, "Hello there," came out like a grunt instead. His heart flip-flopping, he nodded, and left in the opposite direction.

He had seen her a few times during that same fall semester but he was determined not to engage her in any conversation. He was still trying to let go of the embarrassing moment when they had first met. Nevertheless, she'd piqued his interest, so he'd investigated and found out that she was Rozene Bennady, a transfer student from another prominent high school. Thanks to Benson, he had also learned that she was one year younger and a year behind him in tenth grade. Since his high school supported not only brainy but rich students, Benson thought she 'came from money'.

His next close up with Rozene was later that year at his parents' Thanksgiving charity ball at home and their encounter was equally fascinating. She staged what they later dubbed, "The Slickest Escape."

There he was, busy wearing an intelligent look as a senator engaged him in conversation in the grand ball room, when he saw her across the room wearing a knowing smile. Albeit, she was surrounded by fawning young men. He faded in and out of the conversation, wondering how to step away from the exuberant senator, and then, almost swallowed his tongue when he saw her making a beeline for him.

He watched her. Fixated, the same way he'd been the first time he'd seen her. She gracefully sashayed across the floor, her black evening gown hugging her delicious curves and accentuating her movement as it cascaded to the floor. She looked every bit part of this elegant affair. Their eyes connected and he could feel the adrenaline rush between them. She stopped in front of him, smiling.

Oh, man. He all but lost his cool as the faint scent of her perfume filled his nostrils. *Stop the love struck behavior*, he almost hollered at himself, before flashing her

102

a toothy smile. She grinned right back at him before greeting the senator, "Good evening, Senator Cole. How are you?"

The senator gave her a welcoming smile. "I'm doing great, Miss Bennady. Wonderful to see you again."

"You too, Senator Cole." She glanced at Larry, then back to the senator. "I'm soooo sorry but I need to steal my friend away for a few minutes. Hope you don't mind."

Inwardly, Larry chuckled. *She's good.*

Senator Cole smiled at her. "No. Not at all, Miss Bennady." He turned and extended his hand to Larry. "We'll pick up another time. You should think about getting into politics, young man."

"Politics. No way, senator," Larry responded shaking his hand. "But we'll pick up." He then offered his arm to the "gorgeous flower" and they escaped to the balcony on the west side of the grand ballroom. The laughter that started in their bellies quickly made way through their mouths, the minute the door closed behind them. They made their way to the edge of the balcony and held on to the railing, their shoulders shaking with laughter.

Rozene laughed so hard that the water running from her eyes ruined her barely-there makeup. Not that she needed makeup anyway.

And when he got his laughter under control, Larry told her in a dramatic voice, "Thanks for risking your life to rescue me."

She mopped her eyes with tissue from her small purse. "No worries." She grinned at him. "It's not every day I get to be a knightress in shining armor."

"Glad to be rescued by such a beautiful knightress. I'm Larry Kanate."

"I know who you are," she said, smiling, and extending her hand. "Nice to meet you. I am Rozene Bennady."

103

He shook her hand, and held on to it. "The pleasure is all mine, Roz."

"I bet it is," she responded in a slightly sarcastic voice, slipping her hand away from his. She eyed him questioningly. "Only, I never figured you for a cheesy kind of guy."

He gazed at the delicate crease of disappointment on her forehead, unable to understand their affinity for each other. "I don't usually mince words," he told her quietly. "The pleasure is all mine, Roz."

She smiled at him, and indicated her interest. "The pleasure is all mine, too."

His pulse picked up speed as he returned her smile. He was glad for a female that could hold her own in his presence. "Would you like to sit with me for a while?"

"Sure."

He offered his arm and she took it as they walked toward a large royal blue sofa.

"What do you do when you are not studying?" he asked when they were seated.

She was silent for a moment.

He watched her curiously. It was the first time he'd seen her at a loss for words. He leaned forward to peer at her. "Have I rendered you speechless? Already? I'm good."

"Never." She waved his comments away, grinning at him. "Don't know if I should tell you."

"Will I go to prison if I know? You know, I like you and all but that's a bit much to ask on a first date."

She chuckled. "So we're on a date now?"

"The first of many I hope."

"Well, ask me?"

Gosh, she's bold. "Will you date me?"

"But I don't know you. You could be a psychotic killer."

"Listen to your heart."

She laughed – the healthy yet girly kind of laughter, her eyes glistening with joy.

Oh, Man! I could listen to her laughter every day. "So?" he pressed her.

She smiled at him. "I'll date you, Larry Kanate."

He eyed her questioningly. "Did you do a research on me?"

"I didn't really have to Larry. The Kanate goodwill is well-known in this city."

He wondered if he was moving too fast with her. What if she was just after the family fortune? Not that he suspected she was. The air around her suggested that she 'came from money'. *Bennady? Bennady?* Her last name sounded familiar though he didn't know why. Then it dawned on him. She and her brother, Michel were heirs to the multi-billion dollar Bennady International Citrus Corporation.

"Yes. Bennady International," she filled in. "It was nice meeting you. I'm going to head back inside."

He held on to her arm to stop her, then snatched it back as she eyed him as if she pitied him. "No. I don't want your money," she told him, looking totally bored.

Heat rose from his neck to his scalp. "I'm-"

"What? Sorry? All the other girls who threw themselves at your feet want your family fortune. Well, I don't want your money. Neither am I waiting for my parents' money. God gave me a brain and I intend to use it. My family's fortune is great, but I intend to build my own legacy as the Spirit of God leads me."

Larry sat up on the chair. Stunned. Elated. He was feeling all kinds of emotions as he watched her speak. He really liked this girl.

"I'm sorry," he told her sincerely. "That has been my experience and I'm a little tired of it. But I'm glad you intend to follow God's blue print for your life. So do I."

She gazed past him.

"Don't you dare lock me out," he told her.

She looked deeply in his eyes, and he could tell that she was wondering if her personality was too bold for him.

"I can handle bold," he told her confidently. "Bold, brilliant, and beautiful." He smiled at her. "Love a sister who speaks her mind."

She was tickled. "Did you just come up with the three B words? Or, do you say them to all your little girlfriends?"

Gosh, she's quick too, he concluded. *No surprise there. No doubt in smart-talk training from birth.* "Little girlfriends?" He lifted his eyes upwards, before meeting her gaze. "Ignoring that. But what I will say is that, those three words simply sprang from my heart. And I'm going out on a limb here - I dare say, those three words aptly describe you. I want to add a few more, but my heart says wait."

Her eyes brightened. "Thank you." Crossing her legs, she smiled gently at him. "To answer your question, I do charity events during my spare time. My favorite, I would have to say, would be the dance classes at the performing arts center that Mom and Dad established in my name. I have been teaching liturgical dance at the center on Saturdays since I was ten years old." She uncrossed her legs and leaned towards him. "But what I really, really do in my spare time is write, and write, and write."

The joy in her voice made his insides jolt. "That is a beautiful thing. 'The idea is to write it so that people hear it and it slides through the brain and goes straight to the heart.'"

"Awww." She smiled widely at him. "Somebody knows a quote from Maya Angelou. Do you write?"

"No. But I like to read, pretty much a little of everything. What do you write?"

She looked surprised at his confession. He surmised that she thought he only read business magazines. "I write fiction and non-fiction books." Appearing a bit shy, her eyes begged him not to press her.

So he didn't.

"I have not published anything yet," she confessed. "Waiting on the Lord for the right timing."

"And I'm sure He'll let you know when to procced. At least that has been my experience. There's no time like the right time."

She was silent for a moment, before gazing at him. "Thank you."

"Your eyes are amazing. I feel like I'm drowning when I look at you."

Her lips draped to one side. "Then I'll always be your Knightress. My daring escape with you was my slickest to date. Feeling like superwoman right now. I might go ahead and put an "S" on my chest."

Larry laughed out, covering her hand with his. "Please do it. This I've got to see."

Silence fell over them and their eyes locked. They both became motionless, their emotional connection stretching to epic proportion, and instinctively they began to lean in.

"Roz," he heard himself whisper her name, as fireworks went off in his body.

She blushed, and sat up, staring ahead of her.

Slowly, he backed away, trying to regain his composure. He wanted to kick himself for appearing overly eager.

"Yes," she replied, still not looking in his direction.

He cocked a brow. *Yes? Yes, what?* He deliberated, watching her erect posture in anticipation.

"Yes, I will date you, exclusively," she filled in.

His heart climbed into his throat, and the familiar rush of excitement hit him. He wanted to hold her and kiss her until she begged him to stop. He clutched her hands. "Thank you, Roz. I'm going to make it worth your while."

"I'm going to make it worth your while, too." She tilted her head, a soft smile playing on her lips, and he knew his life would never be the same.

He never got to kiss his "gorgeous flower" that night, nor did he try to take advantage of the hug she was willing to give. But that night made history in their lives. That night was the beginning of, "Team La'Roz," as the students at their high school called them. Many other titles followed them - Most likely to succeed. Most likely to marry each other ... early. Match made in heaven. Most multi-talented couple ... and the list goes on.

They attended different colleges but they managed to maintain their relationship. After completing college, Larry worked for a year in the hotel industry, and they got married right after Rozene completed her first degree.

An unwanted slight smile tugged at Larry's mouth. His marriage had been a beautiful part of his life. He'd been proud of many things on their wedding day, but three things in particular ... well, truthfully, four things.

Firstly, he'd gazed at her during their lavish wedding ceremony and he knew he loved her ... and that she loved him.

Secondly, she was his wife. His wife. His heart had skipped several beats that day at that thought. It felt great to finally be able to call her Mrs. Rozene Kanate.

And thirdly, he was grateful that she fitted comfortably into his high-profile life, having been well-groomed from birth.

A Christian? Yes.

Loved the Lord? Yes.

In ministry for God? Yes.

Educated? Yes.

Charming and graceful? Yes.

Drop-dead gorgeous? Yes.

Diplomacy? Yes.

He was grateful too that she understood the protocols for their high-powered social engagements.

Check! Check! Check! He was a happy man.

And, the final reason for his happiness - they had waited to have sex and he couldn't wait to make love with her from sunset to sunrise.

Back then, they were not devoted Christians, but even so, they wanted to honor the Lord in this regard. It was difficult, but they were happy they achieved their goal and it was worth the wait.

At sunrise, he'd stirred, feeling the awesome effects of their unbelievable night. He lifted his head slightly to gaze at her beautiful features, highlighted by the soft glow of the morning light, where she cuddled by his side on the bed.

"Babes. Babes," he called out softly after a while, running his thumb gently over her lips which were swollen from their night of intense passion.

And when she did not budge, he kissed the tip of her nose, before scooping her up into his arms. "Roz," he murmured her name while slowly stroking her body.

He groaned as her hand caressed his cheek before holding his face in both hands and kissing him deeply. "Thank you," she said, when she had had enough.

He smiled down at her before shifting and pulling her onto his chest and wrapping his arms around her. They stayed like that for a little while before she lifted her face to his.

He claimed her mouth hungrily once again.

"You know we have each other for life," she teased, when he'd released her lips.

"Don't know about tomorrow, so I'm getting all of mine today."

"I'm all for that." She grinned at him, her senses on full alert, and he flashed her a suave dimpled smile, his eyes dancing with mischief.

"Husband, you can't keep looking at me like that," she pouted playfully.

"Like what?" he asked, threading his fingers through her hair. "Like you are the most exquisite woman I've ever met." He caressed the small of her back and she relished the pleasure of being in his arms.

"Yes," she murmured, her flesh tingling.

"But, you are. Amazingly beautiful. Love all that makes you, you. I love you," he said, smiling and pecking her lips. "You'll always be the best part of my mornings and my nights."

"I love you too. But what about during the day?" she asked breathlessly.

"Let me think." He rolled on top of her and kissed her slowly.

Gentle moans escaped her lips, and she clung to him.

Lifting his head, he smiled at her. "And the best part of my days."

A shiver of heat rushed down his spine as she traced his strong jawline with her fingertips. "Make love to me, my husband." She was breathing hard now, arching closer, the palms of her hands all over his back, gripping him in desperation. She pulled his mouth down hard on hers, and began kissing him passionately. She was ready to be loved … again. And the pleasure was all his.

Almost a year later, they were both enrolled at Yale School of Management pursuing the accelerated MBA program, and halfway through the program, Rozene broke the news that they were pregnant … with twins. Surprised. Yes, they were.

That seemed so long ago.

But even after nineteen years of marriage, he'd still found Rozene desirable. She not only challenged him intellectually but she was still fine. No. Hot! She had a body that beckoned to his primitive instincts. A body that constantly screamed I-am-yours-for-the-taking. And his appetite for her was still insatiable, and her passion for him had been nothing short of unbridled. The combustion between them could flatten the entire neighborhood. To top it all off, she loved the Lord, and was passionate about the things of God. Well, that was before The Chandler extinguished the flames; before everything blew up in his face.

Larry released a weary sigh, tossing to and fro on the bed to find a comfortable spot in the room where he and Rozene had spent nineteen years, filled with many unforgettable moments. His chest heaved with bubbles of loneliness and moisture filled his eyes, but he was determined not to cry.

CHAPTER 13

Chandler perched on a barstool in Pa'Dada Restaurant and Lounge sipping his drink while sizing up the crowd in an attempt to get his mind off his situation. He had discovered this upscale establishment when he'd moved to Orlando some five years ago. He loved it because he got a chance to hobnob with the restaurant's impressive, affluent clientele. Hanging with the crème de la crème of the community was more his style. And as much as he would like to sweep it under the carpet, what he had been accustomed to from birth.

But this evening, he was not in the mood to socialize. He was a drowning man. His plans to woo Rozene had failed miserably. Truthfully, they hadn't even got off the ground. A frustrated sigh escaped him and he ran his hand over his already disheveled hair as he battled poignant flashbacks of their times together.

There was no communication between them after their hot-hot encounter in Chicago. But that didn't mean she was not always on his mind. He had dated a few other women to get her out of his system but that didn't work. He then literally became a recluse. His only desire - to get home from work and watch her on YouTube or TV. He was constantly on her website and all her social media pages. He'd even taken to re-reading her books.

The unending silence between them was killing him slowly. He needed her and he needed her in a way that was foreign to him. He could hardly believe his own transformation into this supersensitive love machine. Oh, he was warm and fuzzy on the inside … all day … every day. *I carry her in my heart. I long to bask in her presence.* He'd found himself articulating sentimental phrases that he'd previously considered mindboggling, even stupid, when similar expressions were uttered by the women he'd dated.

At one stage, he had glanced at Rozene's profile shot on her Facebook author page, and heard himself breathlessly declaring, "She completes me." Yes, he was in love, hopelessly addicted to Rozene. That day, he scampered through Don's defense and got her number after giving him a story.

Rozene took his call.

Hearing her voice almost sent him over the edge, but he calmed himself. At first, she was against him calling but he assured her he wouldn't call often. Soon, his weekly calls turned daily and they began to develop a relationship of sort. They never met but it was not for lack of trying on his part.

His stomach clenched. *How can she not want us to be together?*

Us? He let out a ragged sigh. *There's no ... us.* First, she had to realize that she needed him as much as he needed her.

Only a few days ago, he'd returned home from his travels to Chicago, where he'd spent almost two months at Renauto's headquarters, leading the team that was developing a new product. Usually, he loved traveling because it afforded him the opportunity to take in new sights. Plus, a change of environment was always good. Now, traveling was like a burden because he had to leave his Ro behind. She was a little slow in accepting their relationship, but he was still hopeful. He had to, for he had already buried his little black book, and once again, "I do" was beckoning in the distance.

Shaking his head, a habit he recently developed to get his thoughts under control, he tried to focus. *Letters to Wives should be out in the fall. I'll turn up at one of her book signings. She needs to stop pretending we don't have*

113

something special going on between us. And if seeing her went anything like the last time ... *Ooh wee!* His breath came in short gasps as his entire body began to relive that moment.

He had cried when he had to spend last Christmas alone, so she promised that they would meet up early in the New Year. She kept her promise when she had to do a book signing in West Palm Beach, Florida, a three-hour drive from Orlando.

On the last day of her book signing, he checked into the same hotel. The anticipation had his heart pounding all day. When he entered her suite, he had to lean against the door to catch his breath, even though his eyes flowed over her from head to toe. Moments later, he followed her to the sofa and they stood there drinking in each other.

He knew her desire for him was strong, for he saw her literally holding her breath before stepping slightly away from him as emotions she had suppressed started to reemerge. She attempted a smile, "How are you?"

An unnecessary question, he thought. *Of course, you can see how I'm doing.* His eyes were raging with desire for her, and he was mentally commanding his hands to stay in place by his side.

"I'm much better now," he said in a sensuous timbre.

"Great." She admired the lean muscles of his fit anatomy.

"No hug. No love for Chandler." He gazed at her in the way he always did - with the longings of his heart on display.

A heart stopping smile lit her face, and whatever thread of control he was holding onto was forgotten, for in a second he lowered her on the sofa and they were doing exactly what they had pledged never to do again.

Beads of sweat formed on Chandler's forehead and slid down his neck, yanking him out of his musing. Shrugging his broad shoulders, he slammed the drink glass on the counter and decided to stop by the gym to unleash his pent up frustration before heading home.

CHAPTER 14

Chandler pulled up to his townhouse in the exclusive gated community of Baladere Estate, and saw that Don's black Lincoln Navigator was parked out front in one of his two parking spaces. He mentally slapped himself when he glanced at the clock on the dashboard. It registered 8:37 PM. He had forgotten, he was meeting Don at 7:00 PM. Thankfully, Don had a key so he didn't have to stay outside.

Don had called him when he was away to find out when he was returning. Since he came home on Saturday, and Sunday was his rest day, he had told Don that he could meet with him the following day. He peeped into Don's car before walking to the patio, with an apology ready on his lips.

He shared a close relationship with Don's family. He liked that because Don was his only brother, albeit half-brother. Although he and Don had never spoken about it, when he was younger, he'd heard through the conversations of relatives that Chandler's mother stole the heart of his father and they had run away together while his father was married to Nadine, Don's mother. By the time Chandler was born, his parents were married and there was never any discussion about Don's mother. Nadine never remarried but she had two other children.

Chandler had heard of Don but had never met him until freshman year at MIT some twenty years ago. Don had graduated from MIT's Sloan School of Management with an MBA and apparently was a stellar student. He was asked to speak at a student forum about his overall MBA experience and its impact on his job.

Chandler was enrolled in the School of Engineering but attended the forum to score points with Varina, whom he wanted to date. He couldn't believe his eyes when he glanced up and saw Don speaking at the podium. Not only were they the spitting image of each other but they sounded alike. Varina stared from Chandler to Don as if she'd seen a ghost.

After the forum, the line to speak with Don was long, so he and Varina waited before walking up to him. His face was priceless, before they all broke into senseless laughter. Ever since that day, he and Don had been close, and remained close even though their lifestyles were like night and day.

"Sorry, man," he greeted, Don with a fist bump. "Don't know where my mind went. Forgot I was meeting you so I went to the gym. Habit. Why didn't you call me?"

"It's okay," Don told him, pulling to the edge of the sofa. "I needed the time to think."

"Sounds serious. But what do you always say? 'God is good all the time, and all the time God is good.'"

Don constantly told him about God's goodness and faithfulness in his life. He never missed an opportunity to thank God for just about everything. However, while Chandler loved his brother, he didn't share his exuberance with this God thing. The only time he'd attended church was when he was invited to a wedding or a funeral.

"You remember that little bro." Don couldn't help the smile that popped on his face. "You're listening to me after all. I'm encouraged."

Chandler smiled at him. "Of course, I'm listening to you. Always have."

That brought much needed peace to Don's heart. Lord knows he needed it for the daunting task ahead of him.

"Hope you made yourself at home," Chandler said. "Back in a few. Need to change out of these clothes."

"Go ahead. I'm good."

"K," Chandler said, walking towards the stairs.

117

Don settled back on the sofa then glanced around Chandler's massive home. It was designed with contemporary living in mind and it accommodated Chandler's dynamic, high-speed lifestyle. Soaring, vaulted ceilings and distinctive wood detailed his home. Shades of yellow along with tasteful green and white accents decorated the furniture and walls.

On the ground floor, the grand, spacious living room expanded to a terrace with an incredible view of a lush landscape. The huge kitchen was a chef's dream, offering sleek state-of-the-art, high-tech appliances and tools. Near the kitchen, an additional room served as a gym.

Upstairs was his home office, two bedrooms and his larger than life master bedroom with two huge walk-in closets. The bathrooms were equipped with Jacuzzi tubs and other delightful amenities.

Raised with an expensive, refined taste, nothing but the best was good enough for Chandler. Nothing was too good for his inexhaustible taste. And why not? He had the resources to accommodate his lifestyle.

Ten minutes later, Chandler re-entered the living room in Army-green shorts and a red polo shirt. "It's about to rain," he said, taking a seat on the sofa across from Don.

"Hope it holds up until I leave."

Chandler eyed him curiously. "What's troubling you? You don't look yourself."

Don wanted to slap the inquiring look off his face. *No need for that*, he told himself, hoping what was about to unfold would calm his fears, and he would put it down to his active imagination.

He looked Chandler straight in the eye. "Did you sleep with Rozene Kanate?"

118

Deny! Deny! Deny! An inner voice shrieked in Chandler's ears. He felt like he was about to pass out. "Yes," he confessed in a voice that he didn't recognize.

The muscles in Don's jaws tightened and his fists ached as he desperately tried to restrain himself. But before he knew it, he'd sprung off the sofa and grabbed Chandler by the throat, pressing him into the sofa. "Are you crazy?" he hissed, his blood boiling. "Why? Why did you have to sleep with her?"

Chandler gasped for air, pushing at Don's hand.

Don released him, but continued to glare at him while they both struggled to regain normal breathing patterns.

Don walked to stare out the window. "I'm sorry, the day I introduced her to you, and allowed you to …" Don stopped speaking as it dawned on him. "You had it all planned," he turned towards Chandler and accused him. "You became a volunteer on the book tour in Chicago for that very reason. Then you volunteered to take her back to the hotel." Don walked back to the sofa and dropped on it. "How could you be so heartless?"

Chandler didn't have a comeback. He remained quiet, feeling a strange emotion … humiliation. When he was finally able to speak, he countered, "I tried to stay away from her, Don, but I couldn't. We only slept together twice. Now she won't take my call."

"Listen to me, Chandler." Don pulled to the edge of the sofa. "She is married. She has a family. Leave her alone before you destroy her marriage and her ministry." He didn't see any reason to inform Chandler about the current state of Rozene's marriage. That may give him hope.

"I'm in love with her, Don," Chandler said quietly.

Don became still. Shocked. Dismayed. Speechless. *Oh, God! Chandler has lost his mind.* How else could he be making that senseless statement? Don closed his eyes for a moment then opened them in the hopes that this nightmare would go away. *No. Wishful thinking.* He was still sitting across from Chandler who was looking for affirmation for his madness.

Man, say something. Anything, Chandler willed Don.

Don tried to calm himself. *Nope. Not working.* "Chandler, have you lost your mind?" he shouted, jumping to his feet. "She is married with kids." *Okay, be calm,* he tried to tamp down his anxiety. "Chandler, listen to me," he began in an overly calm voice, "This is not a good situation, not for you or her. You need to go find a woman of your own. She's already taken."

His eyes flashing with frustration, Chandler stood and threw his hand in the air. "I don't expect you to understand, but I love her. She's always on my mind and I-I just can't have enough of her."

Love her. Don shook his head, silently pleading, *Lord, help.* "Of all the women in the world, why her? Is it because she's unavailable?"

"I wondered about that too, Don, but no. I genuinely love her and I can't see myself with anyone else."

Don walked over to him. His stomach churned at the ugliness of the whole situation. He knew Chandler had a major disconnect because of how poorly he treated women. He was not the sort of man that any woman could pin her hopes on. Chandler had confided in him and told him that his mother had often left him in the care of his nanny to go off on business trips. She was a fashion designer, if his memory served him right. The same held true for their father. He was always away on business, building structures all over the world. Suffice to say, Chandler did not share a great relationship with either of his parents. Truthfully, he had become a loner at heart. And made a genuine loner by Alana, his former fiancée. From the little Chandler had mentioned about Alana - who had convinced him to give up his single life - their relationship had ended in the worst way.

So love was not exactly Chandler's thing. His relationships were short and the minute there was any hint he would have to commit, he was out of there. Don often told him he would settle down when he found someone he couldn't wrap around his little finger. But no, not Rozenc.

"I was trying to help you, you know," Chandler pointed out. "That's how it started."

Chandler's confession caused Don's head to snap upwards. "Help me out! How would that help me?" This he had to hear.

"You'd said that she couldn't reach a certain group of people because she hadn't been on the other side of love – temptation, lusting, unfaithfulness – she was clean."

He watched as Don's mouth opened, and then closed, and then opened again without him speaking.

"I thought I would seek her out," Chandler continued. "You know I have a way with the ladies. Anyway, one night, I was channel hopping and saw her. I couldn't believe all that she was saying, her words were beautiful and she is sooo beautiful. It was amazing to meet her," he gushed. "And, you know what else is amazing?" He clapped his hands together excitedly. "I'm even starting to believe some of the things she's preaching about."

Chandler's countenance fell as he saw the pain in Don's gaze. "I never expected to fall in love with her." His eyes begged for understanding. "I love her, Don."

Don's mind swirled as he looked at the tortured soul across from him. He didn't even know where to begin to fix this situation that was already destroying the Kanate family and could bring down Rozene's ministry.

He looked straight into Chandler's eyes as they searched his for any remote possibility of empathy. But all

Don felt was a dread rapidly rising within. He couldn't take anymore of this twisted conversation. This was a new level of madness.

"Little Bro," Don said with as much empathy as he could muster, "you need to seek counseling for what's going on with you. I always told you, you needed help to deal with your family situation. That is what's eating you up inside."

Chandler did not respond so Don continued, "Rozene is not going to leave her family and her ministry for you. She is deeply connected to her husband and he's a good man." Don observed Chandler's quietness. He was way too far gone to believe anything that Don was saying.

In the past, many times Chandler held the opposite side of an argument with Don, but secretly, he had always trusted and respected Don's judgement. Not only because they were family, but because Don lived an exemplary life.

He exhaled deeply, listening yet not wanting to hear Don out. He hoped this situation wouldn't drive a wedge between them. What he and Rozene shared was different. It was nothing like what he'd experienced with the other women whom he'd dated, and slept with.

"You know, I love you," Don told him, "but this, this situation will not end well. I'll be praying for you. Have a good night."

Don walked across the patio, and then through the pelting rain towards his car. He was oblivious of nature's onslaught; his mind was replaying his conversation with Chandler, a conversation that would probably haunt him for the rest of his life. As the rain saturated his clothes, he urged his legs along but they felt like two huge boulders and now he was shuffling along instead. His heart burned with disgust as he gazed ahead of him.

After what seemed like an eternity, he entered his car and closed the door behind him. He reclined the driver's seat and covered his face with his hands, as condemnation hit him. He took the blows, for putting Rozene in such a position with Chandler. He had failed her and caused the destruction of her family. To think that he'd even given Chandler her cell phone number. What would Rozene think of him when she found out he had a hand in Chandler's scheme?

He was Mr. Fix It, but he felt powerless to fix this situation. Pain zigzagged across his brain but the pain in his heart was not comparable, it was a creeping one. Chandler had betrayed his trust but he felt more like he had stabbed him in the back.

His stomach retched as he started the car and pulled away. Silently, he cried out, "Father, please fix this situation. Only You can." He was quiet for a moment, and then he heard himself saying, "I will lift up my eyes to the hills from whence comes my help. My help comes from the Lord, who made heaven and earth. He will not allow your foot to be moved; He who keeps you will not slumber …"

Seeking comfort in his faith, he began sharing with the Lord of all creation, his failings and disappointments. He was disappointed with himself, and extremely disappointed with Rozene and Chandler.

CHAPTER 15

Chandler glanced at his cell phone and saw that it was 9:00 AM. He intended to speak with Rozene one way or another.

After mulling over his conversation with Don last night, it was too late to call her so he decided to work from home the following day, so he would have privacy when they spoke.

She was the only number under Favorites, so he proceeded to ring her. Holding his breath, he waited for her to answer.

"Hi there!" Rozene answered joyfully.

"Glad it's a happy morning, for somebody," Chandler replied testily.

Rozene bolted upright, almost stopping her car in the middle of the road.

Since the week began, she had been feeling warm and fuzzy with expectation. She had come to the realization that she couldn't hide away forever so she decided to stride out again in purpose. She'd just ended a telephone conversation with Lissan, the Manager of Victorious Women's Shelter, and was expecting a call back. She needed the number of women who would be present for her monthly workshop, so she could pick up copies of her handout from Sarah, her executive assistant.

And now this...

Don't say it, she cautioned herself, as her anger boiled. *When will this maddening chaos cease?*

In the silence, Chandler decided to calm down. "Ro, speak to me, baby."

Rozene drummed her fingers against the steering wheel. "Chandler, I told you to stop calling me."

"I can't do that. I love you."

"I'm not doing this anymore, Chandler. I have to go."

"Why did you tell Don?"

"D-Don," Rozene stammered. "I didn't tell Don anything. Does he know? Oh, Lord," she hunched over the steering wheel in shame. "Lord, noooooo!" she cried out, tears brimming.

"Are you sure you didn't tell him? How would he have guessed?"

Rozene wiped her eyes with the back of her hand, and then gripped the steering wheel as if it was Chandler's neck. "I did not mention anything to Don. I have no reason to, but I'm sure you have plenty."

"And what reasons would I have?"

"You're trying to ruin me. Wasn't that your plan?" she asked, the anxiety in her voice escalating. "Well, you can stop now. Larry and I are separated. Guess, Don told you that too. So if you wanted to destroy my ministry, go ahead." Her eyes filled with tears again, and her brain warned her to slow down as the vehicle took a corner way too sharply. It had rained last night and the road was still slightly wet.

Separated! Chandler knew Don had deliberately left out that bit of information. "That is not my intention. I love you."

Love? Rozene adjusted the volume on her over-the-ear Bluetooth for she must have been hearing things. "Chandler, what is the matter with you? I cannot, will not, be with you again. I have a family. I am married, Chandler, married!" She wiped her eyes, and then gasped loudly as her car skidded towards the guard railing.

"Ro! Ro, are you okay?" she heard Chandler yell.

"Jesus! Help me, Jesus!" she screamed, slamming on the brakes. But her car wouldn't stop, even though everything else in her mind did, so she braced for impact.

Her car seemed to be swirling forever, and she closed her eyes as her vision started to blur. Air seemed to be sucked out of her lungs as the car banged hard against the guard railing and came to a stop.

The thumping of her heart seemed unending as she tried to gather her thoughts. *What?* Her eyes searched frantically as she saw blood on her cream-colored pair of pants ... on her hands. Mindlessly, she was inspecting her hands when a splat of blood hit her sleeve leaving dark red spots. She grabbed her head and a strangled scream emanated from her throat as her hand brushed the wound at the side of her head. Blood ran down her face, and then trickled down her neck. "Help," she called out faintly.

Several heavy thuds caused her to swing her head toward the window and she winced as pain ripped through her body. From the corner of her eyes, she saw the frantic face of a woman mouthing something, but she couldn't understand her words.

Fingers shaking, she managed to roll the window down before slumping over the steering wheel as tiny electric shocks shook her body.

"Hold on," the woman urged her. "The paramedic team has arrived."

Rozene did not look up but she knew the woman was still there. "My head ... my head ... hurts so badly," she murmured.

"We have you," she heard a male voice say before she faded into oblivion.

******

"Mrs. Kanate! Mrs. Kanate!" Rozene heard someone calling her name.

She opened her eyes, seeing all white. She closed her eyes again before opening at the sound of the same

126

voice. "Stay with me. Great. That's it, open your eyes. It's okay."

Rozene stared, unblinking, trying to fathom what was happening.

Two pairs of eyes stared back at her, waiting for her to focus.

"Where am I?" Rozene asked.

"You are in the hospital. You took a nasty blow to your temple," a handsome, young doctor told her.

As bits and pieces of what happened came back to her, she lifted a hand to her temple. "Ouch!" Her head felt tender and there was a bandage around it. "That explains why my head feels like I'm carrying a truck." Her eyes widened and she lifted her hands and inspected them.

"You've not suffered any broken bones. Thank God," the doctor said.

She attempted to smile then grimaced in pain. "Thanks, Dr ..."

"Raymond Reid," he supplied. He gestured with his hand towards the female beside him. "And this is Dr. Renee James."

"Nice to meet you, both," Rozene remarked.

"You too," they responded, smiling at her.

"Did I do surgery?" Rozene's eyes widened for the second time.

"No," Dr. James replied. "We're observing you for the rest of the day. If all goes well, you should be home tomorrow."

Rozene gave them a grateful smile. "Thank you so much."

"You are welcome. A nurse will be here shortly to give you pain medication," Dr. Reid said, pleasantly.

"Thanks, I'm going to need something for sure." Her head was throbbing.

Dr. James turned and smiled at her as they walked to the door. "I read all your books and I love them. You certainly have a way with words."

Joy filled Rozene's heart. "Thank you. To God be the glory."

"You're welcome," Dr. James lifted her hand to display her wedding band, while smiling at Rozene. "I'm looking forward to, *Letters to Wives.*"

Rozene tried not to wince from the trepidation engulfing her heart. If only she had the courage to finish the book. "Great," she said, with a tight smile.

Dr. James nodded. "There's a gentleman from your ministry in our waiting area. He's been anxiously waiting. I told him he couldn't see you for too long. You need to rest."

"You are right on that," Rozene responded, a small smile playing on her lips. She could always count on Don. "Please send him in."

"Will do," Dr. James said. "Your-"

"Did anyone call my husband?" Rozene asked simultaneously. She didn't want any suspicion that her marriage was not intact.

Dr. James grinned at her. "You took the words out of my mouth. He's on his way."

"Thank you," Rozene responded with the bravest smile she could muster.

"Not a problem. Talk with you soon," Dr. James said, before leaving.

In less than a minute, her room door flew open.

"Don, I am -" Rozene paused staring wide-eyed at Chandler for a couple of seconds. "What are -?" She stopped as he quickly pulled a chair close to her bed and grasped her hand.

"I thought you were d-dead," Chandler stammered, tears brimming. "A part of me died. I begged God not to take you from me."

Rozene's heart hammered. She needed to get rid of him. "I'm okay now. But I need to rest."

"I love you so much." His lean fingers lifted her hand to his lips. "Please don't scare me like that again."

His lips grazed the back of her hand. "I won't," she said, while rebuking all the emotions that were rising within her. "Chandler, you cannot be here. Larry is on the way. Please, I'm in enough trouble as it is."

"I won't leave until you promise you'll see me when you're out."

"I will. Now go," she begged.

"Just for you," he said. In the next breath, he lifted himself out the chair and planted a kiss on her lips.

"Chandler don't," she said impatiently, pushing his shoulders with her hands.

A devilish grin spread across his face as his lips hovered above hers. "Kiss me then and I'll be on my way."

"My head hurts."

"Excuses. Excuses," he drawled against her lips. "I'm hearing voices outside. Kiss me."

Annoyed, she gave him a peck on his lips. That was all the encouragement he needed. He kissed her back with urgency … savoring her.

Not good! Not good! Was all that reverberated in her head.

A soft moan of desire gurgled in his throat and suddenly he pulled away. Standing erect by her bedside, his eyes warned her to adjust her gaze.

The door opened, and a female nurse entered and did a double take on Chandler; digesting him in a hot minute before it fully registered that he was not lunch. A smile slipped out as she dragged her eyes towards Rozene,

129

who offered her a slight smile, before focusing on what Chandler was saying.

"… your schedule," Chandler said, looking inordinately please with himself. "Don will take care of it for the rest of the week. I believe he's on his way here. Is -"

"Good morning," the nurse cooed, fake 'professionalism' cloaking her face.

"Good morning," they both responded, and Chandler stepped away as she moseyed her petite, waif-like frame towards the bed.

"I am Nurse Anderson. This won't take long."

"No problem. He was just about to leave." Rozene couldn't help but jump at the opportunity.

"Okay." A sly grin appeared on Nurse Anderson's face as she helped herself to another filling of Chandler.

Chandler stepped back, jerking his gaze away from hers as if he'd been stung by her shameless flirtation.

Nurse Anderson swung her gaze back to Rozene. "How are you feeling?"

"I have seen better days."

"Well, we are going to make sure you are up and running as soon as possible. Let me take your temperature."

Rozene opened her mouth and the nurse placed the thermometer in her mouth. A few minutes later, she removed the thermometer and looked at it.

"Your temperature is good." She offered Rozene a small plastic cup with a white pill. "This is a pain killer. It could make you drowsy."

Rozene nodded. She took the pill from the container and placed it in her mouth, then drank water from another cup that the nurse gave her.

"Thank you," Rozene said, handing the cup back to the nurse.

"You're very welcome. My pleasure to help," she said with exaggerated kindness. Glancing at Chandler, she gave him her sweetest smile. "Don't mean to rush you but Mrs. Kanate needs rest." Her expression indicating, but I'm available.

Chandler was having none of it. He nodded at her before turning towards Rozene, concern coloring his eyes. "Take care of yourself. Everything is under control. We'll talk soon."

Rozene gave him a slight smile. "I will. Thanks, Chandler."

With that, Chandler walked towards the door and opened it. All this time, the nurse took up position to flutter her eyelashes at him. However, when he turned, he had eyes only for Rozene. He lifted a hand to her before closing the door behind him.

The nurse let out a shaky breath, clearly contemplating whether to ask about Chandler.

Instinctively, Rozene's eyebrows arched. "Thank you, Nurse Anderson," she said quickly, and then closed her eyes. She heard the gentle click of the lock as the nurse exited the room.

Rozene let out a sigh of relief, then her heart felt troubled. Chandler was persistent … and slick. *And what was that kiss about?* She scolded herself. She wouldn't even admit she'd enjoyed it. Instead, she jotted it down in the back of her mind as simply a chemical reaction.

Her mind flashed to her conversation with Chandler before the accident. How would Don know, if he hadn't mentioned it?

It was the second time she'd found herself playing the blame game with Chandler. The first time was when she told him he'd given her Chlamydia. She'd called him from the parking lot at her doctor's office.

"I don't have 'The Clam'!" he all but yelled. "And, I hope to God you didn't give it to me."

"I never started itching and feeling abdominal pain until after I slept with you a few weeks ago."

"Again, Ro, I don't have Chlamydia. You must have caught it from someone else … your husband perhaps."

She blew out a harsh breath, disgusted by what he was implying. "Are you crazy? I'm not even …"

"Not sleeping with him, huh?"

Rozene flinched. She couldn't even believe she'd almost said that aloud. Larry was not only a great father and husband, but he was a wonderful lover. She hadn't been sleeping with him because of guilt … and worse now, she didn't want to give him Chlamydia. Well, hopefully she didn't, because Larry had skillfully coerced her into a brief lovemaking session about a week ago. She'd given in because it was his birthday. Anyway, she fully intended to resume her wifely duties as soon as the treatment ended.

"I understand," Chandler drawled, "after being with me that would be hard."

"Don't talk about my husband. You don't know him. He would never do something like that."

"Right," he chuckled.

Still Rozene didn't believe him; she had no reason to. She needed to take care of this venereal disease and get on with her life, without Chandler.

"I'm going to get a checkup and I hope you haven't given me Chlamydia."

Annoyed, Rozene clicked off without saying goodbye.

However, two days later, Chandler called her. "You gave me Chlamydia," he all but yelled.

"I didn't give you Chlamydia, Chandler. I do not sleep around, but clearly you do."

"You gave it to me," he told her angrily. "I almost died of embarrassment getting the medication to cure it."

132

But Rozene didn't care how he felt, even though she could identify with his feelings about collecting the medication. Thankfully, the January weather was still nippy so she went all out to disguise herself - a black hat, sunglasses, and an extra-long, black wool scarf wrapped around her neck - when she'd picked up her prescription one night at the drive-through window at the pharmacy; as if that would stop the pharmacist from recognizing her name.

"I never figured you as the sleep around kind of woman, Ro," she heard Chandler say.

She decided to ignore his statement. "I'm sure you were embarrassed," she said testily. "So was I. But you are not the one telling women to honor their husbands. I have repented before God and I won't be seeing you or taking your calls anymore."

"Why wouldn't you want to see me again? We are perfect together."

Rozene heaved a longsuffering sigh. For sure, she had to get away from him. "Chandler, you know that I am married, right?"

"And?"

Trying not to exhale loudly, Rozene attempted to appeal to his reasoning. "I'm sorry for putting you in this position. Please, I have too much at stake, and I can't do this ... this thing between us. It's not right for God's sake. I'm married. That ought to mean something to you."

"What about your needs, Ro?" he asked softly.

Her lips compressed. "My needs are being met."

"Right. And that's why you're hollering out my name in the heat of passion."

He might as well have slapped her for her hands flew to her flushed cheeks, and she remained quiet.

"Come on, Ro. Don't cut me out of your life."

"I don't want to be this kind of person, Chandler. We both know it's wrong. I love my husband."

"Are you denying that you're attracted to me?"

It's a little too late for that. She was attracted to him but not stupid. "No," she told him with a healthy dose of reluctance. "But, I love my husband, and I already made vows I want to keep. I can't see or speak to you anymore, Chandler. Please, forgive me."

She disconnected the call, hoping this nightmare had ended. However, by the following week, her entire life exploded before her face when Larry found out she'd committed adultery.

The tears running down her neck disturbed her reflection. *Lord, help me.* Fresh tears started and she closed her eyes, trying to repress all thoughts.

Just then, she heard a familiar voice calling her name. She barely wanted to breathe as she opened her slightly puffy eyes. It was Larry.

CHAPTER 16

Larry stood watching Rozene for a moment before calling out her name. Knowing she wasn't the cry baby type, he wondered what could have rocked her world to put her in such a pathetic state. His heart hurt to see her like this ... even though he wouldn't confess this aloud.

He had called her by name and now she was looking at him as if she'd seen a ghost at the foot of her bed. Even with her slightly swollen eyes, she was beautiful. He hadn't been thinking about her in that way these days. He tensed, rebuking his mind for going there.

An effortless stride took him to her bedside. "Are you okay?"

She glowed under the intensity of the tenderness in his gaze.

It had been over six months since she'd seen him and all she could think was, *Oh, what a man?* Bold. Confident. Powerful. In a class all by himself. Clearly, he must have been burning extra time at the gym. He was all decked out in his signature black Michael Kors suit, white shirt and red silk tie with two-tone basket weave marks, which she had helped him choose for a business presentation last year.

A slight smile graced her face as she remembered he usually wore black, keeping it traditional, when he was not in the mood for foolishness. Under normal circumstances, he would let her know who was creating havoc at work.

Most people either loved or hated Larry. No in between. No shades of gray. He was a tough cookie, but underneath that powerful exterior was a soft, sensitive soul with a heart of gold. And she'd opted to love him. She missed him holding her, and missed holding him. She always knew he was right for her ... from day one.

She sighed, wishing things were different.

Larry wondered if Rozene heard him. She was gazing at him with all sorts of expressions on her face, and … a visceral appreciation of his frame. Sure, he was working out more; he was probably in the best shape of his life. Thanks to her, after she'd left, sleeping at night was a struggle so he would go to their home gym and workout until he was dead tired. When that was not enough, he would give the yard a beat down with his running shoes as if he was beating the ground into submission.

"I was asking if you're okay," Larry ventured.

"Yes," she said softly, hoping not to look as love sick as she felt. "Thanks for checking on me. You look great."

"You're welcome, and thanks."

He ignored the look in her eyes and focused on the reason she was in the hospital. Admittedly, he had feared the worst and did get a little scared. Okay, straight up horrified, when the police had called him. He was still her emergency contact. Immediately, he left his office for the hospital, and on the way, he had contacted her parents.

Taking a seat in the chair that was recently vacated by Chandler, Larry flexed his neck muscles to push away some of the tension he was feeling. After all, caring was natural human behavior. "What happened? What did the doctors say?"

Rozene gave him blow by blow details of the accident. Of course, she omitted her conversation with Chandler.

Larry slid back in the chair watching her. She was animated as always, that hadn't changed. *Changed. So much had changed between us.*

She smiled at him and his heart leaped and he had to hold still so as not to squirm in the chair.

"So, they're observing me overnight," Rozene concluded. "I give God thanks that I'm alive and no one got hurt."

"Thank God. Did the police take your statement?"

"No, not yet."

"I'm sure they'll be here soon. Were you using your cell phone?"

She nodded in the affirmative.

He sighed loudly. "You know I don't like when you drive and use-."

"I know. I was using my Bluetooth."

"You need to stop doing that Rozene. What could be so urgent? Are you 911? I'm sure whosoever was calling could wait."

Rozene sulked like a child, murmuring, "I know."

Larry stared at her for a moment, before telling her, "I'll call the insurance company to alert them about the accident and you can do the follow-up when you can."

"Thanks. I appreciate you coming. I know you didn't have to."

Silence.

What could he say to that? *I felt compelled because you are still my wife.* He had no response. Well, except a nod.

He ran a hand across his face, suddenly frustrated about too many things.

Rozene watched him. Since difficulty of speech was not a part of his character, she assumed the worst. *Lord, please, I'll listen to anything he has to say, but no talk of divorce. Oh, Lord, they would have to give me a valium to keep me quiet.* In the midst of her musings, she heard herself ask, "Honey, what is troubling you?"

He exhaled deeply, ignoring her term of endearment. "The children called," and then his voice dropped to a low tone, "they were planning to surprise us

137

next weekend, but they got wind of your accident and decided to come home on Friday. That's after I convinced them not to worry. They wanted to fly in this evening."

Rozene gasped, and then held her head as pain shot through her.

"Should I call the nurse?" Larry asked.

"N-no," she stammered. "Lord, have mercy!" She looked helplessly at him. "That's three days' time."

"They'll call you later. They'll be spending the weekend and then head back on Monday to prepare for the fall semester."

"Larry, please," Rozene begged, "I don't want them to find out about our separation."

"Why didn't you think of that before you ... You know what? They'll find out sooner or later."

Instantly, tears rushed to her eyes and she reached for tissue from the box on the small table near her bed. "I can't tell them right now," she lamented.

"It's been months, well over six months. Don't you think they will be upset that we didn't tell them sooner? They are almost nineteen, I am sure, they can handle it. When were you planning to tell them, Rozene?"

Crushed. That's exactly how Rozene felt. Crushed by his casual attitude. Crushed, he'd already given up on their marriage. And crushed because he had called her Rozene. She was not expecting his usual terms of endearment – Babes. My baby. My love – but at least, he could have referred to her as Roz.

"I-I was hoping ..." she stammered.

Larry's over-my-dead-body look caused the words to dry up in her throat. "Hoping we would get back together," he finished.

"Yes," she choked out.

He didn't respond, but the look in his eyes said it all.

Unable to handle the obvious scorn, Rozene willed the bed to swallow her up. When the silence persisted, she chanced a glance but the eyes that returned her gaze held no promises.

"Please. I need more time. Can I move in for the weekend?"

He was slow to respond. So slow. "And, how would that convince them? There would be no interaction between us. You know how we ... were."

"Please Larry, you could try ... a little. I'll tell them when they come home for Christmas. They would have enough time to spend with both of us. I really don't want them to start the fall semester sad."

"I can't make any promises. Call me when you are out."

"Can you please take me to my parents' home when they release me tomorrow?"

"Are you still concerned about the media? Sooner or later they too will know."

Her mind numbed. The press would have a field day - Another prominent Christian leader fallen. Yes, they would enjoy this salacious story.

Fear welled up in her. "Please pick me up after my release. I'll call you."

He stood up. "Now don't expect me to be all lovie dovie with you out there."

"Okay," she said, without looking at him.

"Tomorrow then," he said moving to the door.

"Larry!" she called out in a strangled voice.

"Yes." He turned to face her.

Courage failed her as she stared into his emotionless eyes. She closed her eyes against the onslaught. She didn't matter to him, not anymore. "It's nothing," she murmured. Her heart was full but now was not the time. She buried her head in the pillow when the door closed behind him.

139

CHAPTER 17

Rozene perched on the edge of her bed, smiling inwardly. *My precious gems are coming home tomorrow.* The children wanted to fly in earlier but she reassured them that she was okay. Nevertheless, they made sure to call every day.

In the midst of her happy thoughts, her mother's words rested heavily on her heart 'You can't make him love you again, Rozie. You have to trust God.'

Larry had picked her up from the hospital the previous day and had driven her to her parents' home. Thankfully, they were allowed to use a private exit at the hospital to avoid the press and some of her loyal readers. Larry appeared grateful too. After all, he didn't have to whip out any fake smiles. He'd even surprised her by willingly playing the role of a caring husband. She was appreciative too that Don had not mentioned anything to do with Chandler and he'd handled the press on her behalf.

She made a final sweep of the bedroom before picking up her purse from the bed. Half an hour ago, with her father's help, she had loaded her personal items in the BMW SUV Larry had sent over.

"I'm trusting You, Lord," she whispered. "I'm looking forward to spending time with my family. Lord, I'm also looking forward to being with my husband."

Excited, yet a bit shaky, she danced slowly around the room declaring, "My hope is in you, Lord." A smile lit her face as she recalled the Scripture, "Thou wilt keep him in perfect peace, whose mind is stayed on Thee, because he trusteth in Thee." And she vowed to keep her mind stayed on the Lord.

A few minutes later, she all but bounced down the stairs and said goodbye to her parents. Then with Bose speakers blasting Darrell Evans' song, "Trading My Sorrows," she headed out on her fifty-minute drive home.

And she was still smiling when she opened the electronic gate to what used to be her haven of tranquility – The Kanate, an impressive two-story home, which was elegantly nestled in the midst of a tapestry of trees, well-manicured lawns, and beautiful gardens. A thing of grace and beauty, aptly described its contemporary French design which captured the allure of past and present times. The classical theme was obvious in the structure - from it gray-blue tiled roof and stone exterior to its magnificent arches, columns, and curved windows. Adding to its appeal, deep contrasts of lights played over the structure making a strong yet refined statement.

She and Larry had had fun times collaborating to decorate their home, around ten years ago. Ensuring that their home whispered elegance yet comfort through its exquisite artwork, handcrafted furniture, unique decor, and all the latest amenities of modern life.

She smiled when she opened the garage, for Larry had left the space closest to the entrance door for her to park. He'd volunteered to leave work early to help her unpack the vehicle, but she quickly reassured him that she would be okay. He was definitely not at home because she noticed the Audi was missing.

As soon as she entered the formal living room, Rozene let go of her suitcase and began to turn in slow trance-like circles, taking in the wonderful feeling of home. *Home.* A quiet sigh of relief left her, easing her soul. Everything she had ever wanted was here. She felt alive and comfortable in her own space again.

She had told Larry to give the house staff the weekend off. And he did. He had also mentioned that Armela, head of the household staff, wanted to see the children. He had assured her she would. Armela had been with the family since the children started middle school.

Almost two hours later, after restacking her personal items, Rozene glanced at the small digital clock on the dresser. Larry should be home in another two hours, if he stayed true to his usual routine. Somehow, she felt he would. She decided to grab a bath and dress into something appropriate before he arrived. She knew exactly what to throw over her curves – a red pleated romper, one of Larry's favorites. *My bed's calling my name*, was all Larry said smiling, whenever she wore it. It didn't matter what time of the day it was, it was "bedtime" and like a sheep, she allowed him to lead her to a greener pasture. She was always happier for it, anyway.

Giggling, Rozene strutted across the grand master suite towards the bathroom. On her way there, she stepped into her huge walk-in closet across from Larry's and located the romper. "Hmmm. I should probably save this for Sunday," she said, looking over the romper. "Yes. Sunday it is."

Instead, she opted for an ankle-length, royal-blue dress and also selected a royal-blue and gold sandals. Dress and sandals in hand, she strolled down the passageway and entered the huge, chic but functional bathroom with its super-cool circular lounge area, his-and-hers sinks and accompanying built-in dressers, Jacuzzi, and shower.

She was placing her dress on the chair near the Jacuzzi when she heard her cell phone ringing. She dreaded hearing the phone ring these days. Chandler was becoming bold in a way that was unnerving. She had eventually opened the envelope that he had sent with Don and saw her ticket for a week's stay in Paris along with hotel accommodation. In a fit of anger, she had ripped up the envelope and its contents.

Walking back to the bedroom, she located the phone in the outer pocket of her purse on the daybed in the lounge area of the room. It had stopped ringing but she noticed it was a private number. Just then, the phone rang again. *Private number?* She wrestled with whether or not to answer, and then decided to. "Good afternoon."

"Afternoon, my love!" Chandler responded joyfully. "How are you, baby?"

"I'm doing well, Chandler," she said stiffly. "Is there something -?"

"Now that's just rude. You're trying to rush me off the phone. You didn't even ask how I was doing."

Rozene shifted from one foot to the other, attempting to control her annoyance.

"Are you still there, baby?" His voice dripped with honey.

"Chandler, do you need something?"

"Yes. You."

Walked right into that! "That's not possible." Ever again, she wanted to add. "If that's it, goodbye."

"I need to see you, Ro. You promised you would see me as soon as you were out of the hospital and I've been waiting for your call. Did you deliberately lie to get rid of me at the hospital? I'm holding you to your word, I need to see you."

His voice grated on every nerve in her body, but she decided to play cool. "I can't see you now. My children are coming home so I'm spending the weekend with them."

"Can I meet them?" he asked eagerly.

"No!" *Are you crazy? Certifiably crazy?* Her heart was still palpitating wildly when she tried to soften the blow. "No ... no need for that."

Chandler sighed, his attempt to be patient obvious. "I'm going to be in their lives so it would be nice for them to meet me." From what he had read on social media, he knew Mason and Madison were attending MIT.

He is on something. That was the only answer that made any sense. "I don't know what you're talking about, Chandler, but I have to go."

"When am I seeing you, Ro?"

"I will call you soon. Bye." Rozene cut off the call before he could respond. Annoyed, she threw her phone on the bed, and was startled as it began to ring. Without even looking at the caller ID, she powered the phone off and dropped it on the bed again. She was gazing at it with hostility when the house phone rang.

She froze. Waves of trepidation ran up and down her spine as she slowly approached the nightstand to inspect the caller ID.

Phew! She grabbed the handset and sank down on the bed.

"Hi, honey," she answered breathlessly.

Larry paused. *That was unexpected.* But then, so was the lurch in his heart rate at her term of endearment. "Your cell is going to voicemail," he told her abruptly. "I was just checking if you made it."

She didn't want to lie so she ignored his statement about her cell phone. And she was most definitely going to ignore his curt tone. "Thanks for checking on me. I unpacked and was about to..." She paused, feeling he had no interest in her next move. Instead, she asked, "Will you be home soon?"

"Another two hours or so."

She paused, noting his tone seemed to ask, *Why do you care?*

In that moment, Larry almost kicked himself, for he'd decided to not be confrontational since they would be under the same roof for the weekend. He tried again. "Is

144

there anything that you need me to pick up? Armela already stacked the fridge but I don't know …"

"I haven't been to the kitchen yet. But, I'll use what is available for the time being."

"All right."

"Okay."

She placed the cordless phone back on its base. *Mercy! He's soooo stiff. I hope this is not how he's going to be for the weekend.* She knitted her brows as her mind swung back to her conversation with Chandler.

The answer came - *Prayer.*

She dropped to her knees at the bedside and prayed for God's continued direction and guidance over her situation.

Shortly thereafter, Rozene strolled to the bathroom, and flipped on the light switch over the Jacuzzi that was nestled in the right top corner of the bathroom. The halo lighting over the Jacuzzi created a relaxing atmosphere that usually made her bath time ritual feel like an extra special treat.

She managed to pry her eyes away from the massive floor-length mirrors which covered most of the walls, and turned on the faucets to prepare for a long, luxurious bath. She picked up her favorite bath gel from the basket nearby, poured some in and then felt the water to make sure it would be lukewarm.

Slipping out of her clothes, she placed them in the laundry basket, and then set the CD player on the intercom to "How Great is Our God" by Chris Tomlin, before climbing into the Jacuzzi. Humming the song, she relaxed and soaked her body. *Perfectly appointed for a time such as this.* She drifted off into prayer as the words of the song permeated her heart.

CHAPTER 18

Larry entered their home with a bit of trepidation in his heart. All day, he'd been uneasy about Rozene moving back for the weekend. Yet ever so often, his body would buzz with a strange anticipation – which he chose to ignore. The last thing he wanted was to be in an awkward situation with her. How was it going to work with them under the same roof, again?

Deciding that he would change out of his work clothes before going in search of her, he headed up the stairs. A corner of his mouth tilted as he strode across the circular landing at the top of the stairs, he knew exactly where she was.

In spite of the four available guest rooms on the second floor, he had no doubt she would be lounging in Madison's room, a few doors down from their master suite. Since Mason and Madison left for MIT, Rozene had been using Madison's room as her private sanctuary. He knew it was because she missed Madison. The two had always been close.

He quietened his thoughts as he opened the door of his study adjacent to their bedroom. After turning on the light, he lifted the strap of his work bag over his head and dropped it on the huge mahogany desk. For a moment, he stared at the large envelope on his desk that was addressed to Rozene. He made a mental note to give it to her before she left on Monday. Taking his iPad from his work bag, he turned off the light, and headed for their bedroom.

After placing the iPad on the nightstand, he sat on the bed to remove his shoes, when something poked his rear. He reached for it and saw that it was Rozene's cell phone. It was off. It was then he noticed her purse was on the daybed.

He knitted his brows thinking it was unnecessary for her to leave her belongings in their bedroom since the children were not yet home. A ragged sigh escaped him as he peeled off his shoes and marched into his closet with them. Dropping them in a box on the floor, he stripped off his socks and shirt, before moving towards the bathroom.

In the next minute, his clothes fell from his hands and he stood in the middle of the bathroom gaping. Nothing prepared him for the picture perfect setting he saw under the soft light over the Jacuzzi. Astounded, his body moved toward the Jacuzzi on its own accord.

Rozene was fast asleep.

The bubbles had fizzed away and he relished the beautiful sight of the only woman he'd known, well other than …

His body shifted as his mind shifted, studying every inch of her with renewed curiosity. Even in her relaxed state, she displayed grace and strength. He'd always loved that about her.

Loved?

Yes, loved.

Nevertheless, his body made sure to remind him that he missed her. He told himself to stop staring but was unable to obey his own command. Breathing deeply, he cautioned himself again, reaching deeper to grasp what was left of his self-control. Stepping slightly away from the Jacuzzi, he gently called out, "Roz."

She stirred and smiled before meeting his gaze unflinchingly.

His heart flipped - twice.

Anticipation tightened his stomach, and he stilled his body that was on the verge of jumping in the Jacuzzi, clothes and all.

Rozene all but licked her lips as her eyes roamed him up and down - his toned, slightly bowed legs, his incredibly sculpted pectorals, his handsome face, and the natural glow of his sun-kissed complexion. Strength and power radiated from him, but it was his compelling aura that held her in place.

Her eyes widened when she saw him move towards her. Then, realization dawned. *Not a dream. Not a dream!* She gasped as a bolt of embarrassment slammed into her chest. In a heartbeat, she pulled her legs to her chest and wrapped her hands around them. She closed her eyes then opened them widely as shivers attacked her body. Her teeth began chattering as the cool water lapped at her body. "To-to-towel," she stammered.

Larry sprang into action, pulling a huge white towel from the rack nearby, and after helping her up, he wrapped it around her. She was shivering so badly that he lifted her in his arms. He grabbed another towel, before quickly making his way to the bedroom.

Rozene clenched her teeth to stop the involuntary shivering. She couldn't remember ever having been this cold. Her face flushed, she tried to hold still as Larry began drying her body on the bed, without saying a word. He finished the task and began massaging her feet with his hands.

"Sor-sorry," she said, twitching now from the sweltering heat that was rising from her feet to the rest of her body.

"No problem," Larry said, not looking at her. He was hanging on to the thin thread of self-control he had left. He wished his body would stop acting so desperate for hers. "Let me get your robe," he told her, moving like he was walking on hot coal.

He'd moved away, way too quickly but it was necessary. He grabbed a hold of the clothes rack near the door in Rozene's closet and instructed his body to yield to the commands of his mind.

After opening several drawers, he located her robes and pulled out a lime green one, then made his way back to her.

Rozene looked at him with apprehension as he was nearing the bed, not understanding why she felt the need to be modest now.

He held up the robe. "Let's get you in this. Should keep you warm."

She did not move but eyed him with a death grip on the towel.

His eyebrows furrowed. "I know you're not trying to hide your body from me."

"I-I ..." She paused unsure of what she was attempting to say.

He placed the robe on the bed then stood looking down at her.

She shivered, blurting out, "Wha-what are you doing?" while eyeing him wildly.

Larry gently reached for her and eased her into a sitting position. *Shivering and mental confusion. Mild hypothermia. More heat.* He sat on the bed, pulled her into his arms and began rubbing her back.

Her heartbeat picking up speed, Rozene knew she couldn't take anymore. "Robe. Robe please.

He eased her off his chest and tugged the towel from her hands, while trying not to get another glimpse of her body.

Right, just what I need, she lamented in her bare-as-you-dare moment. She hoped her breasts were not looking too perky. Goosebumps sprouted on her forearms and she hastily slipped one hand and then the next into the plush robe, grateful for its size. Her heart tripped when she got a close up of his ripped chest. She could only hope she had not made any sounds of appreciation. Instinctively, she leaned her head against his chest then threw her arms around his waist.

Mentally, Larry stiffened, but somehow his body, as usual, didn't get the message. His heartbeat skittered as her hands caressed the muscles on his back before moving up his neck. Her gentle strokes at his neck were threatening to engulf him in an inferno, so he moved quickly.

"Going to get you something warm to drink," he said, while gently easing her from his chest. With that, he literally fled from the room and didn't stop until he was down the stairs and in the kitchen. He held on to the countertop, breathing in large gulps of air.

Scolding himself for his weakness, he poured water in the kettle and put it to boil.

A few minutes later, he felt in control of his emotions when he mounted the stairs with her mug of cocoa in hand. He had no intention of being intimate with her again. Ever.

Rozene could hardly wait for Larry to get back. Thoughts of him widened her smile. She had to make extra effort to calm her palpitating heart when he entered the room. His ruggedness and vitality had always attracted her.

As a pool of heat swirled in her belly, she swung her eyes to his face but she couldn't see his expression, he was putting the mug on the nightstand. Unconsciously, she licked her lips. *Stop gawking.* She knitted her brows wondering how to drum up the courage to drag her eyes away from him.

"Can you manage to sit up?" He met her eyes for the first time.

The screeching of her mental brakes almost stopped her heart when she saw his icy gaze – hard and cynical. She shrank back against the bed seeking distance between them but finding none.

He reached for her, thinking she needed help.

"N-No. I can sit up by myself." She pulled herself into a sitting position and leaned against the headboard. In all this, her body began rebelling at the thought of not getting its duly deserved affection.

She recomposed herself, slightly. "I'll get it," she said, as he moved to hand her the mug. She knew he was looking at her but she didn't meet his gaze, for fear she might start weeping.

"Let me know if you need anything," he said in a formal voice.

"I'll be fine," she reassured him stiffly. "I'm going to move to Madison's room and take a nap."

"Okay." That was fine with him too. She had almost thrown him off balance. Thankfully, he had caught himself and was now back on track. He gathered the towels from the bedside and headed towards the bathroom. He intended to take a shower and hopefully, she would be gone by the time he was finished.

CHAPTER 19

How am I going to fake it? Rozene studied the vaulted ceiling in Madison's bedroom as she assessed her situation. She had no energy to fake it. And Larry's detached behavior only added to her trepidation. She needed a Plan B.

Hauling herself into a sitting position, she pressed her back against the headboard and pulled her knees to her chest. She needed to recharge her batteries, after waking up from an hour of uncomfortable sleep.

Prayer. She was about to stifle feverish despair with prayer, when she heard a light knock-knock on the door.

Grim silence prevailed as she stared at the door, a scowl creeping up her face.

But there it was again. Knock-knock.

She arranged herself on the bed. "Come in."

"I made dinner," Larry said, not opening the door. "Are you hungry? You should be." He'd decided that the least he could do was treat her with respect. After thinking about their recent interaction, strangely, he'd hated to see the look of embarrassment on her face when he didn't respond to her romantic advances.

Rozene paused briefly wondering if she could handle being in his presence. She was a little surprised and embarrassed by his downright coldness towards her earlier when he'd returned with her cocoa. She knew he could be sharp but he was never rude. It was not just his rejection of her starry-eyed advances, but his body language had indicated that he didn't want to share the same air space with her.

"Are you there?"

She pursed her lips. *Must be his I'm-sorry strategy.* "I'll be down in a few minutes."

"Okay."

He was no chef, but since Rozene left home, he'd learned to take care of himself. The house staff continued their weekly job of cleaning and ironing but Larry took on the task of preparing his own meals. Albeit, sometimes he would eat out or order in. Nevertheless, he was thankful that back in the day, he'd always helped out Rozene in the kitchen, so he had caught a few meal preparation tips.

Ten minutes later, Rozene exited the living room into a large circular lounge area, and then veered left to pass through the formal dining area. She was surprised to see the table set for two. Usually, they would eat in the nook between the kitchen and the formal dining room or on the huge patio outside the kitchen.

Larry entered with a covered dish. "You can sit. It's all here."

"Thanks." Rozene mustered a smile before taking a seat at the table, leaving the chair at the head of the table for Larry. He prayed, and then they began to put food on their plates – Grilled Chicken, Brown Rice Pilaf, and Garden Salad.

Oh, the silence. This used to be fun. She waited a minute then took the plunged. "Thanks again for dinner, and everything."

"No problem."

She continued to eat wondering what else to say. Something was definitely sucking the oxygen out of the room. "How's work?" she asked.

Larry wiped his mouth with his napkin. "It's going," he said, attacking the chicken with his knife and fork. He didn't know why he thought he could do this – whatever this was.

Rozene threw another glance in his direction but he was not looking at her. She swallowed a forkful of rice before trying again. "Have you been going to church?" The silence extended so she looked at him again. He was still eating. "I was-"

"I heard you." His eyes glazed over with boredom. "You can stop pretending we are ... Let's just try and be civil towards each other this weekend."

Rozene heard herself gulp. *Civil?* Soon her eyes couldn't hold the tears and they began to roll down her cheeks. Before long, she pushed back her chair and ran out of the dining room.

Tears running down her face, she clutched the wooden beam on the patio outside the kitchen. Her sobs grew louder, more hysterical and she sank to the floor, burying her head in her lap. Her shoulders shook as the pain in her heart grew. *The children will find out and despise me.* Panic welled up within her and she raced out the patio door, collapsing on the ground in the gazebo in the backyard.

Larry reached the patio just in time to see her hit the floor of the gazebo. He wanted to hurry after her but his taut body reminded him that he shouldn't get involved in anything he would regret. He was glad for the motion sensor lights around their home; hopefully, she had not hurt herself.

He approached the gazebo. "Rozene," he called out when he stood behind her.

Sensing his presence, she made an effort to restrain herself. When she felt his hand on her back, she flinched, then sprang to her feet.

"Go away! Just go away!" she yelled at him. "Leave me alone, please." Recognizing she couldn't keep up the tough act, she dropped on the seat, turned away from him and began sobbing again.

Larry leaned against a beam in the gazebo, watching as her sobs grew louder. "Rozene, calm down. Why are you crying?"

Gradually, her sobbing subsided, and when she spoke, there were spaces of silence between her words. "I ... I ... I'm ... a-afraid."

"Afraid of what?"

She rested her back against the seat, not meeting his eyes, for there was no empathy in his voice. "Afraid ... afraid of losing ... you," she gulped, "and-and the children."

One part of him wanted to shout she already did, but he decided not to, afraid he might send her over the edge. He couldn't drum up a response so he watched her hoping she would say something else.

She graced him with unhappy, puffy eyes, and tear-stained cheeks. "Larry, please." She wrung her hands together, "I don't want the children to know right now." She had to convince him not to tell the children - not now, but really not ever.

"They will know something isn't right with us."

"Please try. If they sense anything, please let me be the one to break it to them."

"Okay." He sighed, not looking at her. She expected a lot. Yet, despite the pain she'd cause him, he was willing to handle this weekend for the children's sake.

"I'll be in Madison's room," she said, before walking out of the gazebo.

Larry watched as she quickly made her way to the back patio and then disappeared in the house. He still had not come up with any reason why she'd cheated on him. There was no rationale for it. If she'd stolen, lied, broken the law, slap somebody, sold the house, done anything ... anything but that, he would have taken her back. But no, she played him like a fool after nineteen years of marriage. He was beyond miffed. She had better be glad he loved his children or this weekend would definitely not be happening.

Rozene dropped on Madison's bed, feeling winded. But she took the time to take her woes before God.

"Oh, Lord. You know I made a mess, a total mess of my life. I want to be better, Lord, I pray your will be done in my life as it is established in heaven. God let this weekend be easy for everyone. I pray for understanding between me and my husband. Oh, Lord, cause him to look at me with compassion and love.

Oh, God! Oh, God!" She sobbed, "It breaks my heart when he looks at me as if," she gulped, "as if I don't matter. I feel crushed, crushed and insignificant. His gaze reduces me to naught and I can't breathe when it happens. Lord, I know I caused this situation, but I pray for your grace to walk through this fire. I don't want my family to break apart so I humbly ask you to mend all the broken pieces and put us back together again. Thank you, Lord, in the name of Jesus Christ, I pray, amen."

******

The beeping of her cell phone woke Rozene. She reached for it on the nightstand, and turned off the alarm, wondering why it was set for 2:00 AM. She had meant to set it for midnight, to get up and type a paragraph or two of her new book, *Undeniably Yours: The Journey to Love.* She'd decided to put off, *Letters to Wives* for another season or when she was back in sync with Larry. She had to hope.

156

She checked her cell phone call log and noticed the children had called. She also had a few missed calls from a private number, but no messages. A troubled sigh escaped from deep within as she placed her phone on the nightstand and reached for her Kindle. She began reading Psalm 32, but a few verses in, her stomach began to growl.

"I knew there was something I should be doing," she said, clutching her stomach. Rolling out of bed, she slipped on the matching red robe for her lingerie. Then armed with her Kindle in hand, she headed to the kitchen.

Ten minutes later, she made a cup of cocoa, and then generously spread strawberry cream cheese over two slices of bread. She perched on the stool around the island, and continued reading Psalm 32 while eating.

Larry stood near the kitchen door taking in Rozene, beautifully decked out in her red silk lingerie, her hair tossed behind her back. She had finally finished eating and was now totally engrossed in reading. He wondered if he should disturb her. The last thing he wanted was another bout of waterworks. He had heard when she walked past the bedroom door and decided to investigate what she was doing.

He had felt guilty for snapping at her during dinner. So he'd shared that with Pastor Fotola and he prayed with him. Pastor Fotola, as usual, encouraged him to forgive Rozene and to treat her with respect in light of their mirrored behavior.

Mirrored behavior? There we go again. Mama said the same thing.

Sure he'd committed adultery. But he always hated when Pastor Fotola compared his mishap to Rozene's sin. Not only did he not want to be reminded of it but he felt that his misadventure happened only once, while Rozene's was blatant adultery. Plus, she had pushed him into sin since she'd deliberately withheld her body from him. As

157

anger threatened to explode, he diverted his thoughts to the children. He didn't want to be caught up in a situation where it seemed he had intentionally lied to them by withholding the news. He would not let this situation go past December, not into the New Year. No two ways about it.

He watched Rozene intently. His mind insisted he "X" the spot, but his eyes wanted a snapshot at close range.

"Glad to see you're eating," he said, casually leaning against the door frame.

Rozene mouth gaped and her Kindle fell on the countertop with a thud. *For the love of God, put some clothes on!* Her body perked up as she watched him, dressed in a gray pajama bottom. She squirmed under his gaze as his legs took him closer.

"Sorry, I didn't mean to startle you." He came to a stop at the top of the island and placed both hands on it. His razor sharp gaze trained on her, taking in her nightwear.

His shirtless body set off a hum in hers. "No-No problem."

"What?" he asked, watching her taking him in as if he was a thing to be consumed. It tickled him and a slight smile rose at the corners of his lips.

Embarrassed, Rozene slipped off the stool. "Nothing," she responded, walking towards the refrigerator and taking out a bottle of water. She all but gasped when she was about to close the door of the refrigerator. Larry was standing next to her. She stared at his chest, unable to meet his eyes. "Did you want something?" she asked.

He didn't speak for a while. He was busy mentally photographing her red getup. "A bottle of water, please."

She gave him hers, took out another bottle, and then closed the door. *Are you going to move or what?* He wouldn't, so she moved away but she could feel his eyes on her. She decided not to look at him. What if he still had that icy look in his eyes or worst, scorn? Feeling self-conscious, she pulled on her robe, wishing it was longer, it fell mid-thigh.

She left her bottled water on the island and made her way to the sink with the tea cup and plate she'd used. She washed them, hoping he would be gone by the time she turned around. She took her time to wash the tea cup and plate, and then set them down in the dish drainer.

Larry finished his water and placed the empty bottle on the island. He watched Rozene, taking in her hair and small waist before moving to her toned legs. He knew she was trying to avoid him and with good reason. He hadn't exactly been Mr. Charming, but she had done him wrong. *You did her wrong too*, an inner voice cautioned. *How do you think she's going to feel when she finds out?* He would never tell her. And he was not about to let anyone – not his mother, not Pastor Fotola – pressure him into telling her.

Rozene still had her back turned to him, when she reached for a sheet of paper towel and dried her hands, then dropped it in the garbage bin. Now, she had no choice but to turn around. Was he still there?

Yes. He was still there, leaning against the refrigerator, and watching her as if he had all the time in the world. He didn't even avert his eyes when she turned around. Well, she didn't care. Right now, even if he was going to help her out this weekend, she was not staying in his presence. He had wounded her enough. *No more,* her eyes signaled to him as she walked back to the island, determined to bid him goodnight.

After taking up her bottled water and Kindle, she faced him.

"The children called while you were resting," he said before she could speak. "I told them not to wake you."

Relief hit her. "I noticed they had called. Is everything okay with them?"

"Yes. They are good. Just reminding me to pick them up tomorrow."

She smiled. "As if you would forget. I can't wait to see them."

"Now she looks at me. And wow, she smiles too," he said drily.

After a brief hesitation, she spoke, having swallowed the lump in her throat. "It's just difficult ... all over." She looked away from him. "I try not to look at you because," her voice broke and for a moment she wanted to weep, "you look at me ... as if I don't matter to you anymore. I'm ashamed of what I did to destroy our marriage." Feeling like she would choke, she stilled herself to regain control of her emotions.

"You know it's difficult for me to play a role. How can I look at you the same way? You treated me like a fool because I loved you."

"I'm sorry. I'm really sorry."

The silence stretched on forever.

"So am I," he said, in a clipped tone.

She bolted. But she hadn't made it to the door when strong arms lifted her off the ground. The bottled water and her Kindle fell to the ground.

"Put me down," she yelled, struggling against him.

"Only if you stop fighting."

Winded, she stopped.

He placed her on the ground but his hand still circled her waist, keeping her in place.

"I-I need to go," she said, conscious of their skin to skin contact.

Larry cupped her chin with his hand, forcing her to look at him. "For the children's sake, I promise I'll do the best I can this weekend."

Tears ran down her cheeks and she wiped them away. "Okay, thanks. I-I'm off to bed."

"Pray for me, please," he told her before releasing her.

She nodded and quickly left the kitchen.

Larry closed his eyes for a moment and sent up a silent prayer.

Lord, you know I need more of you and less of me. Help me to do what I need to do this weekend.

He opened his eyes, picked up her Kindle and bottled water from the ground and placed them on the island, before heading back to bed.

CHAPTER 20

"Today's the day!" Rozene threw her hands in the air. Her grin widened at the thought of seeing her children.

She looked over the eight-seater oval table laden with breakfast goodies in the nook, before moving back to the kitchen. She was making omelets, when Larry entered with a loud, "Morning."

She glanced over her shoulder and returned his greeting before turning her attention to the omelet she was making.

"Something smells good." He leaned in with his back resting on the cupboard top near the stove to inspect the omelet.

A whiff of his cologne wafted into her nostrils. "Tha-thanks."

Larry's dark brown gaze ran slowly over her face. He wondered what she was so nervous about. "Need help?"

She stared at him as if she didn't hear him, before pointing to the kettle resting on the stove, then the two teacups behind him. "Pour -"

"Sure." He took the kettle from the stove and poured water into the two teacups.

"Please put them on the table," she told him, composing herself.

She turned off the burner, and then put the omelets on two plates and followed him into the kitchen nook.

They ate, keeping their conversation light, if you can call it that. Nevertheless, several times, Larry felt Rozene's assessing stare. He finished eating and then wiped his mouth with a napkin before meeting her gaze.

She blushed, hastily sipping her orange juice.

He continued to look at her, his eyes questioning her reasons for studying him.

She gulped more of her orange juice before murmuring, "Sorry, I didn't mean to."

"That's hard to believe. You've been watching me ever since we sat down. What is it?"

A slow sigh of regret escaped. "You ... could you be," her mouth formed the rest of the sentence, but no sound came. She tried again, softly, "Could you be more loving towards me?"

"Say that again." He swirled the orange juice so the ice cubes clinked the edge of the glass, then took a sip.

She looked even more nervous.

"Honestly, I didn't hear what you said."

She twitched nervously on the chair. "I-I was saying if it was pos-possible for you to be more loving towards me."

He shifted his gaze for a moment to his empty plate before him. Of course, she was right. He needed to beef up his affection or the kids would know off the bat that something was wrong.

He sighed loudly. Their marriage was now all about keeping up appearances.

"I know I'm asking a lot," she offered quietly.

"Well, you could help by not being so tense and tearful around me. And please quit looking at me with sorrowful eyes. You knew what you were doing with that man. And while I'm at it, stop looking at me as if you want me. You made your choice clear."

Rozene's face flushed with embarrassment. For the first time in her life, she attempted a vanishing act. When that failed, she looked at her plate, murmuring, "Sorry."

A long silence ensued.

Something about her wanting him annoyed Larry to no end. He didn't care either that his body was acting all perky in her presence. He was determined to keep his body under subjection, even if it killed him. His lips tightened as

163

he looked at her. "Like I said last night, for the children's sake, I'll do the best I can this weekend."

Rozene nodded without meeting his eyes.

"Thanks for breakfast. I'll be leaving within the hour," Larry said. "I won't be back to the office until Tuesday but I have stuff to get done on the road. I'm also conducting a resume writing session at the Learning Center, after lunch. After that, I'll head to the airport for the children. Do you need anything?"

"No," Rozene responded quietly.

"Excuse me," Larry said, rising from the table and taking up a handful of plates before making his way to the kitchen.

"I'll get the rest and wash up."

"Thank you," he said before disappearing through the door.

Rozene shook her head in disbelief. *Yes, I do want you,* she wanted to shout. A deep sigh slipped free from her as Larry re-entered the nook.

He stopped briefly at the table before moving on. He needed the strength of the Lord to get through this weekend.

Rozene rose from her seat and absentmindedly cleared the rest of the dishes from the table. After washing the dirty dishes, she took out a packet of fish from the freezer, and placed it in a huge bowl filled with water. She stared at the bowl as it sat where she'd placed it on the cupboard top. Like the packet of fish, she felt like she needed to thaw out. Just chill out. Take it easy. Cooking had always put her in a great mood. Plus, it was always a pleasure to cook for her family.

Family?

Yes, we are still a family. She had to believe that. She was trusting God.

Still deep in thought, she squirted lotion from a bottle near the sink and rubbed her hands together, and then mentally planned her day – spend time in prayer, write another chapter, re-read notes for videotaping session with Don, move out of Madison's room to the master suite, cook dinner, and rest.

She moved to the kitchen window and her breath caught, mesmerized by the lush landscape – the beautiful colors and hues in the backyard. The sun danced through the window, yet she didn't seem to notice. She covered her heart with her hands feeling instantly humbled at the sight before her.

Larry entered the kitchen, and squinted against the dazzling morning sunlight. He stopped at the island when he noticed a fiery halo formed around Rozene's light-brown hair. His muscular legs covered the distance between them and he planted his hands on either side of her, trapping her against the cupboard before lowering his head to kiss her cheek.

Frantic, Rozene whipped her head towards him and found herself in a brief lip lock with him.

Immediately they broke apart.

"Good-goodness!" she spluttered, clutching the sink for support. She could feel her heart pounding in her temple. His touch had scorched her like a brand.

Larry saw her labored breathing. He hoped she wouldn't pass out on him. *How will we ever convince the children we're okay?*

Still shaken, Rozene made her way to the island and sat on a stool. She eyed Larry, with obvious restraint. "What was that all about?"

He lifted his hands and raised his eyes heavenward. "I was just practicing for when the children get here."

"Couldn't you warn me?"

"Why would I? Wouldn't it be natural for me to kiss or hug you? When they are here, do you expect me to tell you in advance that I'm about to touch you?"

"That's different. At least I would be expecting it then."

"I remember a time when you couldn't wait to be in my arms."

Here we go again. "I still can't wait to be in your arms." If it wasn't for Larry's dark piercing gaze, she wouldn't have known she'd said it aloud. It was time to do the vanishing act, again.

Lord knows she and Larry had had their fair share of arguments. They both had strong personalities but they were good at communicating expectations. They were the perfect match, yet the perfect storm. It was a delicate balance but as the years flew by, they had moved towards a more perfect union.

She had no intention of picking a fight now. Not with the children coming home. But what she disliked, was arguing for arguing sake over the silliest, dumbest, slightest thing. There had to be some point to the argument. Now, exactly what was the point of their argument? *Oh, yes – There was a time when I couldn't wait to be in his arms.* Ignoring her rapidly beating heart, she reiterated, "I still can't wait to be in your arms."

Larry stood, looking at her from the other side of the island. *Was wondering where that fire went? Too bad, I'm not going there with you.* "Is that how you're going to be, jittery when I touch you?"

"No. I wasn't expecting you to do so until the children are here."

"Okay then, humor me. Give me a hug."

She knitted her brows, wondering if he was joking. "Please. I know how to hug you."

166

She tried to sound nonchalant, but he knew she was far from it. He shrugged but did not move. "You need practice because you're all jumpy."

Her mouth went dry. "Okay."

Larry stood rooted to the spot. Seconds turned into minutes and he sighed heavily before pushing away from the island and moving towards the door.

"Larry!" Rozene called out in a strangled voice. For all her courageous talk, it was about time she developed a backbone.

He stopped at the sound of the desperation in her voice.

She willed him to turn and face her as she approached, but he didn't.

When they were face to face, Rozene ventured a quick scan, taking in his strong jawline and tempting bow-shaped lips. But his eyes chilled her heart. They were as hard as steel. Nevertheless, a rush of courage engulfed her, and she moved closer to him, and tenderly circled his neck with her arms, gazing at him.

His posture rigid, Larry's icy gaze raked over her face, lingering for a couple of seconds on her lips, before returning to her eyes.

The muscles in her belly tightened in reaction, and her heart skipped several beats under his unflinching scrutiny.

He hugged her lightly around her waist, and she heard the steady beating of his heart - strong yet tender. Passionate yet restrained.

In the midst of her mental deliberations, her body began to relax against his hard frame, and a feeling of rightness filled her. When she tip-toed and buried her head in his neck, she felt tiny tremors rocking his body.

He quickly released her and put her away from him. "Okay," he said in what he considered his most normal voice under the circumstances. "Later."

Without waiting for her response, Larry walked out of the kitchen. The quivering of his stomach testifying that his body had once again betrayed him. His nostrils flared as he stood in the doorway leading to the garage. *How can I still find her desirable after all she has done?* When no rational excuse came, he closed the door behind him.

Rozene slumped down on a stool at the island, bracing back tears at her pity party for one. She was full of pity – for herself and for Larry. His inability to forgive her would forever keep them apart. As soon as the thought formed in her mind, she rose to full height. "No. Not so," she declared loudly. "My God will perfect that which concerns me." *I won't limit myself because of my blunders and failures. It's a new day and it will be a great day.*

CHAPTER 21

Casting a furtive glance at the digital clock on the nightstand in Madison's room, Rozene noted she had two hours to go before Larry arrived with Mason and Madison. Thankfully, she had completed her "to-do" list.

Me time. And she had all intentions of doing that as she moved down the hallway and entered the master suite in high spirit. Smiling, she let out a shout of praise, and began twirling. Suddenly, she stopped. Someone was interrupting her celebration. She cautiously reached for her cell phone on the bed. *Private number.*

"Hello," she answered.

"Ro, at last. Been calling you for the last two hours. Are you avoiding my calls?"

"How can I help you, Chandler? I already explain-"

"Ro, baby, what's with that tone? I'm not feeling the love I know you have for me."

"I need to go. What do you want?"

"No need to be rude. I wanted to know when I'll be seeing you. I need some me time with you."

Rozene closed her eyes and let out a deep breath. He was annoying the crap out of her. "As I explained, my children will be here this weekend," she said slowly as if that would make him understand.

"I will be calling your phone until I get the visit you had promised me."

In a voice that sounded like she was going to the gallows, she said, "I'll see you on Wednesday."

"Wednesday?" He questioned in an incredulous voice. "Aren't the kids leaving on Monday? Why can't I see you on Monday?"

She knew he was guessing. "Because I am busy. It's going to be Wednesday, so take it or leave it. And that's the last time I'm meeting with you, Chandler."

"Wow. Is that how you're going to treat me? And why are you calling it a meeting. Thought you loved hanging out with me."

"It's a meeting. So see you on Wednesday."

"How about Tuesday? I'll make it worth your while."

Rozene all but threw the phone against the wall. "I'll meet with you at six sharp Wednesday evening."

"Yes, ma'am," Chandler relented. "That's if I don't see you before."

Rozene gripped the phone. "No," she said in a tight voice. "We will not be seeing each other before Wednesday."

He chuckled wickedly. "We'll see."

"Bye," Rozene said, disconnecting the call. *Why! Why! Why, Jesus? Why didn't I crucify my flesh?*

******

Almost two hours later, Rozene made her way downstairs to welcome her family home.

Home.

Without notice, bubbles of anticipation and joy surged through her heart. Just then, the doorbell chimed and a wide grin dominated her face. *That could only be Madison. Anxious to get in yet refusing to use her key.*

Rozene swung the door open to squeals of delight as Madison poured herself into her arms and kissed her cheek.

"Mom, I am soooo glad to see you. I missed you." Madison hugged her mother tightly, murmuring words of endearment.

Rozene looked at the spitting image of herself when she was finally able to pry Madison away from her. In a few seconds, Madison was back into her arms. Rozene patted her back. "My baby, so glad to have you home." She rocked her for a moment, signaling to Mason to give her a minute.

Mason would have none of it. His gorgeous dark brown eyes told her that. She smiled at him, marveling how he'd grown even more to look like his father.

"Is there any room in the inn for me?" Mason hollered, dropping two carry-on cases on the floor. "Back away, Madison, my turn."

Larry entered and closed the door, contented to watch the drama unfold.

Reluctantly, Madison relinquished her hold on her mother, but not before telling her, "You smell wonderful and your hair is fabulous."

Rozene was glad she had taken the time to create a soft updo with a loose bun to the back of her head.

"Thank you, baby," Rozene responded before Mason hugged her warmly.

"Yeah, Mom, you look as radiant as ever." Mason eyed her teasingly. "I see the accident didn't do any damage. Dad is clearly doing something right."

Rozene blushed, touching the bandage at her temple. "Behave yourself, young man. I can still give you time out."

"No, Mom, please don't," Mason said, hugging her again.

When he released her, Rozene eyed him, smiling. "Welcome home."

A flash of red caught her eyes and Rozene's heart turned in her chest at the sight of the stunning red roses that Larry held in his hand. A strange cry came from her lips and she covered her face with her hands as tears threatened.

The room was noticeable quiet as Larry held her while she buried her head in his chest. The children exchanged glances and Larry mouthed that she was all right.

"Guess I won't be buying you any more roses," he teased, rubbing Rozene's back.

Rozene pulled away from him, half smiling. "Sorry. Thanks so much, honey. Don't know where that came from." She took the flowers from him, then reached up and lightly kissed his lip.

Larry was still mesmerized by the tiny peck on his lips, when Mason said, "Way to go, Dad. I want to be just like you one day. Mom has it bad for you. But whoa! You're a goner too."

Larry grinned at him. "I would disagree but that would make me a liar."

"Are you two finished having fun at my expense?" Rozene eyed Larry and Mason as Madison hugged her waist.

"All good, Mom." Mason smiled at her, before shifting his gaze to Madison. "Madison, you're not going to monopolize Mom all weekend, are you?"

"Of course not, Mason." Madison grinned at him.

Larry and Rozene watched as a careful sigh of relief left Mason, even though he looked unconvinced.

"You are your Daddy's child," Rozene told him, smiling. She circled his waist with her hand. "And you're as handsome as ever."

"Thanks, Mom." Mason smiled at her. "Must be my fresh haircut." He slipped out of Rozene's arms and posed like he was on the cover of a GQ magazine.

Laughter erupted from everyone.

"You are super fine, son," Rozene said as Mason slipped a hand across her shoulder.

Madison pursed her lips and eyed Mason. "Mom, don't be making his ego any bigger. The girls at college are already doing that."

"Am I missing something, son? We need to catch up."

Mason smiled at her. "Not to worry, Mom. It's all about my school work right now."

"Right?" Madison quipped, before squealing and running away as Mason attempted to pinch her arm.

Larry and Rozene couldn't help but chuckle at the lively banter between their children. "Okay, let's get you all settled in," Larry told them.

Mason grabbed both their carry-on cases and eyed Madison. "You better be glad I love you."

Madison slapped him on the shoulder as he walked by her. "Of course, you do, big brother."

"That's right. You better recognize," Mason said as he climbed the staircase. "I was born before you. I'm your big brother."

"Yes, you are," Madison chuckled behind him, "by all of ten minutes. You would think it was ten years."

"You better have respect for those ten-"

"Okay, you two," Rozene said from the foot of the staircase. "Hurry back for dinner. Ready in fifteen minutes."

"Yes, Mom." Mason and Madison said in unison as they walked across the landing.

Rozene smiled as she watched them. Nothing much had changed between them. They loved each other and had always been close.

After dinner, Larry and Mason washed the dishes while Rozene and Madison prepared dessert and set it up in the family room.

Soon, Madison curled up by her mother's side on the huge plush yellow sofa, eating Peach Cobbler.

"Sorry, Dad, you had Mom to yourself for a long time. I need some me time with her."

Larry knitted his brows. "And she has the nerves to say it." He was stretched out on the matching sofa across from them. "You better be glad you're my child."

Madison grinned at him. "Thanks, Dad. It's just for this weekend. I'll return her soon."

Before Larry could respond, Mason jumped in. "I hope you know I need some me time with Mom too. If you're nice to me, I may even let you have some me time with Dad."

"Nice to you," Madison said sarcastically.

Mason leaned forward from the sofa nearby and rested his bowl of Peach Cobbler on the coffee table. "See, you have no respect for your big brother."

Larry reduced the volume on the huge flat screen TV. "I can imagine how you two are on campus."

"Dad, you couldn't imagine it, even in your wildest dream." Madison spoke with great animation. "He's a mess."

Rozene chuckled. "Is he up to the same thing? He has been chasing away boys from you since elementary school."

"You know I saw that completely different," Mason chuckled. "I'm helping to narrow the choice for her by scaring off the unwanted, no backbone admirers. Big brothers do that you know. Dad, you'll understand."

"Of course, I do." Larry responded. "Madison, let my son do his job."

Madison rolled her eyes in desperation, sitting up on the sofa. "Mom, do you hear this madness. If it was up to Mason, I would be sitting in my dorm room every evening watching TV, and eating TV dinners.

"Come on Madison, you know I'm helping you out. I'm also helping out those long-suffering brothers who you ignore, yet they won't leave you alone. I'm just looking out for you little sis."

Madison shook her head, her ponytail dangling from side to side. "Mom, tell him to stop. I can take care of myself." She shot a plea for help in her father's direction. "Dad?"

Larry looked over at her and smiled, mystified by her energy. Then, it dawned on him. "Seems like there's more to this than you're confessing Madison."

Madison's mouth opened into a perfect O, before she exclaimed, "Dad!" She blushed, burying her face in her mother's side.

"Oh! Looks serious too," Rozene chuckled while Madison poked her side.

"I'm going to let her tell you about that. But this, I'll tell you. While I'm busy chasing away the guys who are latching on to her, she only has eyes for one. That's when she's not busy teaching her praise dance classes. Her girls are doing very well, by the way. Their performances have been outstanding."

"Great," Rozene said. "So glad you're able to continue your praise dance classes." They had always encouraged their children to use their abilities to bless others. "How is preparation for Christmas production coming along?"

A sigh of relief left Madison as she sat up. "It's going really great. Loving the process. We're going to have dance, drama, and hopefully, a bit of singing."

Even as she spoke, Madison felt like choking Mason for 'spilling the beans' like that. Thankfully, her parents were sensitive and knew not to go there with her in the open.

Rozene smiled at her. "Sounds good."

"Great." Larry echoed Rozene's sentiments.

"Thanks. It has been a blessing."

"It sure has," Mason quipped, "in more than one way."

175

Her legs stretched out and crossed at the ankles, Madison eyed Mason. *Just quit, please.* "Yes, it has," she agreed, ignoring his double meaning.

Mason grimace. He had outed her, and realized how appalling that was, even though their parents deliberately did not take it on ... at least for the moment.

"Mason's soccer team is doing well too," Madison remarked. "They have won several competitions. Not only that." She eyed Mason. "He still finds time to ward off all the females that are flocking to him. He's a genius."

Rozene grinned at her. "No kidding."

"But you know me, Mom," Mason said, filled with self-importance, "I'm all focused on my school work and church."

Rozene looked at him. "Is that so?"

"Yes, Mom! School work, soccer, group dates and church. That's all I'm into right now."

Rozene smiled at him. He was so much like his father. All in or nothing. "Okay, son. I know how you do."

"I'm waiting for my special lady, Mom. When the time is right, God will allow our paths to cross. In the meantime, I'm all about the straight and narrow."

Another smile tilted the corners of Rozene's mouth as she gazed at him while he spoke. He always had the potential for a powerful built, just like his father. It hadn't escaped her that his shoulders had broadened slightly. Certainly not problematic for him. And, she expected him to be just as formidable as his father.

"I taught you well," Larry chimed in.

"Yes, you did, Dad," Mason said, stroking his chin with his index finger. "You sure did."

Larry smile at the replica of himself. God's favor was on his family and he was happier because of it. He recalled how he and Rozene were happy, yet almost hopelessly unprepared when the twins were born since

Rozene did not want to know the sexes of the babies. But God had been good. They made it through.

Two hours later, Larry prayed and they all climbed the stairs and bid each other goodnight. Rozene almost jumped as the bedroom door closed with a thud behind Larry. They had not discussed their sleeping arrangements and she was contemplating saying something about that when he spoke.

"You can have the bed."

Rozene turned to look at him and found him looking at her. Neither spoke but she was unsettled by his icy stare. She let out a slow breath before asking, "Where are you -?"

"I'll sleep on the daybed." He moved towards the lounge area in the room.

"Thanks," she said with a barely intelligible mumble. She headed to the bathroom which she knew would always be a safe haven.

Larry was grateful she did not attempt further conversation with him. He was glad to see the children but he was beat. Even though he'd tried his best to appear normal, it had taken more out of him than he was prepared to give. He needed to take a shower and regroup for tomorrow. He stretched out on the daybed, commanding his mind to stay in the bedroom instead of the bathroom.

Eventually, Rozene climbed under the bedcovers, making a point of appearing oblivious of Larry's presence, but in truth, she was aware of all of his movements. She couldn't help it. He was so near and yet so far. She saw him walk to the bathroom and heard him take a shower. Twenty minutes later, he reappeared with a comforter in hand.

She gazed at his athletic frame as he threw the comforter on the daybed before climbing under it. *I've loved him forever*, she thought. Gravity was pulling her body down into a deep sleep, but she turned on her side and

177

drew the covers close to her neck, determined to observe him as long as she could. Nevertheless, before long, a wave of exhaustion carried her away and she drifted off to sleep.

CHAPTER 22

Rozene entered the kitchen, just in time to hear Larry's good-natured chuckles and Madison's snickering as she high-fived her father who was sitting on a stool near the island. "Thanks for being a witness, Dad." She held up a coin. "Some things will never change."

"And some things will," Mason added, looking not too happy with his hands covered in soap at the sink. They had just tossed a coin to determine who would wash the dishes. He'd lost as usual. "Don't think I'll be washing dishes all weekend. Just this time."

Madison grinned mischievously. "No need to toss the coin again. You always lose, so prepare to do dishes all weekend."

Mason gave her a threatening look. "You would like that, huh?"

"Well, good morning," Rozene greeted them. "Thanks for waking me up."

"Oh, Mom!" Madison shrieked with delight. "Glad you're up. Dad said not to wake you, you're tired. The good part is we get to spend most of the day together while Mason and Dad go off by themselves, and we'll meet up for early dinner. What you think?"

"I'm still at - you didn't wake me up for breakfast."

A murmur of, "Ohhh," came from everyone, and Madison and Mason moved to group hug her.

"Come on, Dad," Madison encouraged.

A look of horror crossed Rozene's face but Larry had no choice but to participate. Soon, the children wiggled out of the embrace and he found himself cuddling Rozene. His heart tripped as Mason spoke, "Dad, kiss Mom and make up. It's your fault. You're the one who told us not to wake her."

Larry felt Rozene go still in his arms.

179

His hand cupping her chin, he lifted her face to look at him. It was time to show her what she'd been missing. Without thinking, he kissed her ... slowly and deeply. She clutched his shirt, lifting her chin higher as he took her over the edge, and explored her mouth in a dance she would always remember. When he lifted his head, she was panting. He brought his lips within an inch of hers again, and her lips instantly parted. It was then that Larry remembered the children. You could hear a pin drop. *Note to self*, Larry thought. *Not the kind of kiss you do before the children.* He needed to divert attention away from his little mindboggling performance. That was one lesson that didn't go as intended. The blaze between them almost derailed him, if he was going to be honest.

"I'm going to get your breakfast," he told Rozene, acting as if nothing happened.

She nodded, avoiding his eyes and then held on to the island to steady herself as he released her.

He looked at the children who were busy sending silent coded messages to each other. "Get back to work," he told them jokingly.

"Yes, sir," Madison hollered, holding back laughter.

"Daaaad! You go, Dad!" Mason exclaimed, grinning from ear to ear.

"Attempt at humor noted, son." Larry wagged a finger at him.

"But Dad, no one is laughing," Mason responded cheekily.

Larry rolled his eyes, telling him, "Give it a few minutes to settle in. They'll get it."

That silenced Mason, who gave Madison the "evil" eye. She was snickering loudly.

Larry moved towards the microwave and warmed the sausages they had left for Rozene. As he poured boiling water on the cocoa in her favorite cup, he wondered what on earth had possessed him to kiss her like that.

Rozene sat quietly at the island, calming her frayed nerves.

Soon, Larry set her breakfast before her.

"Thanks," she said quietly, unable to meet his gaze.

"You're welcome," Larry said. "Enjoy."

He shook his head as he looked across at the twins who were snickering until their shoulders were shaking. "Look at you two. What are we going to do with them, Lord?"

The twins snickered even more. "Sorry, Dad," Madison said. "It's Mason's fault." She bumped Mason with her hip. "He's talking crazy."

Larry shook his head from side to side. "Be ready within an hour, Mason" he said before walking out of the kitchen.

Some forty minutes later, Rozene managed to get her body temperature under control. She stared at herself in the mirror on the dressing table, wondering what on earth had possessed Larry to kiss her like that. Not that she didn't enjoy it. It was simply troubling considering how he'd been treating her since she'd arrived home.

Her cell phone started to vibrate, and she glanced at it on the bed, but decided to ignore it.

Larry poked his head through the room door. "We're leaving. We'll all meet up say three o'clock. You and Madison can decide on the meeting spot and text or call us. Do you need to get that?" Larry asked pointing to her phone.

"No. I'll return the call later." Thankfully, the phone stopped vibrating.

"Okay," Larry said moving away. "We are off and running."

"We are right behind you," she said, grabbing her purse from the bed. She reached for her cell phone. *Private number.*

"Are you okay, Mom?" Madison asked.

Rozene jumped. She was so busy wishing Chandler away that she didn't see Madison enter the room. She gave Madison a slight smile. "I am now. Looking forward to our time together."

"Me too."

Just then, her cell phone began to vibrate and she glanced at the screen. *Private number.* She fixed her gaze before looking at Madison. "Baby, I'll meet you downstairs. Give me a moment, I need to take this."

"Okay, Mom."

Rozene was waiting for the door to close behind Madison when Larry entered the room. Her knees went weak, and she stared wide-eyed at him, her mouth gaping.

Larry stopped in his tracks. "Is something wrong?"

"No! No."

"Are you going to get that?" he asked, moving towards the lounge area in the room.

"Yes."

Rozene's palms began to sweat as she silently urged the phone to stop vibrating, and it did. But her relief was short lived, it started vibrating again. She decided to answer, because the last thing she wanted was to raise Larry's suspicion, any further.

"Hello," she answered cautiously, moving towards the door, and hoping to get through it before Larry finished what he was doing. Out of the corners of her eyes, she saw Larry walking towards her and had to stop herself from running. In the back of her mind, she heard a response from the caller.

"Who is this?" she asked.

"It's Don. Happy Saturday! You seem busy. Did I call at a bad time?"

Relief hit her and she leaned against the door post, and glanced up to see a puzzled look on Larry's face. She ignored Larry's expression and focused on her conversation. "Hi! Did you change your number? I know you called before. Sorry, I was getting ready to head out."

"No, I didn't call before. And no, I haven't changed my number. I'm using Derek's phone. Ran out of the house and left my phone. My son has me running all over the city before he heads back to the university. But enough about me. You ran across my mind so I was giving you a shout out. I know the twins are here for the weekend. Hope all is going well."

"Thanks, Don. We are doing great. Glad to have the children home. Such a blessing. We are hanging out today." She glanced at Larry who was motioning for her to walk and talk at the same time, and she did.

"I like the sound of that," Don told her.

Rozene smiled as she descended the stairs with Larry. "Will be fun."

"You know if you're having any issue with Chand-"

"Don, thanks, but-"

"I'm serious. Just let me know."

"Let's talk about that another time. I have three pairs of eyes looking at me crazy."

"Okay. Talk with you soon."

******

"Mom, thanks for your patience while we visited the center." Madison smiled at her mother, three hours later. They had stopped for lunch at a deli. "Thanks for trusting me to help with managing it even though I'm away."

183

"The pleasure was all mine. The girls were amazing as usual. You know, I'm thinking of changing the name of the center to yours."

"Mom, nooo. The performing arts center carries your name. What would grandmama and grandpapa think? It was a gift from them to you."

"All right, let me put some more thought into that. But it's totally your baby now. You have been doing a great job with it."

"Thanks, Mom. But please don't change the name."

"Okay, that's on pause." Rozene smiled at her. "You ran me ragged today. All that shopping, running from store to store."

Madison feigned a look of shock. "Oh, Mom, not you. You're always filled with so much energy."

"Yes, but my poor feet."

"A little rest will get your feet feeling like normal again." Madison smiled, encouraging. "Our dancers' feet covered a lot of ground. I wish you would start dancing again."

Rozene waved Madison away. "You're kidding, right?"

"Mom -" Madison paused as the waiter placed their meals before them. "Thanks, Joey."

Joey smiled, telling her, "You are most welcome!" before taking his leave.

"Mom, you're the one who told me folks can dance at any age. Have you changed your mind?"

Rozene wrinkled her nose. "Let's pray before you take me to task." She prayed, then told her, "No. Haven't changed my mind. Dancing is such a fun activity. Everyone should dance, no matter the age."

"Now you're talking, Mom. I'm picturing a mother daughter dance. Can you see it?"

"I walked right into that one. Sadly, my eyes were open so no excuse will suffice. Yes, I can see it, in the distant future."

Madison smiled, and then took up her sandwich. "There's hope then. I can work with that."

"It may cost you a bit, but you can always hope."

Madison was quiet for a moment and Rozene knew that she had something important to say but couldn't get it out.

"What else is going on with you? You told me how great your classes were. I heard about your praise dance classes, but is there something else that Mom needs to know."

Madison blushed. "I'm in love, but it's complicated."

It was Rozene's turn to feign a look of shock. "Complicated?"

"Of all the guys to fall for, I had to fall for one who doesn't seem to be aware I exist."

"Say it ain't so," Rozene teased.

"Mom, he acts as if he doesn't know I have strong feelings for him. While I on the other hand, I'm all smitten." She grabbed her chest. "I want to tattoo his name on my forehead."

Rozene smiled at her with understanding. After all, she and Larry did fall in love during high school, at a tender age according to her mother. "It can't be that bad. He's probably trying to get himself together; you are quite a tough young lady you know."

"I hope not that tough." Madison sighed. "His name is Tyler. And Mom, when I tell you he loves the Lord, I mean he genuinely loves God. He's the youth leader at the church Mason and I attend but he's also studying Civil and Environmental Engineering at MIT. He has another year left in school."

This is serious. Rozene watched as Madison glowed as she spoke. This was the first time Madison had ever confessed about being in love ... ever.

"Mom, I love him endlessly. My code name for him is HC - Hot Chocolate." A girlish giggle escaped her lips. "I said that out loud, didn't I?"

Rozene chuckled. "You sure did."

"Mom, he has such a great heart for people and he is an amazing speaker," Madison gushed. "I went to youth service one Friday evening and he spoke about love. He said, 'Please don't say, I love you unless you mean it. Love is an action word. Saying, I love you comes with action, responsibility, and commitment.' He blew me away in that service."

"Are you friends? What's going on?"

"Yes. We are friends. We are together on all the church's outreach programs and he helps me whenever the dancers minister at church or at another venue. He volunteers to operate the music, and set the stage, and whatever else needs to be done. He's always there even when Mason can't help because of his soccer practice or something else. But, Mom, it seems he only wants to be friends."

"Did he say that? How old is he?"

"No, but his body language says it all. He's all of twenty two," she said dreamily.

"Have you been praying about it?"

"Yes. I love him, Mom."

Rozene smiled at her. "It's going to work out for your good, baby. Continue to commit the situation to the Lord and let him lead you. We'll get to meet him in December, right?"

"I hope so. Oh, remember, you promised to do a session with my dancers when you and Dad pick us up in December."

"Yes, I remember. The appointment is on my-" Suddenly, the color drained from her face as she looked beyond Madison into the eyes of Chandler. Ignoring her you've-got-to-be-kidding look, Chandler moved towards her. His stylish white Ralph Lauren shorts and navy polo shirt enhanced his eye-popping, jaw-dropping allure, causing heads to turn in his direction. In the distance, Rozene heard Madison's voice pulling her away from her straying thoughts but before she could respond, Chandler arrived at their table.

"Mrs. Kanate, great to see you," he flashed his charming, megawatt smile, extending his hand to her. "How are you?"

"Mr. Peynard. I'm doing great." Rozene had no choice but to shake his hand, after which she quickly return it to her side. She didn't bother to ask how he was doing, but that didn't deter him. Neither did her cool disposition. She stilled herself as he opened his mouth to speak.

"Doing really great myself," he mentioned, oozing pure joy. His dreamy eyes confirming - now that I see you. He looked at Madison. "This must be Madison. So nice to meet you at last."

Madison shook his hand, clearly puzzled. "Ah, nice to meet you too," she said extending her hand.

Chandler shook her hand and then released it, but not before telling her. "Heard so many great things about you."

Madison smiled, sending an eyebrow lift in her mother's direction.

"Mr. Peynard at one time volunteered with my book tour team." Rozene hastened to clarify. "Thanks so much for helping out," she told Chandler, her expression telling him to buzz off.

He flashed her a sensational smile. "You are always welcome. Anything for you, Mrs. Kanate. If you ever need

187

me, you know where to find me." He smiled at Madison. "Nice to finally meet you. Forgive me for disturbing your lunch."

Madison returned his smile obviously taken with his charm. "No problem. Nice meeting you too."

"Have an amazing day," Chandler said, before leaving.

"You too," Madison responded, while Rozene nodded her thanks.

Rozene released a breath she didn't realize she was holding. "Now, where were we?"

Madison's eyebrows shot up. "That was strangely disturbing. Nevertheless, that is a fine man, Mom."

Rozene maintained her cool. "Is he? Let's talk about your Mr. Fine."

Madison gave her a look that was between something isn't quite right and what are you not saying? "Yes. Tyler is fine but it's not just about his physique. He's the kind of husband that I see …" She paused as her mother's cell phone began to vibrate. Rozene looked at her phone in the pocket of her purse but made no move to retrieve it. "Are you going to answer, Mom? It could be Dad."

"Right."

Indeed, it was Larry who wanted them to meet up for dinner at 4:00 PM instead of 3:00 PM.

"Okay, honey, that time is good for us too. We are finishing up lunch. Then, we'll do our much needed manicures and pedicures before joining you guys."

******

Later that evening when Mason and Madison decided to spend time with their friends, Larry reminded them to also visit Armela, whom he knew would be overjoyed to see them.

After the children left, communication between him and Rozene was pretty much non-existent. He spent most of the evening hibernating in the study.

Around 9:00 PM, Rozene closed her laptop and was gathering her papers to clear the lounge area when she heard the bedroom door open and then closed. Larry entered the room and stood looking at her.

"I'm moving out now so you can relax," she told him.

When she finally piled all her stuff together, she placed them on the table in the lounge area. She turned and found him still looking at her. Unnerved, she decided to speak. "I'm going to take a shower." *That sounds like an invitation.* Showering together was a part of their usual routine ... well, most times at night before they went to bed. "I mean, I'll take a shower, then you can get the bathroom."

His eyes twinkled with laughter. "I see."

She hurried pass him to get to the bathroom, but stopped in her tracks when he spoke.

"Mason asked if we were okay. He said something was different about us. I tried to play it off but I don't think he bought it. He told me there was some kind of weird vibes around us."

"Oh, no!"

"It would help if you stop acting all nervous around me. At dinner, you were not your best self."

"I'm trying, Larry. It's just that I feel so ... so un-undeserving of your affection. And then, it's hard because I know you don't care for me anymore."

"I did say that I would try for the children's sake but every time I come near you, you freeze up. You need to relax. This was your idea, remember?"

"I'll try harder," she said, escaping to the bathroom to stop the flood of tears.

A loud sigh of sadness escaped Larry as he plopped down on the daybed.

Half an hour later, while Larry showered, Rozene slipped under the bedcovers, and began praying. She was grateful that despite her mistake, she still had her family. Before long, she fell asleep, only to be awakened by loud knocking on the door. Frightened, she flew back the bedcovers and sat up on the bed. "Who-who is it?"

"Us, Mom." Madison's voice floated in the room.

"Give -" Words left Rozene's mouth as her eyes landed on Larry who was strutting toward her, all manly and powerful in a black silk pajama bottom. She was sure her jaw dropped. It sure felt like it. Her eyes met his darkened gaze, and for a moment her breath halted. When his eyes shifted to her body, she realized her red lace lingerie was on display, and quickly flopped backwards, pulling the bedcovers over her body.

"I'll get it," he told her in a huskily voice, pulling on the nightshirt in his hand.

She watched as his legs swung into motion. She was in for another sleepless night, peering at him on the daybed, while wishing she was in his arms. Then in a panic, her head whipped towards the daybed. *Phew.* Larry had cleared it.

Larry opened the door, "Come on in."

The twins poured in, climbing on the bed.

Madison smiled at her mom. "We came to pray. Lord knows, Mason needs it."

"And you don't," Mason threatened Madison with his eyes.

During Mason and Madison's going-ons, Rozene shot a panic stricken look in Larry's direction, as anxiety knotted her inside. Usually in the bedroom, they had always prayed with all four of them lying side by side and holding hands on the huge bed.

"How were your visits?" Larry asked.

Rozene attempted to relax her face and made room for Larry on the bed but to her surprise, he slid under the bedcovers. She tried not to tense at their skin to skin contact for he had not buttoned his nightshirt.

Larry patted his chest and she rolled to rest her head on his chest while wrapping a hand around his waist. *Oh, Lord, this is good.* She snuggled deeper into his chest, her smile hidden from his vision. She almost moaned loudly when he began to caress her hair during the twin's happy banter about the visit with their friends and Armela.

Larry tried his best to hold back the warmth that was shooting from his toes to the rest of his body. Then, he realized he had to hold back more than his amorous feelings. All on their own, his fingers had begun stroking Rozene's hair. He shifted a bit, and then draped his hand across her shoulder.

It was then that Larry noticed the deafening silence. "I'm hearing you," Larry told Mason who was speaking before he actually faded from Larry's thoughts.

"Dad, you haven't heard a word I said since Mom rolled on your chest," Mason accused. "And Mom ..." The twins collapsed on each other laughing.

Rozene's eyes fluttered. *What have I missed?* "Did you say something, Mason?"

Mason pulled himself together, clutching Madison's shoulder. "Mom, Dad, what's going on with you two? We were barely gone a year and now we are back to find this kind of weird dynamics between both of you. It's good, weird, and different, all in one."

"We weren't gone that long," Madison chimed in. "I know you're used to being here all by yourselves but you've got to let us in. Like we were."

"And here I was thinking you would be gone forever," Larry teased.

"Dad!" Madison exclaimed, squeezing his foot before releasing it.

"No such thing," Rozene said, smiling. "You will always be our babies. Come on over and let us pray."

As usual, Mason lay beside his Mom while Madison lay next to her Dad. They took turns praying.

An hour later, after chitchatting, the twins bid them goodnight but not before Mason teased, "Mom, don't bring more babies in here."

Rozene was momentarily stunned.

Madison laughed so hard, she bowed over and even Larry let out a loud chuckle.

"You're on time out," Rozene threatened Mason.

He ran over and kissed her cheek before walking away with Madison who was still snickering.

"You're still on time out," Rozene yelled as the door closed behind them. She nestled closer to Larry and half buried her face in his shoulder. Her hand was warm on his chest, Larry made a pathetic attempt to move away, then stilled when she began to rub her cheek against his shoulder. She tilted her head to look up at his face, and placed a soft kiss against his jaw.

His heart thumping, Larry watched as she ran her fingers over his rippled chest.

"I love you so much," she murmured.

His eyes tracked the descent of her fingers on his stomach, and when the heat of her fingers burned against his skin, a low guttural sound burst from his lips.

At the sound of his pleasure, she grew bolder. Smiling up at him, her fingers toyed with the cord of his pajama bottom.

He tensed to keep his composure. "You will have to excuse me." His voice cool, despite his rising temperature.

192

No way was he going to be sidetracked by her beautiful body ... or by his reaction to her. Plus, his conscience would not allow him.

Embarrassed, Rozene rolled away from his chest, her back to him. Dread and a sense of inadequacy swept through her. She tried to calm her mind but when she couldn't get a handle on what had just transpired, tears flowed freely down her face.

Larry eased himself off the bed and walked over to the daybed. Every nerve in his body taut, begging him to return to the cozy spot. He held his head high. *Will not, even if I have to twitch for the* rest *of the night.*

CHAPTER 23

My family is still intact. Rozene smiled inwardly as she hunched over her laptop on the bed, typing away. Her gaze shifted to Larry who was stretched out on the daybed watching CNN. He was engrossed in the show. She took a breather and lay back against the pillows, and before she knew it, she was sending up silent praises for the great worship service they'd attended that morning. They had left church before the service actually ended. She and Larry had decided to go that route since they hadn't been to church in a long time, and definitely wanted to avoid the wagging tongues.

After leaving church, she and Larry had visited their parents with the children, before taking in the world renowned Cirque du Soleil show and heading home.

Rozene heard knocking on the door. "Come in," she yelled, glancing over at Larry who was still deep in the discussion.

The twins appeared, ran and sprawled out on the bed before her.

Rozene eyed them, teasingly. "At least try to make me miss you when you're gone."

"Sorry, Mom. That was Madison's idea."

Madison sighed, and then pursed her lips at Mason. "Why can't you behave like a normal young adult, Mason? Come on, let's try that again."

They both exited the room and closed the door. They knocked but Rozene did not respond.

Larry strolled to the door and swung it open. "My children." He grinned at them, and they group hugged him.

"Oh, Daddy! Our Dada!" Madison exclaimed. "Thank God for you!"

"At least somebody wants us," Mason added.

They both looked at their mother who was setting aside her laptop on the nightstand. She turned and opened her arms to them. "Come and give your Mama hugs."

The twins were delighted, burying themselves in her arms.

"My babies. I love you." She kissed each of them on the forehead.

Larry observed them from where he sat at the foot of the bed. "Hold still, let me take a pic. He retrieved his cell phone from the daybed and took the picture.

"Nice," Larry said, looking at the picture, and then moving in closer so they could view it. He chuckled. "The babies aren't babies anymore."

Mason and Madison began to grumble in disagreement.

"You'll always be my babies," Rozene offered, smiling.

"Thanks, Mom," the twins said in unison, cleaving to her side.

Larry smiled at them. "Is it prayer time?"

"Yes, Dad, but ..." Madison eyed her father, squeezing both her hands together. "Dad, you know I'm all about school and my ministry right now but I really, really like this guy." She paused to gauge his reaction.

"Say more," Larry said, observing he was the last to know.

"His name is Tyler. He's actively involved in church and he has another year left in school. He is pursuing a Civil and Environmental Engineering degree. The thing is - we do a lot of church activities together but that's about it. His focus is definitely not on me in that way, even though we chat about everything else."

"Have you been praying about it?" Larry asked.

"Yes, Dad. But, I'm asking you and Mom to please pray for me." Her eyes filled with tears as she hugged her mother's side.

Larry briefly touched her feet. "Fear not. You only want God's best for you. What is yours is yours. In the meantime, continue to work alongside him and observe him. Make sure he is who he is portraying himself to be. Don't forget you are precious to God and to us. Any great God-fearing man would be happy to have you in the right season."

Madison heaved herself from her mother's side to hug her father. "Thanks, Dad. He reminds me so much of you."

"You are welcome, baby girl. Thank you. That's a great compliment." Larry smiled at her as she returned to her mother's side. "Are you sure Mason isn't threatening him under the quiet?"

"Dad, no!" Mason hollered, knitting his brows. He just had to declare his innocence, especially with Madison becoming unglued like that. "I actually like the dude. He's okay and he loves the Lord. We have a growing friendship, but he's private. He has never mentioned Madison and I get the feeling I shouldn't ask. You know how hard it is to find men like us Dad, so if Madison found someone like us, I'm seeing the green light."

Larry high-fived Mason. "We are pretty special."

Rozene and Madison could only shake their heads.

A few minutes later, after they prayed, the twins were about to leave the room when Madison asked, "Mom, I've been seeing re-runs of your TV program. Are you planning to do new ones?"

"Yes, dear. We'll have new ones showing this coming week and I'm doing more tapings next week."

"Great. Looking forward." Madison smiled at her before leaving with Mason.

An hour later, Larry was roused from his deep sleep on the daybed by a shriek. "Roz," he called out.

There was silence.

He turned on the lamp on the table nearby and glanced around the room. There was no sign of Rozene so he hastened to the bathroom and found her sniffling while running water on her hand at the sink.

"What happened?" He came up behind her to inspect it, and then grabbed her hand to apply pressure to the spot that was bleeding.

The concern in his voice made her heart thrash about in her chest, despite the burning sensation from her finger. "It hurts," she lamented, tears running down her face.

"Don't cry. It's going to be okay," he told her softly.

She groaned as his hand worked to stop the bleeding. "Shhh," he said gently. "You're going to be okay."

She could feel his chest on her back as he leaned over her. With his lips close to the nape of her neck and his breath warm on her cheeks, all thoughts of pain flew out of her mind, and she relaxed against him.

Larry lowered his head to inspect the wound on her finger and the smell of the perfume behind her ears filled his nostrils. He stilled. "You'll be fine. I'll wipe it with peroxide, and then put a Band-Aid on it."

He felt her shiver and goosebumps rose on her arm, as her finger started bleeding again. "You'll be fine," he encouraged, running water over her finger while applying pressure. "Relax."

Rozene closed her eyes and leaned against Larry's shirtless body while she took slow relaxing breaths. He made her feel safe. She turned her head so that it rested on

197

his shoulder, and then she snuggled into the crook of his neck.

The heat of her breath on his neck sent a warm current flowing through Larry's body, and his heart bottomed in his chest. Immediately, the hairs at the back of his neck stood on end.

Kiss me, she willed him. It had been a while, and she was no stranger to his kisses, and right about now, she needed one. The taste of his lips would be the perfect cure for the pain ... and the excruciating pain in her heart as well.

Larry knew exactly what she wanted. It was the same thing he wanted. He had long passed denying that. But he was not about to give in. "What happened?" he asked.

"Slammed my hand in the drawer at the sink," she said, her voice but a whisper as if she couldn't quite catch her breath, "and, and a piece of the wood got stuck in my finger. I had to pull it out"

Larry quivered slightly as her voice vibrated in his ear. He desperately needed an out.

Noticing that blood was no longer flowing, he turned off the tap and bent slightly to inspect her finger again. "I think you'll live," he teased.

She turned quickly and tilted her face towards him. "Thank -" She paused at a loss for word.

He had shifted too, and their lips were a breath apart.

She gasped softly, anticipating the coming moments.

Her ragged breath tickled Larry's lips and his body responded feverishly, and instinctively, he pressed her against the sink.

Her eyes widening, Rozene clutched his shoulders. She couldn't breathe, couldn't think.

Everything stood still.

Everything.

She opened her mouth to speak, but couldn't summon any words.

His fervent eyes were locked on hers, for what seemed like an eternity, and he didn't show any signs of easing up from her. And she didn't want him to. He'd always wanted her, with a passion that threatened to overwhelm them both. Just that thought caused her to become even more breathless and a guttural sound came from her throat.

Instinct held Larry steady. For even as his body responded like it had a mind of its own, some part of his brain knew he shouldn't go there. He stepped away from her, letting out the breath he was holding.

"Peroxide," he said, moving towards the First Aid kit on the wall.

He took his time taking out the bottle of peroxide, a Band-Aid, and cotton. He couldn't be bothered to deny how his body responded to hers. After nineteen years of marriage, his body was on auto pilot. And it certainly didn't help that she was decked out in his favorite white lace and mesh teddy.

He closed the First Aid kit and approached her, forcing himself not to swallow hard as her eyes raked him up and down.

She was still standing where he'd left her. He drew close, and stood in front of her. He placed the Band-Aid on the sink and dabbed peroxide on the cotton. "Give me your finger," he said after corking the bottle of peroxide.

She held out her hand and he wiped her wounded finger with the cotton.

"Thanks," she said softly, as he wrapped the Band-Aid around her finger. She shifted position, her leg brushing against his and as their eyes met, he had to fight to keep from leaning down and kissing her.

However that was short-lived. His expression became stone cold as images of her and her new man rushed to his brain. His bow-shaped lips turned up, before coolly telling her, "You will have to excuse me. Have a good night." With that, he turned and walked out of the bathroom.

Rozene was too stunned to speak. Overwhelming loneliness swept through her and tears she could no longer hold back, rushed down her face.

CHAPTER 24

The sound of chuckles jolted Rozene awake. She squinted against the morning sunlight filtering through the curtains, trying to make out the figures huddled at her bedside.

"Mom, wake up. We're leaving," Madison said.

Rozene's eyes widened. "Oh, my, gosh! What time is it?"

"Don't worry, Mom," Mason said. "Dad told us you're tired."

Rozene's brow furrowed. "Where is he?"

"He's putting our stuff in the car."

"Stuff? You raided the house."

They grinned at her.

"Yes, the usual stuff," Madison filled in. "Although I tried not to take all your jewelry."

Rozene sat up against the pillows. "Just don't leave us with only the clothes on our backs."

Mason jumped in. "Madison intended to do that, but as usual, I had to save the day."

"Right," Madison quipped, rolling her eyes.

Rozene smiled at them both. "Do you need any money?"

"No," they said in unison.

"Dad gave us money. Plus our monthly allowances have been more than enough," Mason said, squeezing his mother's hand. "Thank God for generous parents."

"And full scholarships," Madison chipped in.

Rozene looked at them and couldn't help but thank God for her blessings. "I know I've been up late every morning since you've been here," she told them. "I'll make it up to you both. I promise."

"It's okay, Mom. It's the first time, so we forgive you." Madison flashed her an encouraging smile before looking at Mason. By now, Rozene knew the signal. They had something to say and they hadn't decided who should say it.

"What is it" Rozene prompted. "Just say it."

"Mom, is everything all right with you?" Madison asked. "You seem rather edgy. Are you sick? Is there something we should know?"

Rozene knew she must look a mess after last night's debacle. She was thankful they were careful not to mention her swollen eyes. "No," Rozene responded. "I am well. I have a couple of issues working out, but other than that, I am fine."

The twins gave each other the signature look again. Madison gave Mason the go ahead. "Are you and Dad okay? We noticed a change in the way you're relating."

Rozene paused to choose her words carefully. "Dad and I are going through an issue." Her countenance fell further, if that was possible. She gathered herself. "It's my fault so I'm trying my very best to fix it. Please pray for us."

The twins eyed each other and nodded. "We will, Mom," Madison said, knowing they shouldn't press their mother any further.

"Try and cheer up though, Mom," Mason added. "You look broken."

"I will. I love you both. Hugs, please."

They both hugged her tightly, breathing in her enduring love.

"I'll see you downstairs in a few," Rozene said.

After the twins left, Rozene brushed her teeth, combed her hair, and then put on her robe before making her way to the garage. She found Larry leaning against the SUV, deep in thought while waiting for the twins.

A smile curved her lips as her mind flashed back to their goodbye kisses on the hood of whichever vehicle he would be driving before he left for work in the mornings. But those memories dried up fast as what transpired between them the previous night overwhelmed her. She gave herself a pep talk to keep from running back to the bedroom.

"Good morning." she called out to him.

He eased up and glanced at her. "Morning." He didn't make an attempt at further conversation. It was best. He hated who he was becoming in her presence.

"Sorry, I'm not coming to the airport with you. I wanted to but it's a little too late now."

He nodded.

She fought against the impulse to stare at him, but couldn't resist it. So, she let herself admire him as he stood there with his hands in his back pockets, showing off his impressive physique. He was decked out in a black polo shirt that fitted his toned torso like a second skin, tapering near the black leather belt that looped through his black jeans.

Larry's eyes shot to his brows as he watched Rozene. He wondered if she knew she was drooling. Even that, he couldn't understand.

Just be cool and smile, Rozene told herself when her eyes returned to Larry's face. But all her intentions to act blasé disappeared when her puffy eyes met his cold steely gaze. Completely mortified, light beads of perspiration speckled her forehead, and her eyes brimmed with tears.

Larry swallowed hard. Her expression was haunting and wary, cutting into him. And he hated to see her cry. He shot her a warning glance. "The children will be down any minute."

"Okay," She wiped her eyes with the back of her hands. Then she remembered he was off work until tomorrow. "Will you be coming home after you make the airport run?"

"Yes," he answered in a monotone.

She linked her fingers at her chest. "Are you going to be busy when you get back?"

"What is it, Rozene?"

"Can I speak to you when you get back?"

He took his time to answer. His expression asking, *What do we possibly have to say to each other?*

Heat rushed to her face, and she turned away from him.

Swallowing his bitterness, he responded, "Yes."

"Thanks."

"Please wipe the sadness off your face, even for the children's sake."

"Okay," she said, straightening her shoulders as the twins arrived.

She smiled and hugged them. "I love you. Call me every day."

"Sure, Mom," Mason told her, giving her another squeeze. "I love you."

Tears filled Madison's eyes as she hugged her mom again. "I love you so much."

Rozene squeezed her tightly, telling her, "I love you more." Rozene released Madison, and then hugged her again when she saw her tears. "We'll talk every day," she reassured her, putting her at arm's length. "I know you're going to miss us and we'll miss you too. We'll see you both in December."

"Thanks, Mom," Madison said, giving her another squeeze.

"Okay, let's pray," Larry said to them.

"Yes, Dad," Madison responded, walking with her mother towards Mason and her Dad.

Larry prayed and the children hugged their mother again.

Seeing them leave reminded her of what was important ... her family. *Lord, please! Please, Father, I don't want to lose them. Please make a way of escape for me.*

CHAPTER 25

The Lord will fight your battle, Rozene reminded herself. She had just finished praying with her mother and was about to meet with Larry in their home library. *The library of all places.* Clearly, it was all about the business for him. She would much rather meet in the bedroom.

As she made her way downstairs, she began shoring up herself with scriptures.

"For God has not given us a spirit of fear, but of power and of love and of a sound mind."

"And we know that all things work together for good to those who love God, to those who are called according to His purpose."

She took a deep breath and prepared herself as she came around the corner on the ground floor and entered a passageway. The library was in full sight.

Larry sat patiently waiting for Rozene. He almost went to pieces as he watched her in the rearview mirror when he drove away with the children for the airport. She looked as wounded as a lost puppy, begging for affection.

He missed her spunk and the way everything seemed balanced when she was around. He wasn't looking forward to their conversation, but he intended to hear her out. *Lord, help me to hear her heart, and help me to express myself with clarity,* he prayed silently.

Rozene entered the lounge area in the library with an air of quiet confidence. After greeting Larry, she took a seat on a plush turquoise three-seater chair across from him. She sat up on the chair and tipped her head back, taking in his serious expression. Not a problem. She was accustomed to his intense stare. It had popped up more than a few times in their marriage.

She humbly lowered her eyes.

Larry watched her keenly. Mentally, he grudgingly admitted that she looked repentant. He hoped she'd read him correctly - *Say what you need to say and let me be.* He had gone through many fires but this one was as hot as heck.

"You have something to say?" he asked.

She nodded. "Larry, nothing I can say will excuse what I have done to our marriage. My behavior-"

"We're done here then," he told her, pulling forward on the chair.

"No, no," she begged. "I still need to talk with you."

He settled back in the chair, his gaze trained on her.

She gripped her hands in her lap. "My behavior is inexcusable, and I am so sorry. The first time I came in contact with Chandler was last fall at my three-day writers' conference and book tour in Washington, D.C. I didn't meet him officially. He was in the audience and -"

"So that's when the lust started?"

She squeezed her fingers together. "Please hear me out,"

"No need," he said pointedly. "I know the rest of the story. You've been sleeping with him since then."

"I slept with him twice."

His eyes turned stone cold. "Twice. Twenty times. One hundred times. I really don't care, Rozene. You have a husband. That's what I'm here for." He glared at her, not even realizing he'd pulled forward on the chair. "You know what kills me. I was running around the house jumping through hoops to sleep with you, my wife. And my wife was busy getting some everywhere, from a random stranger."

Rozene's eyes brimmed with tears. "It was not like that."

"Listen!" Larry stood up and marched towards the door. "I don't have time for this."

Rozene ran before him and blocked his way. "Larry, please, just hear me out."

He tried to go around her but she blocked him.

"Please," she cried out, burying her head in his chest. "I'm sorry. Please, please, just listen."

He was still for what seemed like forever, but she was not about to give up. The whole world closing in on her, she wrapped her arms around his waist and clung to him, her tears drenching his shirt. "I love you. Please don't do this."

Larry slowed his breathing as she nuzzled against him. "Let go of me," he told her roughly.

"Larry, please," she begged, still hanging on for dear life.

"Let go of me, Rozene," he told her firmly, tugging on her hands.

She released him, dropping her watery eyes to the floor as she stood before him. "Please," she begged again.

A long moment of silence passed as Larry struggled for composure. He slid his hands into his pockets, and regarded her. "Okay," he huffed out. Walking back to his chair, he lowered himself in it, staring straight ahead.

She sat beside him with her legs turned towards him. "Nothing happened in D.C.," she told him. "But he was at my book tour event three weeks later in Chicago."

She looked at Larry who seemed like he wanted to be anywhere but in his current position. He was now looking at the door as if any moment he would bolt.

Larry sighed heavily, leveling the full force of his gaze against her. "So that's why you were faking sick in Chicago? You were never in the mood for intimacy."

She was quiet before she decided to put on her big girl hat. "Yes. But -"

"I see."

"I wasn't faking my sickness. I felt sick because of what I had done. Guilt was eating away my soul. I was in prayer for the entire weekend."

Larry chuckled in disbelief. "In prayer? Isn't that what you should have been doing before you got yourself into that mess? What's the point of telling others to pray when temptation comes upon them, when you yourself can't even do it? Isn't that the height of hypocrisy?"

Rozene looked away as tears rushed in. For she remembered the lively Bible Study she'd conducted at church, and the in-depth discussion on 1 Corinthians 10:12 - "Therefore let him who thinks he stands take heed lest he fall."

"You know, Rozene, you talk a good game. You said you were in prayer all weekend, yet you had to go back for seconds. He was that good." Larry stood up, unable to take any more. "Well, you can both have each other."

Rozene jumped off the seat. "Larry, I'm not seeing him anymore. I told you that long ago. It is over. Has been over. Honey, please, I want our marriage. I was just in a bad place after the kids left. I didn't realize how much their lives were a part of mine. I had begun to feel lonely and ..." She looked away, wiping her eyes with her fingers.

He folded his hands across his chest. "And?"

She took her time. "I wondered ... I wondered if I was enough for you."

He shook his head in disbelief. "Enough?" He could hardly find the words to express how ridiculous that sounded.

"Yes, Larry. The children were a huge part of our lives and with them gone, I didn't know if I could handle all of you. And ..."

"I have been waiting to hear what is behind that 'and'."

She became quiet for a moment, even though her eyes were brimming with tears. "And, I did put on some weight, in case you didn't notice."

Larry looked at her - the girl whom he had loved from the day he saw her in high school – trying to make sense of what she was saying. He couldn't let go of the images of her that he'd stored in his mind – her wild intelligence, her love for humanity, her joy for giving, and the way she pushed and overcame any and every challenge that came her way. She always lived to fight again because she always relied on the Rock of Ages.

She was unmovable.

Filled with integrity.

Always above board.

A woman of grace.

A woman of God.

He was always stunned by her beauty, whether she was asleep or awake. He remembered waking up many mornings and he would lie there watching her sleep. She was divine. She was still the best part of his ... every day.

Her tears weighed on his spirit, and his anger evaporated.

He cupped her chin and used his thumb to wipe her tears away. "Don't cry."

Her eyes widened and she hyperventilated as she pleaded with him. "I don't want to live without you. Please don't ma-make me."

"Shhhh." He released her face but didn't say anything for a while.

"Lar -"

"Rozene, I have always loved you, just the way you are." His tone was kind, yet restrained. "I don't care if you put on weight. In any case, what weight gain are you talking about? It's barely noticeable. What I desire most, is for you to be healthy and happy. You were always the most beautiful girl in the room for me. You always had my love, my heart, and my eyes."

He looked at her without saying a word. For all the boldness he possessed, he was struggling with what he had to say to her. Yet, they had always been frank with each other. So he took his time.

"Rozene, you need to face the reality of what you did. It would have been better if you had pleaded temporary insanity."

Heat scorched her face and she looked away from him, unable to suppress the bleakness in her voice as she asked, "What do you mean?"

"What you are doing now is catching a reverse," he told her. "You've deliberately tested the waters and realized the grass is not greener on the other side." A hollow laugh escaped him. "Can I tell you, it never is," he said in all seriousness. "You were caught up in your own lustful thinking. You saw that man. Obviously, he saw you too. You knew he wanted you. It must have surprised you, that you wanted him. Sadly, you were only testing the water, because you know you have it good at home. On the other hand, he wanted more. Little did he know you would never, ever give up your family for him."

Rozene attempted another vanishing act.

"Did I get it right?" he asked.

She did not respond.

"I know you heard me. Did I get it right?" Larry insisted, already knowing the answer.

A fresh wave of tears assailed her. "Lar-Larry, please."

"Please what, Rozene? He had a craving. You got the same craving. And clearly, you accepted his invitation to the treat, because we wouldn't be here now." The intensity in his voice cut through the air. He eyed her. "I get it. Why can't you just admit the truth? Am I right?"

The truth will destroy him. She hung her head in shame. Truthfully, Chandler took her by surprise, and before she knew it, she was off the grid. He'd been a thorn in her flesh for a short spell, but clearly long enough to wreck her life.

She swallowed the lump in her throat as she caught Larry's eyes. No fooling him. He knew her too well. She mumbled something inaudibly at first, tears trickling down her cheeks, before finally quietly answering, "Yes."

Shock held Larry immobile for a second, as her response echoed unendingly in his heart. His mouth opened but nothing came out. He couldn't speak, which probably was a good thing.

"Larry," Rozene choked out.

But, he didn't respond. He turned away from her, stress knotting his throat and he blinked back tears.

Instinctively, Rozene grabbed his arm. "I'm sooo sorry."

He recoiled, causing her to quickly remove her hand.

A long silence followed, and her tears continued to fall but not a sound escaped her lips. Then, she began to sob loudly. Minutes passed and her sobs stopped and the only sound in the room was her deep gasps for air.

Larry felt disconnected and disoriented at the same time. "Do you love him?" His voice cracked into a hoarse whisper.

"No!" she gasped. For she realized, she'd fed her carnal desire by looking and looking, until the desire to touch took root, and before long, she'd reached out and not only touched the fruit but bit it. Since then, her daily cry had been, *Lord, teach me to hate sin.*

Larry didn't even realize tears had escaped until he was drying his eyes. He was startled by what he'd revealed to her. But little did she know that her response briefly

212

stopped his heart. He didn't have to ask, for he already knew the answer, but he was hoping she would insist that Chandler had forced her. But no. She wanted that man … even if it was for a hot few minutes.

A deep gnawing hurt crawled from the sole of his feet to the crown of his head, before igniting his heart and residing there. He needed to flip the switch to pull his dull senses back to reality. He felt like he was in a fiery furnace with no clear escape route.

He closed his eyes briefly, trying to clear his head. Then something hit him. He'd always accompanied her to her events but he'd been busy for her last couple of tours, so how did this man get close to her?

"How did he get close to you? Is he related to someone on the book tour team? Thought Don kept security tight."

Rozene pursed her lips then answered truthfully. "He's Don's half-brother."

"My good, Lord!" Larry jumped away from her. "The Chandler." He ran both hands over his face as he tried to contain himself.

Rozene gulped. "Lar -"

The hollow laugh that came from him silenced her. He stopped laughing abruptly, his eyebrows shooting to his hairline and staying there. "Never met the man but his reputation precedes him," he told her slowly.

Rozene's gaze dropped to the floor.

"I know Don would never tolerate this in his shop," Larry continued. "I've heard enough." Long strides took him near the door.

"Lar -"

He paused in the doorway but did not look at her. "It's best that we don't see each other or communicate for that matter."

"Don't say that!" she cried out behind him. She froze as he turned towards her.

He cleared the gravel from his throat. "Have a safe trip back," he said, before moving on.

Overwhelmed and filled with regret, Rozene's knees buckled. Her screams of anguish pierced the air as she doubled over on the floor, clutching her stomach to quell the pain of her broken heart.

CHAPTER 26

Larry did not look back. He couldn't save Rozene from the pit she had dug for herself. The same pit he was trying to crawl out of. Truthfully, he needed saving himself. He couldn't breathe.

Once he cleared the library door, he ran as quickly as his legs could take him down the corridor. Panting, he took the stairs two at a time.

A few minutes later, his heart pumping out of control, he burst through the door of the study, slammed it shut, and crumpled against it. This time he couldn't hold back the dam as his tears broke free. His shoulders shook violently and his sobs grew louder and turned into hoarse, heartbreaking gasps. He stumbled blindly toward his desk but couldn't make it, so he collapsed on the sofa nearby, weeping inconsolably and convulsing.

The hurt was like a ton of bricks and he felt ridiculously inadequate to carry them. He was tired of being strong. Tired of pretending that everything was all right. Tired of pretending he didn't care. Just tired ... of everything. He had fallen into a pit of nothingness.

Fresh tears ran in an endless stream down his face and he allowed his tears to flow for he realized his marriage, as he knew it, had come to an end.

A little over an hour later, Rozene knocked on the door of the study but no response came. She knew Larry was in there. Throughout the course of their marriage, it had been his place of refuge, the one place where he could find solace.

She quietly entered the study and found him stretched out on the sofa. His eyes were closed but she could tell he was not in a deep sleep. She noticed the pieces of tissue on the floor beside the sofa. *Was he crying?* She knew her husband tried not to have too many regrets. The only time she'd seen him cry was at his father's funeral. He cried at the funeral but wept inconsolably in her arms that night. He regretted that up to his father's death, he'd not forgiven him for the way he treated his mother. She'd accompanied him to grief counseling with Pastor Fotola. He pressed through, and eventually managed to forgive himself.

Even though Larry had tried hard to conceal it, she could clearly see the pain in his eyes when he'd speed walked out of the library earlier. She had to try again to convince him that their marriage was worth saving.

"Larry," she called out softly.

He stirred but did not open his eyes.

"I'm leaving," she told him. "Wanted to say goodbye."

"Okay," he said in a monotone, not opening his eyes.

The silence stretched on, and he knew she was staring at him. Feeling at a disadvantage, he opened his eyes and swung his legs off the sofa and sat back. Then every coherent thought stopped as his bloodshot eyes beheld her frame. She was decked out in a red pleated romper, her hair falling delicately over her shoulders. *She came to win the war.*

Rozene gazed at him, unable to comprehend that this was it.

Tortured, Larry shut down his mental deliberations. "Was there something else?" His eyes were cold as he looked at her questioningly.

"Larry -"

"No more, Rozene. I'm done talking." His brows slammed together as he pushed away from the sofa and walked towards the huge window.

Rozene stared at his back, as he gazed out the window, his hands in his pocket.

"Why are you dressed like that?" he asked sternly, not looking around.

"Like what? I'm more than covered. It's a halter top but I'm probably the only one wearing a romper near to my knees. Not sure why I'm explaining this to you. You've seen me in this a thousand times."

"I don't know you to go on the street like that."

"Who's going on the street? I'm going straight to Mom and Pop. In any case, I'll have my jeans jacket with me."

Stop this nonsense, Larry scolded himself, still staring out the window. *Are you going to tell her what to eat next?* He glanced over his shoulder at her. "I'm all talked out. Have a safe trip back."

"I need to say something to you."

"You have more to say? Thought you said it all," he scoffed, propping a shoulder against the wall near the window while continuing to stare outside.

"Exactly! I said it all. Why don't you say what's really on your heart, Larry? Tell me, you hate that I gave myself to another man."

He didn't move. "Yes. I hate that you gave yourself to another man. Is there something else you need me to say before you leave?"

"Larry -"

Then something inside his heart broke. "How could you?" he hollered, giving her his full attention. "Betray me. You of all people. I-I gave you everything. And, if you had asked for Mars, I would have spent my days and nights finding a way to give it to you. Now, all I have are images of you and that man."

"Larry, I'm deeply -"

"You killed me! You killed everything in me! Emotionally! Physically! Spiritually!" His hands clenched into fists as he glared at her. "I've never, never, felt so hurt

217

in all my life. You, you," he choked out, "you broke my heart." Acidic tears spilled from his eyes. "You broke my heart." He clutched the wall for strength.

She rushed to him, and touched his shoulder.

"Don't you touch me," he growled, shaking off her hand.

Her heart broke as she watched him struggle to regain his composure. "I'm sorry," she murmured quietly, wishing she could hold him.

It took him a while but Larry reclaimed some semblance of mental order. He wished she would just leave … leave him in peace so that he could crawl under his bedcovers and nurse the hole in his heart.

"Lar -"

"I'm done talking."

"I know I hurt you but -"

"Hurt? You have no idea," he spat out. "You destroyed our marriage. I was looking forward to roaming the world with you. I was looking forward to us ministering together. Yes, Rozene, I was looking forward to us. You don't get it, do you?" He stared out the window again.

She moved closer to him. "I want to make us better but you're not giving me a chance."

He all but hissed his teeth. "You make it sound so simple. You are not the one having to deal with nasty images of you and that man. You are not the one wearing a crazy, fake smile when anyone ask, 'How's your wife?' So, please spare me."

"I'm not trivializing my behavior but you need to stop visualizing what Chandler and I did."

"I cannot just shut down the images. You are my wife," he charged.

"I'm your wife. And I want to make things better." She clutched her heart. "Lord knows I do."

"Lord knows I do," he mimicked.

"Yes. He does," Rozene stated softly, but firmly. "God Almighty, the creator of the universe has forgiven me. I have forgiven myself and," she gulped, "I would have forgiven you, Larry. I'm not saying it would have been easy but I would have forgiven you."

The honesty of her words slammed into his chest. That caused him to pause, and for a moment he stared at her, remembering his own sinful behavior with Gabrielle. Sadness threatened to overwhelm him, and he said quietly, "The envelope on the desk is yours. Please read and sign the documents, and return them as soon as possible."

Rozene's head swung towards the desk then swiveled back to Larry. Her mouth gaped, "I'm NOT signing those documents."

"I've been more than generous, and if you want more, please feel free to dictate your terms."

She advanced upon him, her eyes flashing defiantly. "I'm not signing."

He eyeballed her. "What more do you want from me, Rozene? The terms of our divorce are in your favor, and I said, if you want more, by all means take it."

She shook her head slowly back and forth, and then moved closer, angling her head to look up at him. This time her body was almost touching his. "I'm not signing. I don't want things. I want ..." She paused, her voice tapering off softly, "you."

Her words stunned them both momentarily into silence. Uneasy stillness hung in the air like a fog.

If indeed her words were meant to solicit compassion from him, she scored a perfect ten ... even his body acknowledged it. He backed slightly away from her, fighting for control.

She turned her head away so he wouldn't see the tears forming in her eyes. "I-I want you," she whispered, as if the confession had frightened her.

219

Again, the room was deafeningly quiet as she waited for his response. When none came, she moved closer to him. He could feel her breath on his chin as she told him, "I want you."

He was sure his body stirred.

Despite his anger, his resistance had crumbled. He wanted her. No. He was desperate for her. His eyes traced her face before settling on her lips. He drew in a harsh breath and in his mind, he had backed away from her but in reality, he had backed her up against the wall with his arms wrapped tightly around her. He groaned when her lips parted, for he had all but lost control.

She capitalized on his signal. "I want you," she said softly, for she knew he needed to hear her say it.

Her stare was intoxicating, and the urge to touch her was overwhelming. The memory of what it was like to be truly loved hit Larry like a thunderbolt as he gazed at the flicker of hope and simmering heat in her eyes. Eyes he had lost himself in on many occasions. Before he could stop himself, he touched her hair, smoothing it away from her face. Not long after, he was touching her face, feeling her soft skin beneath his hands.

She purred, turning her face into his hand and kissing it.

"Hmmm," came from his mouth and echoed in the room.

His pulse accelerating, Larry crushed his lips to hers, and she kissed him back, as if he held her very existence in the palms of his hands.

His back now against the wall, Larry paused to catch a quick breath, when an inner voice started scolding him. *Stop it! Stop it!* His body was enamored but his mind was clearly not. They were taking advantage of each other, when they had serious issues to work out. But one look at Rozene settled everything. *I need her.*

Trying to compensate for his earlier roughness, he gently kissed along her jaw and cheek. "Roz," he murmured her name, raining soft kisses up and down her throat.

Then, he restrained himself and lifted her.

She heard him muttering something indecipherable, but heard "bedroom" somewhere in the mix. When he started kissing her again, she realized they were still in the study, near the door.

A low groan rose from the back of her throat as tiny tremors shook their bodies. Her entire body feverish, she gripped and clawed at his biceps.

Suddenly, Rozene felt as if Larry's lips were angry against hers, like he was reprimanding her for something. When he finally released her lips, she sagged against him, tears burning her eyes. She dared not look at him, afraid to confirm her suspicion.

His hand tilted her chin to meet his eyes. "Did he make you feel like this?"

Her eyes widened when she realized what he'd asked. "Wha-what?" she stuttered, staring up at him.

He didn't respond. Instead, he kissed her greedily, swallowing up her protest, and then her whimpers as she writhed with pleasure, clinging to him.

"Did he make you feel this good?" he murmured, while dropping feathery kisses along her shoulder.

Her chest heaving, she fought back the urge to scream. "You're being crazy," she said, pushing away his head.

"Did he do this to you?" In one smooth movement, he pinned her wrists above her head and began grinding her against the wall.

She puffed out his name in surprise and delight, instinctively wrapping a leg around his hip to keep him in place and obtain more of the sweetness that was building. It felt so good.

Rozene's sweet voice calling out his name was like music to his ears. He had always loved the way she said his name with oh, so much passion. The way her body responded to his touch always catapulted him to a state of euphoria, like he had done something epic. Not that it mattered now, but he allowed himself to enjoy the ride.

As wave after wave of sensations rocked her body, Rozene closed her eyes, remembering he liked having her like this, soft against him. "Please," she begged, having dragged her lips from his to take much needed gulps of air. It was then that she noticed he'd gone still. She gazed into his eyes, and that gave her reason to pause completely.

"Did you say that to him too?" he asked against her lips. He drank in her soft gasps.

"Let me go," she choked out, pushing his taut chest with her hands. He stepped slightly away from her and she eased away from him.

"Please don't do this," she told him. "I know you need me -"

"Sleeping with you is not an option," he told her firmly, halting her in her tracks.

She averted her eyes. "Then tell me wha-what you want." A sob escaped her and she paused, "and I-I'll do it."

"Nothing," he responded. "Nothing at all."

"I told you I'm sorry a million times. My moment of weakness -"

He held up his hand. "Moment of weakness? That was a habit. Just sign the papers. Please."

The sharpness in his voice pierced her heart, and a broken sob emanated from her throat. "Larry, please. I love you." She looked away from him feeling strangely vulnerable.

"The tongue without the heart is of no significance, Rozene."

"I'm sorry," she choked out.

"Sorry?" His tone was filled with incredulity. "I bet you are, now. He looked at her for a moment before walking out of the study. *It would take the faith of Job for me to go back into our marriage.* Yet, a cry came from the depths of his heart - *Increase my faith, Lord.*

CHAPTER 27

Chandler clutched the windowsill like a lifeline as his stomach plunged to his feet. That was not the way he saw the evening going. By now, his lips should have been hot on Rozene's and she would be pleading for more of him. She was pleading all right, but not exactly in the way he thought she would.

Peering blindly through his living room window, he tried desperately to compose himself. Yet, he couldn't. It was hard enough for him to think she didn't want to be with him, but to actually hear her say it...

No. He didn't want to hear anymore of her speeches about finding someone else. And about the good Lord providing a wife for him. *Yada. Yada. Yada.* Enough. She was a cosmic killjoy, sucking away the very breath that he needed to stay alive.

He had begged her on bended knees to be with him, but she remained resolute. She gave him no wriggle room. She wanted her husband. *She chose him ... over me.* And just like that, she had stripped away his confidence, and unraveled his universe with two words - 'It's over!' Her voice echoing in his sanctuary, in the very place where everything was supposed to be safe and secure for him.

Not realizing he had closed his eyes, Chandler opened them and squared his shoulder. *Maybe if I begged one last time ... just one last time.* He needed to fight for what he believed in, right? Frustrated by his own lack of self-control, he swiftly brushed away the single tear that had rushed down his cheek with the back of his hand.

As the pampered child of overprotective, even though absent parents, he had wanted for little in his life. Yet, for the second time in his life, what he desired - what he longed for and consistently dreamed about - was seemingly impossible to attain. She did not give him a single thread of hope. Yet, he had to hope.

His love for her had changed him. With Rozene it was not about sex, he actually loved her. He didn't realize how difficult it was to love someone when the love was not reciprocated. Now, he fully understood why some of the women he'd dated hated him when he didn't respond in like terms to their confessions of love in the relationship that they had orchestrated in their minds.

Not that he was into breaking women's heart on a whim. Before he engaged in relationships with them, he'd always been upfront about what he needed. No strings attached. No emotional baggage to complicate the situation. Nothing permanent. Only sex ... and definitely, no hassle. Yes, he had been upfront.

In any case, women might grumble about him being a Casanova, but that had never deterred any of them from hopping into his bed. And if they agreed to his terms, he would hop right in with them.

Rozene gazed at Chandler's back as she stood behind him. She knew she had 'knocked the wind out of his sail'. But, she had to. He was head strong and determined, but so was she. She wanted to be left alone. However, she hoped she hadn't pushed him too far over the edge, causing him to do something outlandish. Lord knows, he seemed desperate enough.

She stepped back. She didn't like how he was making her feel. More than ever, the only thing she wanted was to be left alone so she could pull her marriage back together again. She sent up silent prayers as she moved further away from him and sat at the edge of the sofa.

Chandler turned to face Rozene, his demeanor resolute. He had tasted heaven, and no way was he giving it up, not without a fight. He moved to sit next to her.

I can take him down. Rozene adopted a ready-to-charge posture, in case Chandler made any surprise moves.

"Give me your hand," he said.

Her bravado flew right out the window. Her heart was beating so hard she thought he could hear it. "Why do you -?"

"What do you think I'm going to do? Break it." He dropped his gaze to the floor. "I need, I need a little of your strength to share something with you."

Seriously? Rozene wanted to beat her head against something. Anything.

"I won't hurt you, if that's your concern." His voice broke. "I-I ..."

Rozene gazed at him, wishing she was not in her current position. Nevertheless, she extended her hand to him, and he placed it on his knee and covered it with his own.

"I love you," he told her earnestly. He held up a hand as she began to protest. "I didn't know I was capable of loving anyone. The last time I thought I was in love was around sixteen years ago. Her name was Alana." He smiled to himself. "She made my days worth living, and lived we did. Every minute we spent together, I fell deeper in love with her. I was almost twenty-two years old but I knew I wanted to spend the rest of my life with her." He let out a hollow laugh. "Of course, I proposed. Why wouldn't I? Everyone thought we would get married anyway."

He shifted a bit to settle back against the sofa. "We planned a lavish wedding; over-the-top, in my estimation. My parents wanted a grand occasion, so they threw us the 'wedding of the century' as mom dubbed it."

Chandler sat up, to make sure Rozene was paying attention.

She was. *Left that poor girl at the altar, didn't you?*

Chandler sighed at her expression. "You think you know me, huh? I did not leave her at the altar, Ro. She left me at the altar," he said, casting an accusatory glance her way. "She did not show up and neither did the best man."

Rozene felt a tug on her heart strings. "That must have been hard for you to deal with. I'm sorry that happened to you. When you extend your love to someone, there is never any assurance that it will be reciprocated."

"Sorry?" He looked at her with slight disdain. "But you're doing the same thing. You throw back the love I have for you in my face."

"Chandler, I'm married, and I have a family. What I felt for you was lust. That's not love. 1 Corinthians 13:4-7 describes exactly what love is - It is patient and kind and -"

"Whatever, Ro." Anger rushed through him. "You can pretend all day long but you cannot deny that what you feel for me is real."

Her eyes narrowed defensively as she decided to be frank with him. "I'm not saying that I didn't feel some sort of ... passion for you but that's not love. Yes, passion is a part of love; but love takes time. It's intimate and -"

Chandler chuckled loudly. "After all that whooping you do when we're together - you say that's not love. You had fooled me. You don't look like the type to fake it," he said sarcastically. "Just so you know, all my moans and groans were for real."

"Why do you have to take it to that level?" Displeasure laced each word.

"What level? I'm speaking the truth."

She watched him keenly. He'd never been angry with her but now he was. "Look, Chandler, I'm not here to fight with you. I'm sorry that I led you to believe that I was in love with you. I have never been in this situation before -"

"Situation?" He thundered incredulously. "Situation? Is that how you plan to remember our relationship?" He watched as guilt spread across her face. "Yes, I said relationship. We had a relationship." His gaze ripped into her. "While you are busy putting our situation in File 13, this is how I'll remember it - I loved you but you used me. Yes, Ro. You used me. It took me years to build up the courage to love someone, to trust someone. I thought we were going somewhere with our relationship. You led me on and made me love you. I trusted you, and in a few seconds, you've crushed my heart, like it was nothing. "

The painful memory he would carry because of their situation gave her more than a few anxious moments. She studied him, torn between wanting to comfort him and wanting to slap him. She angled her head and met his gaze with a challenge of her own. "Chandler, aren't you tired of playing the blame game?"

She stood up and looked down at him. "From day one, you knew I was married. I never told you, ever, not one time, that I intended to leave my husband." She held his gaze and her eyes began to fill with tears. "Chandler, please try to understand. I cannot give you what you want."

Frustration mounting, Chandler stood abruptly, folding his arms across his chest, hostility in his gaze. "Say what you want, but you and I both know that our relationship evolved into something beautiful." Cold laughter rolled from his mouth. "Silly of me to even think that thought. How dare me? What would possess me to think that Mrs. Mighty Prayer Warrior would want to stay in my chamber forever? You sure had me fooled. You had one intention - to satisfy your needs and get back to your ready-made family and holy living. Didn't you read where the good book said, "Do not commit adultery?" His jaw tightened as the words erupted from his mouth.

Instinctively, Rozene stepped back, speechless for a moment. He might as well have slapped her. She allowed her tears to fall as a pang of guilt hit her in the stomach. "I'm sorry. I had no intention of hurting you. But, I can't love you the way -"

"Right." He glowered at her. "So you're just going to grovel, begging him to take you back?"

Reeling from his words - because she knew that was exactly what she had to do - more tears spilled from Rozene's eyes. Larry was hard, unapologetically so, but she would never stop trying. She intended to use every avenue to win back his love.

"Yes. If that's what it takes," she croaked out, the tension in her chest almost stopping her breathing.

"How the mighty has fallen." The hiss in his voice was a firm reminder of his feeling towards her.

Fury rose within her and she grabbed her bag from the sofa, and swung past him towards the front door.

He caught her by the arm and turned her to face him. "Don't leave here like -"

"Let go of my arm," she insisted, threatening him with her eyes.

"What can I do to make it up to you?" he implored, releasing her arm. "Don't leave here like this."

His suave, velvety voice would make any woman swoon, but Rozene did not utter a word. She steeled herself from becoming putty before him as his eyes twinkled seductively at her. She took it all in - His smoky bedroom eyes, his easy-going, gorgeous smile, his fit physique ... *Just sinful.*

"Ro," he attempted to engage her heart once more, soft and beseeching. "Make love with me one last time." His eyes were dark with desire as they met hers.

Her heart jolted in her chest and her purse fell to the floor with a loud thud.

In the commotion, he pulled her to him.

"Don't," she pleaded with him, pressing her palms against his chest.

Ignoring her protest, he rubbed against her, reveling in the warmth their bodies created. "I know you want me."

"Chandler, stop," she said firmly, pushing him away, but he yanked her back, holding her firmly against him. She wriggled, attempting to get away from him, but instead of being turned off, it turned him on.

"Tell me you want me." His voice was deep with need.

Fear tightened her chest. "Stop it."

"Stop struggling," he told her, annoyance then disappointment washing over him as he released her. "You never struggled before."

She backed away from him. "I can't, Chandler."

"Can't or won't?"

His eyes rested on her supple bosom, which rose and fell with each breath she took. Eventually his eyes pierced hers and the raw desire was like an intimate touch, causing her breath to quicken. She closed her eyes, to prevent herself from being sucked in. In that moment, Chandler scooped her up and they fell in a heap on the sofa.

Her breath halted in her throat. "Get off me!"

"Shhh," he murmured, raining kisses over her face. "I know you want me." He dragged his mouth down her neck.

"Don't," she said, her breathing panicky, as she moved her neck out of his reach. However, her sharp gasps of breath and movements against him only served to further his excitement. He gazed at her lips ready to partake, and definitely ready to tame her.

"Don't do this," she begged, her voice choked with fear.

He observed the fear in her eyes and the desire in his eyes faded into oblivion. He laughed for a few seconds, and then became silent. *When have I ever had to beg for sex? Never. Not in this life.* He rolled off her and rested his head next to her shoulder. "Let me hold you for a minute." He wrapped an arm around her waist and lay motionless.

Rozene's body felt numb, several emotions spiraling in her head. She didn't even realize she was crying until her hand moved to wipe the tears from her face.

Soon, Chandler heaved his body from hers. He watched as she quickly gathered her purse, knowing he'd traumatized her, but he didn't care.

"Take care of yourself, Chandler." Her voice was uneven, and her hands were shaking as she smoothed her hair.

"You're lying to yourself, you know," he muttered, his eyes stark with pain.

"I'm done fighting with you." Yes, all the fight had gone out of her. She was even planning to stop fighting herself for her stupid mistake. "I wish you the best. Bye."

But Chandler didn't move, he sat gazing ahead.

Hurrying away before she received anymore unwanted conversation, Rozene walked through the front door, and closed it behind her. She was well aware of how foolish it was to have risked a short term relationship with him. She understood his fear of losing her, but truthfully he never had her. *Hopefully, one day, he'll smile again.*

Half an hour later, Chandler left his townhouse. He straightened, welcoming the cool evening breeze that hit his swollen eyes. He couldn't think about her anymore.

Willing the throbbing in his head to go away, he pulled the hood of his sweatshirt over his head and scurried the distance to the main entrance gate of the subdivision while allowing his vision to adjust. The second he exited the gate, he started running. That seemed to set him free.

He ran hard, with his head and shoulders thrust forward. His breath came out in short pants, tearing at his throat, but that was not enough to stop him. Sweat mixed with tears, ran down his face. For miles he ran, with no particular destination in mind; seeing nothing, feeling nothing, hearing nothing except the pounding of his feet in sync with the pounding of his heart ... nothing mattered anymore. Running was sufficient in itself. Hopefully, his run would halt the madness that was closing in on him.

CHAPTER 28

Guilt gnawed at Larry.

Guilt. Guilt. Guilt. He couldn't rid himself of it.

His eyes landed on Rozene's picture on the console table in the oval entryway and his breath caught in his throat. He closed his eyes to suppress the anxiety that flooded his stomach as he waited for Pastor Fotola's car to pull up to the front door.

Since his last encounter with Rozene in the study, he had awoken each day with a nagging feeling of guilt from the memory of her statement - 'God Almighty, the creator of the universe has forgiven me. I have forgiven myself and I would have forgiven you.' That day, he'd secretly watched as Rozene left their home with her shoulders slumped and her feet dragging.

He had savored the sweetness of the blame game for so long that he was having difficulty accepting her statement, even though he knew it to be true. Now, he experienced a deep sense of loss and an equally deep vacuum of hopelessness in his heart.

Last night, perched on his bed, he had cried, no, bawled his heart out, while reading 2 Samuel 12 - Nathan's Parable and David's Confession. He was particularly overcome with grief when he read verse seven, "And Nathan said to David, You are the man! ..." He had stumbled out of bed onto the floor and mirrored King David's confession, ""I have sinned against the Lord.""

He couldn't continue living like this ... no, not anymore. He had to tell Rozene the truth and deal with the consequences of his sin.

The doorbell rang and he hastily wiped damp palms on his pants before opening the door.

"Larry, my good man," Pastor Fotola greeted him with a firm handshake.

"Good to see you, Pastor."

Larry closed the door. "Let's talk in the living room."

"Okay."

Larry led the way. "Thanks for coming on such short notice."

"No problem. I'm always here for you."

"Thank you." Larry exhaled deeply, motioning with his hands for Pastor Fotola to sit on the sofa across from him.

"It can't be that bad," Pastor Fotola said encouragingly.

"I have really dug a hole for myself," Larry told him, his hands resting under his chin. "Gabrielle is still not speaking to me. I've lost my wife. I cannot afford to lose my children."

Pastor Fotola watched him keenly. He knew he could speak frankly with him. "What is really happening with you, Larry?"

"Since Rozene left the other day, I have been feeling guilty. Guilty about everything. I have been praying the Scripture, 'Create in me a clean heart, O God, and renew a steadfast spirit within me,' over my life. I know I have to make a change, and I want to make a change. I would like Roz to come on home so we can be a family again. But I am terrified to tell her about my infidelity, and I'm equally terrified she'll eventually find out."

Pastor Fotola crossed his legs and sat back on the sofa, silently thanking God. "I'm glad you didn't allow the enemy to hijack you. I'm taking it you have forgiven her."

"Definitely," Larry said, without hesitation. "And, I have forgiven myself. Now, I want to apologize to Roz for how I treated her. I want to tell her the truth about what I did, that I committed adultery too."

234

"That's good, Larry. You're doing a good thing. If you're going to build afresh, truth is the best way to go."

Larry wiped his hands over his face. *Yes, truth is the way to go.* He'd been bold and brave all his life, negotiated amazing deals at the boardroom table, yet he was having heart palpitations every time thoughts of confessing to Rozene hit.

"What are you afraid of?"

A brooding expression cloaked Larry's face. "I'm afraid to lose her."

"I understand. But, Larry," Pastor Fotola called for his attention, "only God knows the outcome. Lean on Him and allow Him to instruct you."

Larry squeezed his trembling hands together. "I don't want to lose her."

"I know you don't, so let us trust God. You are doing what is right. Go with God, step by step. Stand in faith, and let him guide you."

Larry nodded thoughtfully. "I will."

They were both quiet for a moment, and then Larry choked out, "Do you think she'll forgive me? I couldn't -" He folded his lips to prevent them from trembling.

Pastor Fotola rushed to his side and patted his shoulder. "I don't have all the answers, but this I know, you can trust God. Don't waste your energy trying to figure out how Rozene will react. Pray for the right timing, the right words, and a heart that's receptive to the leading of the Holy Spirit."

Larry nodded with understanding. It was just what he needed to hear.

"Focus on what you need to do to come into your new season," Pastor Fotola continued. "'…whatever things are true, whatever things are noble, whatever things are just, whatever things are pure, whatever things are lovely, whatever things are of good report, if there is any virtue and if there is anything praiseworthy - meditate on these things.' God needs you, you and Rozene."

"Thanks for the reminder." Larry smiled inwardly. "I will trust God. I have to."

All this because he missed the aroma of Rozene's presence. She was the missing ingredient in his life. *I can live without her but my life is better with her in it.* He needed her to be properly balanced. She was supplying something he didn't even know he needed.

"Great. Let's firm this up by agreeing in prayer," Pastor Fotola said.

"Yes. Thank ... you," Larry managed to say. "Thank you for allowing God to use you to bless me."

"You're welcome. It's going to be all right." Pastor Fotola squeezed his shoulder, then decided to lighten the moment. "But you know," he chuckled. "In my line of work, you can't last on personality alone."

Larry couldn't help but chuckle too. "That I understand."

"Good to see you laughing, Larry."

With that, Pastor Fotola began to pray, knowing that Larry's and Rozene's hearts were under the influence of the Holy Spirit. *Let the sealing begin, Lord,* was his heart's cry.

CHAPTER 29

Larry closed his eyes briefly and replayed the first line of his speech in his mind. If he could get that line out, and get it out with the sincerity that was in his heart, he would be well on his way to celebrating a victorious Saturday evening.

After slipping on his tuxedo, he took a last look, squared his shoulders, and left the bedroom. A few minutes later, seated in his car, he uttered a short prayer, before driving away.

Only God can fix it, an inner voice reminded him.

He nodded, smiling and ordered himself to relax.

He would be a good twenty minutes early, but he wanted to make sure he was ready to deliver the speech of a lifetime. He knew she would be ready for him, so he wanted to make sure he was ready for her. *For after all, a man must be big enough to admit his failures, learn from them, and correct them.* In any case, this particular failure had had him in chains for far too long. Now, it was time to break free.

Fifty minutes later, he greeted Cedrick Somack, the new chief security officer at the electronic entrance gate to the super exclusive Abella, a French Restaurant and Lounge which was owned by Benson, his cousin. Cedrick greeted him by name, clearly taken with himself for remembering the clientele of the prestigious restaurant.

And perhaps rightly so. Abella offered unique contemporary French dining experiences that tantalized the taste buds, leaving memories that would linger forever … well, that's if you could get a table.

Larry remembered Benson's ecstatic expression when he insisted that even the most discerning palates would enjoy an exceptional dining experience. 'An investment in yourself that just won't ever dissatisfy,'

Benson had said. And the restaurant did live up to the hype from all the great reviews in top chef magazines, and on social media.

Larry smiled as he drove through the gate, and then through another entrance into the heart of the breathtaking location. Marked by elegance and luxury, the magnificent off-white and gold building, borrowed generously from modern French architecture.

The name Abella was fitting, Larry concluded, once again.

Benson had met his wife, Abella, some ten years ago while he was studying French cuisine in Paris. He was so taken by her beauty that he named the restaurant after her. When she told him that her name meant breath, Benson didn't skimp on cost for he was determined that every detail, even the minute features of the restaurant would be designed to 'take your breath away'.

And so it did. This stylish "playground" which the rich and famous frequented for private parties and events, had become a hot spot. Filled with unimaginable treats, this exclusive setting was the perfect place for many celebrities to enjoy relaxing moments while sipping aperitifs before dinner.

Larry slid from behind the steering wheel of his Audi and walked up the steps to the lobby as the valet parked his car. The glass doors to the lobby swung open. The young woman who greeted him looked more like a model than a receptionist. Her eyes widened under two carefully plucked eyebrows, and she smiled at Larry with a set of even white teeth. "Mr. Kanate, good evening. Pleasure to have you here, sir."

Larry smiled at her. "Thanks, Jordanne." The staff badge on the lapel of her trendy black suit indicated her name was Jordanne Bratten.

"Please come with me, sir. I'll take you to your table."

"Thanks." Larry followed her through the lobby, oblivious that he was turning the heads of several female guests.

As he remembered, the lobby was gorgeous. Just perfect - open, immaculate, and welcoming. Beautiful arrangements of fresh flowers were intricately incorporated and the pleasing fragrances they emitted, delighted his senses. Luxurious marble floors and chandeliers grabbed attention as they moved from the lobby to a bank of elevators that took them to a private dining room.

Impressive. Larry briefly glanced around the cozy yet quietly sophisticated room. Piped instrumental music filled the room. He reprimanded himself for not taking up Benson's offer to visit anytime he wanted to.

"I hope it's to your liking, sir. We have prepared all that you've asked for."

"Yes. Thanks, Jordanne."

"You are most welcome, sir." Smiling, she left the room.

Larry walked to the spacious lounge area and reclined on the white, overstuffed leather loveseat, which was set before a coffee table with a beautiful, tall floral arrangement and a gold tray with two wine glasses and champagne in a gold-trimmed wine chiller.

The room was a little too dark for his liking, so he found the remote sitting on the entertainment console near the huge flat screen TV. He tried several shades of lighting before reaching his desired goal. He wanted to see her clearly, when she entered the room.

Moving to the dinner table, he inspected the two dozen red roses he'd ordered. A smile popped on his face. They were perfect.

By his watch, he had a few minutes to spare and what better use for them than to continue lifting up the situation before the Lord.

"Father, in the name of Jesus, I thank you for this time in my life. God, I thank you that your grace and mercy continue to abide with me. Thank you that your favor goes before me. Grant me wisdom as I speak, Lord. Help me to speak with clarity, yet humility. Prepare Rozene's heart to hear my heart, Lord. Help me, Lord, to hear her heart. And, God may understanding prevail as we share together. Lord, my life is in your hands. In the name of Jesus Christ, I pray, amen."

Soon, Larry took up the flowers and positioned himself in line with the entrance door.

He didn't have to wait long.

He heard Rozene's joyful, "Thank you" as the customer service representative opened the door and closed it behind her.

CHAPTER 30

Sweet instrumental music filled her ears as Rozene entered the room. Her skin felt warm in anticipation of the meeting. The moment was here.

She moved from the doorway and Larry had to stop his jaw from dropping. Her long white dress hugged the curves of her lithe body and was setting every nerve in his body on fire. Yes, all of them. He silenced his inner voice - the one that was screaming, *Hot! Hot! Hot!* As he watched her gliding towards him.

Of course, he remembered this one-of-a-kind gown. Two years ago, they had attended an Oscar de la Renta fashion show in Nashville, Tennessee, and she loved the gown so much that he had secretly purchased it for her. He knew she was holding it for a special occasion.

It was difficult not to zone in on her slight cleavage, but when his gaze lingered there, he quickly zipped it back to her face.

He was thankful that he came prepared ... in the full armor of God. Every piece - loins girded with truth, the breastplate of righteousness ...

He was still busy shoring up himself, when he noticed with satisfaction, the wild uncertainty that leaped from her eyes.

She had called begging for a meeting so that they could come to some sort of consensus on the state of their marriage. Of course, he'd agreed. He too was on the verge of asking for a meeting.

He drew a deep breath, remembering that she played to win but so did he. He knew she came armed with another apology for her moment of weakness but was she prepared to handle and understand his moment of weakness?

Rozene stopped abruptly and began looking around the room when she discovered he was watching her with a guarded, yet approving gaze. *Well, at least, he likes my dress.*

Now it was her turn to take him in.

She swung her eyes back to his, taking her time to soak in his appearance. He didn't flinch. Not that she expected him to. *Oh, Lord, he looks gooood.* This tall, powerful, debonair, all-male creature, in his edgy, perfectly-fitted, black tuxedo. Only he could pull off such a stylish cut that defied traditional rules.

Her stomach tightened as their eyes met. Her head angled slightly upward as he moved towards her. He looked full of confidence, and in the depths of her heart, she felt hopeful.

"How are you? Thanks for coming," he said, circling her waist with a hand and lightly kissing her cheeks.

"I'm good. Thanks for having me. Good to see you," she said, fidgeting in his embrace. When he released her, she glanced at her gown, and then eyed him. "You said dress up, but I wasn't -"

"You look gorgeous. It's a great fit." He admired how the material accentuated her flawless, caramel complexion.

"Thank you," she said, breathlessly staring at him, and hoping for good news. *Please, Lord, favor.*

"Did you have any trouble getting here? I hope not."

She watched him. His eyes were sharply focused as he spoke, as if he was on a mission. "No problem. Everything went well."

"Great. These are for you." He handed her the flowers, and experienced the joy of the beautiful expression of gratitude on her face.

"Thank you."

He flashed his drop-dead, gorgeous smile, highlighting his miniature dimples. "Just thinking about you. Enjoy. And you are welcome." He touched her elbow. "Let's eat."

She nodded and he escorted her to the table. She smiled all the way there. The sudden show of civility destroyed the tightness in the air between them.

"Thanks," she said, when he pulled out the chair for her.

Standing next to her, he said quietly, "I hope you don't mind, I ordered your old favorites. If you don't want them, then we'll ask for something else to be prepared."

She smiled up at him. "Tell me you included Soupe a L'oignon and Coquilles Saint-Jacques. Anything else with that is great."

"I sure did. And I know you like Cheese Soufflé." He grinned back at her. "I'll tell them we'll be ready for dinner in ten minutes." Sitting down across from her, he used the small iPad on the table to indicate just that to customer service.

"Would you like a glass of wine? Hot beverages are available too."

"A glass of wine, please."

"Sure." He moved to pour it. "How has your day been?"

"Good."

He smiled as he handed her the glass of wine. "I can tell our conversation will be exciting this evening," he teased.

Her insides knotted nervously as he took his seat. Then she decided, *I've had enough of this. No need to wine and dine me to disappoint me.* "Have you made a decision?"

He paused, looking disappointed before responding, "Let's talk about that after dinner."

"Okay, no problem," she said, wishing she hadn't jumped ahead of herself. "The children called this morning. Told them we were having dinner this evening. That Mason had to remind me not to bring more babies ..." When she realized where she was heading, she blushed, mumbling, "You know, Mason."

A soft smile tugged at the corners of Larry's mouth. *A show of unity usually works at a time like this.* "I hope you told him to mind his own business. We got this."

Her eyelids fluttered as his smile caressed her face. *That smile. How can I respond to that?*

Saved by the bell. Literally.

"Come in," Larry said.

Two customer service assistants, laid out their dinner on the table, and made sure that they were okay before leaving.

After Larry prayed, they began to eat.

The steam rising from the Soupe a L'oignon made Rozene's mouth water. She took a spoonful, blew on it a little before swallowing rapidly.

Larry grinned at her. "You're enjoying your soup."

"Oh, it's so good."

"It is," he agreed. "Have you finished the book you were working on - *Letters to Wives*?"

She eyed him, before dropping her eyes to her plate. *Why did you have to mention that?* "That's on pause for right now. I wrote another book, *Undeniably Yours: The Journey to Love*. Just completed the final edits so it should be out within the next month. I have several promotional activities lined up for it."

He avoided asking why, *Letters to Wives* was on pause. *Why cause her additional stress?* Plus, he already knew why. Instead, he said, "Great. Can't wait to get my copy."

"As usual." She smiled at him. He'd always been her greatest supporter.

The rest of the dinner passed in a haze of small talk and laughter. They made a subtle effort to bolster each other, discussing everything from the children to the latest news headlines.

Hope reigned in Rozene's heart as Larry's eyes gleamed with appreciation when she spoke. He chuckled often, his lips curving into a knowing smile.

Before long they were sweeping their dessert bowls clean.

"This was really good," she said, surveying the table. "Thank you."

He caught her gaze. "Would you like me to arrange a take-home box for you?"

Her heart began to beat faster at the care in his voice. "Thank you."

For a few seconds, he gazed at the delight in her eyes. "That, I will do," he told her before lifting the iPad from the table and began typing. "It should be ready by the time we're leaving." He placed the iPad on the table. "Let's move to the sofa."

She nodded nervously, although she didn't know if it was from the flicker of desire that she saw in his gaze or from the knowledge that things were coming to a bump.

He pulled out her chair, and gently took her hand in his, and she offered no resistance. Her hand encased in his, they walked silently to the loveseat and sat on it. They were still holding hands, his eyes locked in her gaze, when the faint noise from the change in tempo of the music broke the silence.

She smiled slightly, and gently removed her hand from his. *Just tell me,* she wanted to yell. Her stomach

245

wavered as her bravado faltered. She was unsure what to expect, even though the evening was going well. She fidgeted with her fingers, looking everywhere but in his direction.

"Look at me," he said softly, ready to bare his soul.

Her eyes glistened with uncertainty, and tears burned behind her eyelids. *Lord, help me to be strong. I can't walk away from him another time.* She gripped her trembling hands in a ball at her chest.

Larry decided to move speedily. A lot was at stake, but he was undecided on the approach. Her legs were restlessly bouncing and he wanted to hold her. But, he quickly decided against that. After all, she hadn't heard his story yet.

"Roz," he said quietly, taking her hands in his.

She didn't even realize she'd closed her eyes until she felt his lips on her knuckles.

This was not the planned route but Larry desperately wanted to remove the petrified look on her face. "I'm sorry," he said. The raw emotion in his voice came through his sweet caress as he kissed hands. "I never stopped loving you."

Confused, she swallowed the lump in her throat, gazing at him in awe. *Kissing hands isn't what you do when you're breaking up.*

Unable to help herself, Rozene smiled at him.

Larry leaned in to plant a gentle kiss on her forehead. He released her hands, and sat gazing at her.

She could barely take it all in. *Tell me I can come home,* she willed him.

He could see her wish in her expression. He had to tell her she could come home so she could relax and be attentive.

"I love you," Larry told her softly. "Please come back home. I really miss you."

Rozene cried out in relief, burying her face in her hands and began sobbing. All her pent-up emotions bubbled over and her sobs became louder and louder.

Larry cradled her in his arms. "It's going to be all right." He kissed the top of her head. "Roz, please don't cry. You're breaking my heart."

She buried her head in his chest, breathing him in. "Thank you for taking me back."

Guilt racked Larry and he eagerly responded. "Don't say that. I took way too long. I'm going to spend the rest of my days making it up to you."

"Thank -" Her voice broke and tears ran down her face "Thank you. I love you so much." Her chin quivered. "I never stopped loving you." She wiped her face with the back of her hand and then wrapped her arms around his waist.

Larry wrapped an arm around her, and used his other hand to brush her hair away from her face.

"I'm sorry," she whispered, tightening her arms around him.

"We are going to be okay." Larry gathered her against him as he reclined deeply in the sofa. His lips gently touched the top of her head and he stroked her back with infinite tenderness.

"Hmmm," she murmured. His hands felt wonderful on her back, and so did the soft fabric of his tuxedo under her cheek.

Larry wished he didn't have to tell her about his infidelity but knew he had to. He sent up a silent prayer for help, while projecting a coolness that was far from what his troubled heart was feeling.

Fifteen minutes later, Rozene lifted herself out of Larry's arms. She smiled weakly at him, her eyes were red from tears. "You have made me the happiest woman in the world. Thank you." She laced her fingers together under her chin.

He considered her and once again, guilt racked his insides. *Tell her now*, an inner voice pressed him. Instantly, he sank to his knees before her, and grasped her hands.

She looked at him puzzled as he kissed her hands. "I love you. I'm so sorry for what I put you through." His voice broke a little and her heart loved him more.

She caressed his cheek. "It's okay. I did take you by surprise, you know."

He cleared his throat and spoke again. "I love you with all my heart but I've not been -"

"You stop it. I'm grateful you took me back." Her hands grasped his face, and as he opened his mouth to speak, she kissed him.

She craned her neck, desperate for his kisses and he kissed her back, instantly molding her body into his, and pressing her against the sofa. She was kissing him into mind-numbing bliss, when he remembered that he still had not confessed his infidelity. He dragged his lips from hers, breathlessly telling her, "Need-need to talk -"

"Talk later," she told him, grabbing his face again. She crushed her lips into his, simple aching for more of him. Her fingers held the back of his head to keep him in place. *Dear Lord, he feels good.*

Moments later, with reluctance, she released his lips and leaned against his chest, panting heavily. Even though they had kissed each other breathless, Larry knew it was not as long as she would have liked. He pulled away just enough to smile at her.

Rozene sat up and smiled back at him, her eyes glowing with passion.

Her need was as great as his. Yet, he couldn't. At least, not until he had confessed. "You are so beautiful,' he told her passionately. His fingers skimmed over her cheek. "I could love on you all day. But, there's -"

"Stop. I love you!" She laughed softly, leaning in and kissing his lips.

His face softened and in a heartbeat, he forgot the task at hand, and silently returned to what he craved - kissing her full lips, before trailing wet kisses down her neck. *My. My. My. Delightful.* He pulled back and looked down at her, he didn't have the heart to go further. But neither did he have the courage to destroy her moment of bliss.

She looked up at him, willing him to capture her mouth beneath his. But instead, she saw the flicker of indecision in his eyes. She couldn't quite understand it. Was this happening too fast for him? She pulled away from him, but still held his hand. His eyes were dark with desire, but the uncertainty was still there.

Larry watched her eyes dancing with yearning, yet there was a glimmer of fear there too. Fear of rejection, no doubt. "Roz, please -"

She quieted him with her finger to his lips. "Don't," she told him, nodding vigorously. "Don't explain. Let's take a rain check on that." Her eyes shined with tears. "I love you and I know you love me. Let's ... leave it there. Agreed?"

He was silent for a moment before nodding in agreement. He would tell her another day.

She removed her fingers from his lips. "Let's pray for each other and our marriage going forward."

Yes, I'll tell her another day. Why spoil this beautiful moment? He gave her a soft dimpled smile, taking her hands in his and kissing them, before he began to pray.

CHAPTER 31

Rozene was pleasantly surprised at the ease at which things fell back into place with Larry, when she moved home the following day. He had been most attentive to her needs - helping her to unpack then picking up fruits, while she slept for two hours. He used every opportunity to give her his undivided attention or gently touch her, and at times, she saw his lingering gaze which caused her insides to churn happily. He seemed genuinely pleased to have her back home. He served her dinner in bed when she awoke, and by night fall, he had disarmed her with his love.

Well, almost.

While she was accepting of his light touches and warm gestures of intimacy, she still felt unworthy, and undeserving of his love. Partly too, because of the indecision she'd seen in his eyes when they had met at Abella. *What was that all about? Second thoughts?* Even though she could never tell by his current behavior. *Probably had a chance to mull it over.*

That evening, she decided to hide in Madison's room, telling him she was going to finish up a chapter. However, she spent an hour re-writing the same paragraph because her thoughts were focused on her new season. Frustrated, she powered down her laptop, prayed, and decided to face the music.

She cautiously entered their bedroom and closed the door behind her. She glanced around and saw that Larry was nowhere in sight. As she moved towards the lounge area, she heard sounds in the bathroom. A grateful sigh left her body and she sat on the daybed so she could see him when he entered the room.

Larry heard movement in the bedroom and knew Rozene was there. He wondered if she was okay and if coming home was overwhelming for her. She had still looked a bit tense even though he had done everything possible to make sure that she was comfortable. When she had said she needed to finish up a chapter, he knew she just needed a little time to get herself together. He had waited for her to shower with him, but when he didn't see any sign of her, he decided to shower and then talk with her to see why she was running scared.

He was running scared too … if she only knew. He had packed up the idea of telling her his little secret. She was already troubled and he had no desire to aggravate the situation any further. Plus, he had already confessed and repented of it.

A few minutes later, he entered the bedroom looking for Rozene when he heard her soft gasp.

Rozene's heart whipped to and fro in her chest, and her mouth hung open, as Larry's legs moved closer. How could he just casually stand there in his black boxer brief that seemed to be painted on to him?

He walked over to her, smiling. "What's up? Was wondering where you were."

Unconsciously, a sigh danced from her lips, as she slowly regained her wits. She glanced at him and found a pair of startlingly warm brown eyes assessing her in return.

An exhilarating, yet familiar sensation passed between them and he leaned down and placed his hands on either side of her while flashing his pearly whites. "What are you so spellbound about?"

She blinked rapidly and her mouth twitched as she gazed at him wondering how to respond. She licked her lips nervously, and then broke their stare to catch a closer glimpse of his gorgeous physique. He was magnificent.

He allowed her to leisurely peruse his body and when she had had enough, he said, "You keep looking at me like you've never seen me." He pressed a kiss against her forehead, and then nuzzled his nose against hers.

251

Shaky giggles escaped her and impulsively, she grabbed his face, and planted a quick kiss on his lips, before releasing his face.

He gasped against her mouth, before leaning deeper to brush his lips lightly against hers. He continued to graze his lips against hers, tickling her.

Eager for more of him, she clutched his face and kissed him with unbridled urgency as heat ignited in her core.

Taken by her outburst of passion, he sat on the daybed and gathered her up against him, and allowed her to devour his lips before kissing her until it took her breath away. Eventually, he lifted his lips slightly from hers, and her half-lidded eyes gazed at him as she panted.

He chuckled softly against her mouth, the heat of their kiss, still lingering and sizzling through him. "I love you." The words seemed to float from his lips.

"I love you, too," she whispered, nestling her face against his neck.

He could feel her smiling and he closed his eyes, inhaling her scent.

Guided by instinct, he let out a deep, slow breath, and gently eased her away from him.

She looked at him, her surprise and slight annoyance evident. Her lips parted questioningly.

"I'm all yours when you are ready," he answered before she could ask. He knew she was not mentally ready to give herself to him. There was no rush anyway. As much as he yearned for her, he knew it was better to put his desire on hold. Mustering all of his strength, he walked away from her.

Rozene watched, unable to take her eyes off him as he headed towards the bed. Frustrated, she quickly moved to the bathroom.

Forty minutes later, she donned another of his favorites - a royal blue mesh barely-there teddy with a blue satin bow at her breasts. She remembered that he loved it - for the color, but mainly because the split at the front allowed easy access.

She stared at her reflection in the mirror at the sink. Apart from the undeserving feeling that refused to let her go, she was still having self-confidence issues over her body. She was not usually this obsessed with her body, but since the children left, she had come to the realization that she was not the size she'd once been. Clearly, little exercise and the years of sitting and typing her books did not help. Of course, Larry's healthy body also gave her reason to pause.

She made a few turns and inspected herself. *Not bad*, she concluded. She had gained a bit of weight, but mostly on her breasts. They seemed to be spilling from her teddy.

She whispered a prayer, asking God for direction, all the while hoping Larry would be asleep by the time she climbed into bed. Of course, she wanted to make love with him. Desperately so. But each time she looked at him, she felt guilty all over again for what she had done to him. Thankfully, she was blessed with a forgiving husband. A smile curved her lips. For that, she would always be grateful.

Her smile widened as she recalled her mother's words, 'Handle your mistakes without regrets. Enjoy the present with confidence and grab a hold of your future without fear'.

Engrossed in her thoughts, she stared at the mark at her temple that the accident had caused. It had healed well and was paling out, thanks to a cream that the dermatologist had given her. She patted her face with a small, white towel and then hung it on the rack near the

253

sink. *Fear has no place in my life. Lord, thank you for favor. Every time.*

"Thought you had fallen asleep in here," Larry said from behind her. He smiled as she wheeled to face him. "I knocked and didn't hear a response."

"Sorry. Didn't hear..." She stared at his ripped torso and happy thoughts danced across her mind. She clenched her hands at her side to keep from touching him.

"What's going on?" he asked quietly.

She nibbled her lips, wondering how to tell him it had nothing to do with him.

"Give it to me straight. I can handle it."

"It's ..."

"Roz, you can tell me." He held on to her hand as she looked away from him. "It's okay. Tell me."

She gazed at him, all choked up. "I constantly feel guilty every time I look at you. Guilty for what I did to you ... and our marriage." She held up her hand to stop him from speaking. "I know you've forgiven me, but it's still a struggle for me. I didn't want to be that kind of person." She wiped her eyes with the back of her hand.

"You are not that kind of person," he squeezed her hand reassuringly, before resting it on his chest.

With a sharp intake of fear and delight, she felt his heart hammering away.

"Babes, my heart beats only for you. I love you."

Her eyes and her heart fluttered in unison. "I love you too."

Enjoying the feeling of her hand on his chest, she gazed at him and found his eyes slowly exploring her body, until they came to rest on her lips.

Something about the tenderness in his gaze made her feel beautiful. She was glad she was wearing his special teddy, and by the look in his eyes, she knew that as much as he liked seeing her in it, he would prefer her out of it ... as quickly as possible.

Her eyes still holding his, she released the bow at the front of her teddy, and felt the cool air on her skin as her teddy opened. She almost giggled at his sharp intake of breath. "I'm all yours when you are ready," she said softly, arching towards him.

He continued to gaze at her, wondering if she was truly ready. The last thing he needed was sex out of gratitude. That would kill everything in him. He would rather wait.

Sure he desired her ... her touch, her kisses, and her passion. And right now, she was maddeningly hot - gazing at him with her striking eyes. He cleared his throat in the wild hope of clearing his head. Then, all on their own, his fingers began threading into her hair. She gripped the sink behind her, and threw her head back to give him full access. His hand wandered across the delicate inside curve of her neck and he watched her shiver with delight.

He gazed in awe at her breasts ... admiring them ... memorizing every inch. *36C.* That he couldn't forget, even though they had gotten fuller, with her slight weight gain. *Not that I mind. Not one bit.* "Mm hmm," escaped his lips.

The husky longing in his voice caused warm tremors to shoot through her.

"I missed these," he said softly, a full smile gracing his lips. Then in a fluid movement, he cupped her breast, his fingers sinking into their softness.

As if in sync, they both moaned in pleasure.

And they miss me too, was all he could think.

"Larry," she purred softly, her heartbeat thundering in her ears.

He pulled away from her and gazed into her eyes, and instinctively, she moved her body forward, her hands gripping his shoulders.

255

But, he was unhurried - in awe of the gorgeous flower before him.

"I need you." Rozene shuddered in anticipation. Her mouth felt dry, as parched as a desert landscape. And she was getting hotter by the second.

He pulled her firmly against him. Her heartfelt plea touched his heart. In that moment, he recognized something - a longing in his heart that mirrored hers. "I need you more."

Her lips parted softly. "Then have me."

"That is my only intention." A smile tilted the corners of his mouth for he knew how she liked to be touched, and he intended to touch her ... everywhere.

Her breath caught as he lifted her. She hugged his shoulders purring in anticipation as he made his way to the bedroom.

******

A faint light seeped through the curtains as Rozene watched Larry sleep, his head cradled at her breasts. His body rose and fell with slow breaths and she felt the warmth of his hands on the small of her back. Memories of their night together flooded her, and a smile burst across her face. They had explored each other without limitation and he had made her swoon and chant in languages that were incomprehensible.

He is mine again, she thought, a grateful smile curving her lips. All in all, it was perfect - maybe even too perfect. She nestled against him, and before long, she was fast asleep.

An hour later, the stillness of the morning woke Larry. He shifted slightly to gaze at Rozene as she slept, lying on her side, and facing him. His heart smiled. Her lips were slightly swollen from their night of passion, but she looked well-loved ... and satisfied.

Their amorous night stirred his soul and he would have a permanent, blissful smile on his face for days to come. He leaned in and gave her a quick kiss before gently brushing back strands of hair that had fallen over her cheek. She did not stir. His hand glided over her breasts and when she still did not stir, he bathed her breasts with gentle kisses.

That brought Rozene back to the present with a loud gasp followed by even louder moans as her body reacted instinctively. Near hyperventilating, she clutched his shoulder for support as tremors racked her belly.

"You're up," he whispered, kissing her neck, and cheek, and then her eyelids.

He gazed at her in the same way he always did and she came apart. "Kiss them again," she whispered hoarsely.

A smile emerged on his lips. That was all the encouragement he needed. He kissed her passionately before fulfilling her request. Soft sounds swirled from her throat, and she eagerly lifted her chest to meet his lips. Whimpering loudly, her head jerked back against the pillow as he trailed butterfly kisses down her chest. The subtle gasps that escaped her increased his growing passion, but he knew that enough was enough. There would be other days.

"Shhh." He kissed the top of her head before cradling her trembling body against him. When her body began to relax, he rolled her over to hold her in a spoon position.

She kissed his fingers and a moan passed his lips.

"Stop it," he said, holding her tightly as he worked to slow his breathing.

She chuckled softly when she realized what he was doing.

257

An hour later, he kissed her head and climbed out of bed. "I have to go," he told her, sadness evident in his voice. "Told them I'll be in late. I'll be back as soon as I can get away. I have one meeting I need to attend."

She attempted to sit and groaned in pain, every muscle in her body protesting.

"Hard night," he grinned at her.

"Hard, but great night." She looked at him boldly as she finally pulled herself into a sitting position. "Thank you."

"Thank you too. And don't worry, your secret is safe with me." He winked before strolling off to the bathroom. "Back in a few for prayer."

"Okay," she murmured with a languid stretch, while watching him leave the room. She couldn't imagine her world without his passionate kisses and his ability to bring common sense to any situation. Without question, every situation.

She couldn't wait for him to return for their prayer time. Later, she had a few things up her sleeve. She giggled, rolling back and forth, and her cheeks warmed thinking of the delicious things she would do to him.

The corner of Larry's mouth did a slow slant upward as he entered the bathroom. He had felt her eyes on him. Little did she know he had seduction plans of his own.

CHAPTER 32

Rozene rested against the wooden railing on the back patio and breathed in the fresh morning air, while watching the rays of sunlight peeking brightly through the trees. She smiled thinking the sky was a pretty blue, mirroring her joy and gladness. She felt in alignment with nature, fully aware of the enduring love of an Almighty God who clothed His creation with majesty.

Her shoulders rose a tad bit as she closed her eyes and took in more of the crisp air, before starting to hum "Amazing Grace" with her face tilted. At the end of the song, she opened her eyes, and glanced around the patio. *Life is good.*

She walked towards the breakfast which Armela had laid out on the table for her and reached for her mug of cocoa. Cradling the mug in both hands, she gingerly blew in it, before sipping.

She couldn't help but send up another prayer of gratitude to God. Her recent season had been long, hard, and grueling, but God had sustained her. Indeed, He had purified her in the midst of the fire. Now, she and Larry had returned to normalcy at home. She was back on schedule doing more TV tapings, promoting *Undeniably Yours: The Journey to Love*, attending charity events, and writing another book, *Give Me You.*

After breakfast, she called to check on the children and then she called Sarah to confirm that she had no morning appointments, so she could work from home, for a few hours.

Three hours later, Rozene grabbed her purse from the passenger seat and alighted from her Blue Water Metallic BMW. She walked through the full-height glass doors of Rozene Kanate Ministry and stopped to chit-chat with Sienna, the receptionist, in the gorgeously decorated foyer.

The foyer was adorned with white vintage furniture with gold trimmings and stunning shades of blue accent pieces. The soft light in the ceiling illuminated the area, creating a dazzling white setting whether day or night. The foyer's natural elegance created the perfect entryway to access the various offices and rooms of the ministry.

Soon, Rozene left Sienna and walked across the intricately patterned gold and white marble floor, entered the elevator and punched the number five. She greeted Sarah and was barely settled behind her desk when Don knocked and walked in.

"Good afternoon," she greeted him.

"Good afternoon to you too. Aren't you looking rested, bright-eyed and bushy tailed." Don smiled at her.

"Yes. I have good reasons. You know God has been super good to me."

"As always. But you have that extra glow, created only by looove." His smile widened. "Just don't set the place on fire."

"You know that's going to be hard but I will definitely try to hold it down."

"That's the least you can do," he told her, still grinning.

"You're in a great mood. What's up?"

"Everything is going well. You and Larry will be the last couple to be interviewed for the marriage series. Glad he'll be able to make it today."

"Oh yes, looking forward."

"After the team put the series together and we get the green light from you, Marianne and I will be taking a vacation. Heading to Europe."

"Don that's great. You are both so deserving of that. Take all the time you need."

He eyed her, raising an eyebrow and they both started laughing, since the entire staff knew that they were her hands and feet. Above all, they understood her heart.

"You know I don't mean that right?" Rozene chuckled. "I'm only being brave."

"Don't worry. We're only taking two weeks."

"You can take more, you know."

"I know, but there is much to do. We'll take more time in the summer."

"Sounds good to me."

"If you need anything while we are gone, Kelvin and Marcia will be your go-to people, as usual, if you're okay with that."

"Yes, that's fine. Have Sarah put them on my calendar. I haven't spoken to them since we did their TV taping for the marriage series, a week ago."

"Yes. I'll do that. We'll be ready as soon as Larry arrives. After the taping, I was hoping we would look at the calendar of activities for the rest of the year, and next year."

Rozene grimaced, gazing at the folders of papers and books on top of her desk. "I was hoping to sort through my mails and emails. Let's talk about it after ..." She paused smiling, upon hearing Larry greeting Sarah. "Let's talk about it after the TV taping," she continued, looking at Don who was grinning from ear to ear.

He shook his head. "You have it bad. Really bad."

She smiled. "Guilty as charged."

Some fifteen minutes later, hand in hand, Larry and Rozene took their seats on two plush, royal-blue chairs in the studio.

"You better stop looking at me like that," Larry leaned in and teased quietly. "Your staff is probably thinking we were up to no good in your office."

261

She squeezed his hand that was resting on the arm of the chair. "That's your fault, giving me those beautiful red roses ... that's a lot of roses." She smiled at him. "Mind you, I like them, they are lovely. Just that ..." Her eyes saddened as her voice trailed off.

"It's okay. Don't succumb to that feeling. I buy you flowers because you are my gorgeous flower."

She flashed him a captivating smile. "Thank you. I love you."

His eyes twinkling, he returned her smile. "I love you more."

"Well, if you too love birds are ready. We can get cracking," Don told them from across the room.

Larry and Rozene smiled at him.

"Yes, we are," Rozene said.

Don signaled with his hand and the team took up their places to begin taping.

"I hope you both got a chance to review the questions," Don told said, taking his seat as chief interviewer on a matching, royal-blue sofa in front of them. "I have a few that I didn't email to you, but I think you will be all right."

"Yes, we'll be okay," Larry responded.

"Here we go." Don nodded their readiness, and the taping began.

Half an hour later, they took a break from taping to have a cool drink and refresh their make-up. When Don indicated they were ready to proceed, Larry and Rozene took up their seats.

"Welcome back to our marriage series, "Promises of Forever," Don began. "Designed to strengthen and enrich even the best marriages. Thank you, Larry and Rozene Kanate, for all that you have shared on the heart of your marriage. We have already discussed God's purpose and plan for marriage, the roles of the husband and wife."

262

He smiled at them. "And we touched on intimacy. Now for the hard stuff. Let's talk about communication and conflicts in a marriage. As you know, Marianne and I recently celebrated twenty-five years of marriage. It has not been twenty-five years of pure joys, because we've had many, many conflicts." His smile widened. "Clearly, we have resolved them. We are still together."

They all burst out laughing.

"Happily so," Don hastened to add, still chuckling. "Rozene, I know you are working on a novel – *Give Me You* – which will comprise some of the challenges, some of the hard things that couples go through. Talk to us about some of those hard things."

"Sure, Don. By now, most of our viewers would have known that Larry and I met in high school and started our relationship after an epic rescue, when I had to save him from a particular gentleman at my parents' charity ball."

"An epic rescue, indeed," Larry chimed in, smiling.

"Yes." Rozene returned his smile, touching his hand. "And it was my pleasure, hon."

Tossing his head back, Don chuckled. "That's your story, huh?"

"Yes, and I'm sticking to it." Rozene grinned at him. "Anyway, Larry and I decided we wanted to be best friends. That was not always easy because we both have strong personalities, although I would say his personality is more dominant. The good thing is that we enjoy each other's company and that kept us in check.

But, I also believe that we both didn't want to risk losing each other. We had to learn to listen to each other. Communication is very important in a marriage." She gazed tenderly at Larry, who was hanging on to her every word. "We had to hear each other's heart and we had to learn to compromise, and support each other. Now, I know

263

it sounds easy, but it is a hard thing to do. So, each person in the relationship has to dig deeper in God and ask for strength, to do this. I would say to every couple going through any kind of conflict – take it to the Lord in prayer together, listen to each other, compromise, and if necessary, call in an unbiased third party like your pastor to help sort out the situation." She looked towards Larry, indicating that he needed to pick up.

"Every marriage relationship is continuously moving,' Larry added. "The couple is moving closer or drifting apart. I hate to say, the natural inclination is for the couple to drift apart, especially if reality doesn't match the vision they have in their heads. So, the individuals in the marriage need to pay attention to each other. As we stated earlier, to have a successful marriage, God must be in the center of that marriage. I want to echo what Rozene said, it's important to enjoy your spouse as both friend and partner. And, you do want the very best for your friend."

"Would you agree then, that a part of loving is giving sacrificially to the other person?" Don asked.

"Certainly," Larry said emphatically. "Each person will have to give sacrificially for the good of the marriage. Love is a beautiful, powerful emotion. Yes, it is great to be in love. 'You're holding heaven in your arms,' according to Celine Dion's song. It is that good." Larry laughed. "Can I get a witness?"

"Amen," Rozene grinned, lifting a hand, while chuckling, "yes, it is, hon."

Smiling, Larry continued, "Yet, loving someone requires dying to self in a way that so few realize. Love is not just about the passion that I feel for my wife. Love is based on a continuous concern for her."

Larry chuckled knowingly, before adding, "Sometimes in the midst of a conflict, I secretly remind myself of the definition of love – 'Love suffers long and is

kind; love does not envy; love does not parade itself, is not puffed up; does not behave rudely, does not seek its own, is not provoked, thinks no evil; does not rejoice in iniquity, but rejoices in the truth; bears all things, believes all things, hopes all things, endures all things. Love never fails ...'"
He glanced at Rozene who smiled tenderly at him.

"We have come a long way, hon," Rozene said. "It has not been easy but we are definitely more considerate of each other. Also, because of our love for the Lord, it strengthens our marriage."

"We have learned through the years to help each other," Larry jumped in. "For instance, if I am getting too ugly in our heated conversation, Roz will remind me of Proverbs 15:1, 'A soft answer turns away wrath, but a harsh word stirs up anger.'"

"Yes. Yes," Don agreed. "Nothing like the Word of God to bring things back into perspective."

"At the end of the day," Larry added, "we both thrive for a harmonious relationship. We are at our best when we are at peace with each other; and we are leaning on Jesus." Smiling, he reached across the arm of his chair and held Rozene's hand. "You know what I realize, even more so these days – I love my wife with all of my heart. I loved her from the first time I laid eyes on her, and I wanted to make her happy, even if it meant sacrificing some things."

Rozene smiled gratefully at him. "I love you too, hon," she told him softly, as he stared into her eyes that were filled with love for him.

A quiet calm filled the studio and for a moment, no one moved.

"That was simply a beautiful moment folks," Don pressed on. "And there you have it - Love works best when we love each other with genuine affection, and take delight in honoring and preferring each other." He smiled at Larry

265

and Rozene. "We wish you many more years of togetherness."

"Thank you," Larry told him, as he released Rozene's hand.

"We have a few minutes before we take another break," Don said. "I have a burning question from a Twitter follower - Can a couple learn to love again?"

Simultaneously, Larry and Rozene looked at each other and smiled ... a smile of thanksgiving, before letting out a resounding. "Yes."

Suddenly, Larry's eyes welled up with tears. "Yes, you can learn to love again. And I dare say, it's even better the second time round."

Rozene gazed at the man who still had the power to make her heart beat rapidly. "Definitely better the second time round."

"Thank you, Larry and Rozene." Don smiled at them. "We'll be back shortly to hear more about learning to love again."

As soon as the cameras were turned off and the crew started moving about, Larry smiled at Rozene, his dimples pronounced. "I love you," he whispered. "I want to share how God extended his grace and mercy towards us."

Excitement clothed Rozene. *A man with a powerful testimony. No resistance here.* "Sure, hon, I trust you." A proud look shrouded her face. "I love you too."

When the interview resumed, she intended to listen ... listen to her husband's beautiful renewed spirit.

CHAPTER 33

"Thought we were leaving the cold weather behind," Mason remarked as his Dad pulled away from Orlando International Airport to head home.

"You thought wrong," Rozene said, smiling in the passenger seat across from Larry.

"And that wouldn't be the first," Madison quipped.

"You still mad at me, baby sis."

"Why would you think that?" Madison asked. "Guilt?"

"We're experiencing a cold front outside, and inside this vehicle," Mason announced, throwing a glance in Madison's direction.

She ignored him, fixing her gaze through the window.

Larry glanced at the twins through the rearview mirror before turning his attention back to the road. *Can't live with each other and cannot live without each other.* He smiled inwardly, before mentioning, "We haven't had a December like this in a long time,"

"But this weather is still much better than the one in Massachusetts – Cold, crisp, and white," Rozene said. "And windy."

"Yes, it's like that," Madison agreed, "but strangely, I like it." She glanced at Mason who was waving an 'olive branch' at her. Ignoring him, she focused her gaze on her parents. "I'm eternally grateful, Mom and Dad, that you attended my Christmas Production. Mom, you had my dancers star struck."

Rozene smiled. "Really. Even after I -"

"Yes, mom, even after you tried to put them at ease. It was hard to get over your presence. Your session with them was great though."

"Mom, you know what else has been great," Mason piped in. "Your TV programs. Wow! You sure made an impressive comeback. I even found myself watching re-runs. Can't wait to see what else will be showing."

"Yes, Mom," Madison agreed. "They have been inspirational on a new level. Mason and I have been discussing them. The one on forgiveness simply moved me to tears."

"Praise God. Glad you like them. God is good."

"Yes, He is. It's great to see you and Dad back in sync too," Madison added. "It's just wonderful all around. Thank God."

"Thank God," Rozene agreed while Larry nodded, adding, "Glad to have you both home for Christmas."

In unison, the twins responded, "Great to be home," and a comfortable silence settled in the SUV.

But not for long.

"Are we going to talk about the elephant in the room?" Mason asked mischievously. "Forgive me, I meant Tyler. What do you call him? Mr. Chocolate? No. Hot Chocolate." He chuckled loudly. "What do you think, Mom and Dad?"

"Really, Mason? Really?" Madison lashed out.

Mason eyed her. "Why are you so uptight? I'm trying to get their take on the situation. I know it's important to you." He was quiet for a moment. "I joke about it sometimes, Madison, but I want the best for you. I already told you I approve of the guy."

He tickled her side.

"Stop!" she yelled.

"You know I mean you well, right?" He poked her in the side when she didn't respond. "Right?" he asked, setting to poke her again.

"Okay. Okay, I know you do. I'm supersensitive because I don't know what direction it will take."

"I understand," he told her quietly. "But remember, I mean you well, okay," he said, offering her a fist bump.

"Okay." She bumped her fist to his.

He smiled at her. "I think Tyler is a bit overwhelmed with the family legacy. It was even more obvious to me when he met Dad and Mom. I think he likes you a lot. Give him time," Mason suggested.

Madison smiled at him. "Thanks, big bro."

"That's why I'm here." Mason returned her smile, knowing she would get back at him.

Rozene and Larry glanced at each other with raised eyebrows because Rozene had indicated as much to Larry. In the meantime, they would continue to commit the matter to the Lord.

******

Christmas passed in a haze of bliss for the entire family. Armela had helped Rozene to prepare Christmas dinner, of which, all the in-laws, siblings, and their children came to partake.

Almost a week later, Larry stood on the balcony outside their bedroom, soaking up the cool evening breeze. He deliberated whether or not to go back into the bedroom and help Rozene, who was getting dressed for the Church's New Year's Eve banquet. She hadn't been feeling well since she woke that morning, so he hadn't planned on attending. He'd even communicated that to Pastor Fotola. He didn't mind one bit though, because attending the event was not something he wanted to do anyway. However, by the afternoon, Rozene had recovered and was determined to be present.

A frustrated sigh slipped free. His conscience was killing him since he still hadn't confessed his infidelity to Rozene. He'd come close to telling her the truth a few

269

times but his heart palpitations strongly warned him against it. The truth would change everything and he couldn't risk that. He was sure she could see the guilt in his eyes. He'd even caught her watching him curiously a few times. Then, it could be his imagination, but Pastor Fotola kept casting accusatory glances his way. Now, he wished he hadn't mentioned his little secret to him.

But someone was also haunting his thoughts - Gabrielle. *Would she ever see Jesus in me?*

His interaction with Gabrielle had been nonexistent until two weeks ago, when he saw her in Talpher Supermarket. He was having a conversation with Don and Marianne, when he happened to glance down the aisle. He knew he'd done a double take, because he had to ask Marianne to repeat what she was saying.

Gabrielle was engrossed, peering at something she'd taken from the shelf, and he wanted to go to her before she saw him. He couldn't wait to excuse himself from the conversation, which was getting on his last nerve anyway. Marianne was quietly hinting that she was glad he had forgiven Rozene, that 'forgiveness was a part of the Christian duty.' He wanted to shout, Yes! Yes! Yes! For the love of God, I know; that's why I forgave her. But for the sake of the cross, and Marianne and Don's friendship, he'd kept his cool, nodding politely.

In the midst of that, he sent a signal of sorts to Gabrielle, and she picked up on it. He could feel the air between them crackling with intensity as Gabrielle suited up in full battle gear. Mental combat was inevitable, and Gabrielle saw the intention in his eyes before they shifted back to Don and Marianne.

He glanced at Gabrielle again and saw her chin come up. She stared him straight in the eyes before recoiling and mouthing a passionate, "No". When she wheeled her cart and headed in the opposite direction, he knew he had to hurry or he would lose her.

As soon as he got away from his conversation, Larry hurried across the aisle in the direction where he'd seen her go, and boy was she in a hurry. He yelled her name, and made a dash down the aisle, but she seemingly disappeared. He even stood at one of the exit doors and scanned the parking lock, but she was nowhere in sight.

That night before he went to bed, he had said a special prayer for her, hoping that their encounter hadn't shaken her too much and that she was finding help dealing with what had transpired between them.

Later that week, he had taken it upon himself to call her, and that conversation did not go well either. He was grateful she had answered his private number, and answered the phone cheerfully.

"Gabrielle, please don't hang up." He had to beg, because he was desperate to speak with her.

"What do you want?" she asked, firmly.

He pushed past the annoyance in her voice. "I'm so sorry for what I di-did to you." His voice broke, but that was not a surprise to him. What he had done to her was wrong, and while he knew he couldn't undo the past, he wanted to make sure she knew how sorry he was. "I just wondered if we could meet and talk."

He knew she was fuming ... no, she went ballistic. "Larry, you already told me you're sorry. There won't be any meeting."

"I really feel bad about my actions, Gabrielle. I have never done anything like that in my entire life. My Pastor thinks it's a good idea to meet with you, preferably face to face."

"Larry, I told you there will be no meeting. Stop calling my phone or I will report you to the police." With that she disconnected the call.

The phone fell from his hand with a thud on the desk. He pushed the chair away from the desk, feeling scalded by the intensity of Gabrielle's animosity towards him. He shed a few tears that Saturday morning in the study.

The cool evening breeze brought Larry out of his musing, and he took the time to breathe. Grateful to still have his family intact. Inwardly, he smiled, and kept smiling. *Now that's something to smile about.*

He heard movement behind him and turned only to have his breath halted. "Babes, you look gorgeously edible." *Jaw-droppingly stunning!* He strolled purposefully towards her.

She grinned at him as he admired her eye-catching black evening gown. His eyes lowered to the bodice of her dress.

"Am I showing cleavage? Tried to tuck everything in."

He smiled at her. "No. You're good, but they are looking fuller." He held up his hand as she began to protest. "You know I like them, no matter the size." He hugged her, nuzzling his nose against hers before gently pecking her lips.

A soft sigh escaped her lips, and she angled her head for more. His soft kisses were pointblank delicious and addictive. Her entire body tingled with anticipation, and she grabbed his shoulders.

Panting, Larry lifted his lips from hers. "Do we have time?" He nipped her lips to encourage her.

A low moan escaped her. "I wish," she said, still holding his shoulders. "Rain check, please."

His mouth thinned in mock displeasure as he released her, slowly. "You're no fun."

"We'll see about that later."

"Uh-oh. Can't wait."

"Did I say that out loud?" she asked, batting her eyes before moving back to the bedroom.

He followed her. "You sure did."

"Then I will make good on it." She walked over to the dresser mirror, and then turned from side-to-side in front of it.

"I'm holding you to it." He stood behind her, watching closely as she leaned forward, and reapplied her lipstick.

"It's a done deal. And you make it easy. You're looking mighty fine yourself."

He placed his hands on the dresser, trapping her between them. "Thanks, babes." He dropped soft kisses on her shoulder, whispering an apology for causing her to have to re-apply her lipstick.

"Oh, my," she murmured at the first contact with his heated lips.

"You are good for me. Can you tell?" he asked, nipping her neck between lingering kisses.

She squirmed, pressing closer to him as his voice tickled her ears, for she knew exactly where he was going. "You know I want to, but we better stop before we miss the banquet." She watched him in the mirror and he made a face at her, refusing to budge, and instead pressed her against the dresser.

Grinning, she playfully whacked him on his hand. "Naughty man. Play nice. Save all that for later."

"Yes, ma'am." Stepping to the side, he adjusted the jacket of his black tuxedo in the mirror, flexed his muscles a few times, before smiling at himself. "Ready when you are, madam."

She burst out laughing. "You're the man."

"Yes, I am." He offered his arm, which she graciously took. Tonight, he was attentive and passionate, and she was perfectly content with that.

******

Almost two hours later, after eating, they were roaming around the banquet hall, meeting and greeting. As Rozene spoke to a few of the ladies, she glanced around the hall for Larry and saw him in an animated discussion with Deacon Watson. She smiled at him and he returned her smile, signaling as usual, by touching the back of his neck, that he would be ready in a moment.

Just then, Pastor Fotola approached Larry and she was sure she saw anxiety in Larry's gaze. Strangely, she felt the need to rescue him. She politely excused herself from among the ladies and motioned to him.

He arrived by her side and hugged her waist happily. "Ready?"

"Nope. Try again?"

He looked at her puzzled. "What?"

"Felt the need to rescue you."

"Me? Why? From who?"

"Pastor Fotola."

"Pastor Fotola?" A strange glint appeared in his eyes before he quickly masked it with a chuckle. "You're ready to leave, huh?" He poked her side. "You made me a promise. Don't think I forgot. I'd like to get started."

She let his avoidance slide. "I hate to say, but me too."

Larry swallowed hard. "Play nice."

She grinned at him. "I'll try. Give me a moment; need to use the restroom."

"Don't be long. I'm holding my breath."

"You may not want to do that," she chuckled, sliding out of his arms. Later, she would ask Larry what was happening between him and Pastor Fotola. She knew that Pastor Fotola had counseled him through the period of their separation and understandably so, he and Larry had a great relationship. But now something was not right between them.

Come to think of it, these days, Larry was in a hurry to get home after church. Forget the meet and greet after church, which he was always so gung-ho about back in the day. 'We have to fellowship after church. That's where true ministry takes place,' Larry would say. However, since they had started going back to church, Larry couldn't wait to get to the car as soon as church ended. She'd put it down to him not wanting to answer too many questions about them being absent for such a long time. So, she was cool with that.

Now that she thought about it, something was definitely going on. At Christmas Sunday service, Larry was almost in a tizzy to get away from church after that foot-stomping, hand-clapping, worship service. She cornered him, well … attempted to corner him, when they were changing out of their church wear.

"Why are you always in a rush to leave church these days?"

He slipped off his shoes. "No rush."

If she didn't know better, she would have thought nothing of it. "You're in a rush. Trust me, you are."

"Babes." He cocked a brow at her, his trousers sliding down his legs and pooling at his ankles. "Why do you keep saying that?"

She almost lost her train of thought when he stepped out of his trousers and began moving towards her while peeling off his shirt. "Just saying," she said in a low voice, gazing at his sculpted torso.

He hugged her waist with one hand while the other massaged her back. "It's nothing, babes." His touch ignited a firestorm in her core and she felt his excitement as he pulled her closer, giving her a feel of his hard abs.

275

Unable to help herself, she stood on tippy toes to kiss his lips.

Yes. She'd let it pass.

After dinner that day, she reminded him that Pastor Fotola had asked him to resume his duties as the church's operations director. He told her he was still praying about it.

Although she was sure her eyes screamed disappointment, she held her peace. In her estimation, his attitude was a bit nonchalant. Nevertheless, she had shoved the whole thing aside, vowing to get back to it later. But, it had slipped her mind. Now, here it was again.

Rozene reentered the banquet hall and glanced around for Larry. He was still in conversation with Deacon Watson. She located Mason in the midst of a group of young ladies and told him, she and Larry were heading home. She moved towards Larry, and when his eyes met hers, he hastily excused himself and headed in her direction.

He smiled as he approached her. "Ready?" he asked, taking her hand.

"Sure," she said, returning his smile. "Mason and Madison will head home later."

Together they strolled to the exit door, greeting other attendees on their way. They were making their way through the parking lot, when they came face to face with Pastor Fotola. *Oh God*, Larry almost hollered out.

Rozene felt Larry's hand tighten over hers.

"Well, hello again," Pastor Fotola greeted them, smiling.

"Hi, Pastor," Larry responded in a cautious tone.

"Pastor Fotola," Rozene smiled at him warmly. "Great event, wouldn't you say?"

"Yes, it was. Glad you were able to make it."

Rozene knitted her brows and Pastor Fotola clarified. "I'd spoken to Larry this morning and he mentioned that you were not feeling well. Glad, you're better."

"Yes. Much better. Thank you."

"Stop by my office sometime," Pastor Fotola said. "It has been a while since we had a chat."

Rozene almost squirmed from the pressure of Larry squeezing her hand. She shifted her fingers and he released the pressure.

"I will," Rozene assured Pastor Fotola.

"Well, have a good night," Pastor Fotola said.

"You too!" They both said in unison, before continuing across the parking lot.

An awkward silence settled in the car as they drove home.

"What's going on between you and Pastor?"

Larry felt like his heart plummeted to his knees. He wished she wouldn't ask. "Nothing," he responded quietly.

"Exactly!" Rozene said, staring at his profile.

He took his eyes off the road briefly to glance at her. Even though he couldn't make out her expression, he knew she was staring at him.

"Is it about you not taking up your position at church?" Rozene asked. "No … It's more than that. You two had a great relationship. Does it have anything to do with me?"

"Why would you think that?" In his mind, he sounded like he was on edge.

She was silent for several seconds and Larry began to fear she'd seen through his façade.

"So you do admit that things are not right between you two."

"Don't want to talk about it, Roz," he told her as he pulled in the garage.

"Are you hiding things from me Larry? That is a dangerous precedence."

He turned off the engine, and slid from behind the steering wheel.

By the time he arrived on her side of the car, she'd already opened the door and stepped out.

She eyeballed him. "Come here."

He took two hesitant steps and stood before her. "I don't want to fight with you."

She put her arms around his waist. "I don't want to fight with you either. But you need to sort out whatever is going on between you and Pastor."

"I know, babes. I know, and I will."

She kissed him lightly on his lips, and caught his sigh of relief in her mouth. She giggled against his lips as he pressed her against the car.

"Are we going to celebrate the New Year or what?" he asked.

Her heart rate spiked. "I'm all for a great celebration."

The joy of the moment delighted his senses, and he groaned with pleasure. "Then, let's take the celebration upstairs."

CHAPTER 34

Larry smiled at Rozene after stopping the car in the driveway at Chateau de Kanate. "Thanks for a great evening out. Dinner was superb. Benson and Abella were extremely happy to see us. In fact, thanks for a wonderful day."

"You're welcome, hon. Celebrating you is always my pleasure. But celebrating your birthday, you know I had to bring my "A" game."

His smile widened as he took off his seatbelt. "I love how you started with devotion as usual. That was quite a prayer, you prayed over my life. Thank you." He reached across and gently kissed her.

"You're welcome," she mumbled against his lips, while caressing his cheek.

He eased back and then looked at the gold watch on his hand. "I like my gift. Plus, the massage was hmmm, hmmm good. You clearly had some training done to get it right. And lunch - with all my favorite foods - was so great. At one stage, I thought I had eaten my fingers. But I'm glad you took in consideration my dietary regimen." He smiled wickedly at her. "We cannot speak of what happened after lunch."

She laughed poking his side. "No, we won't."

"We won't," he chuckled. Then, he was quiet for a moment. "Thank you."

"You're welcome, hon, anytime. I love you."

"And I love you," he said, smiling at her. He was about to open the door when he turned to look at her. "Stop looking at me like that," he teased. "Didn't I fix you up before we left home?"

She tilted her head to the side. "You sure did."

"Ohhh," Larry shouted playfully. "You said that out loud."

"I did?" She dazzled him with a naughty smile. "Thought that was all in my head."

"Lady, you are going to wear me out."

"You're always the one initiating, I'm only taking a leaf out of your book."

Larry shook his head, clearly amused. "The pleasure is all mine," he drawled, winking. "The evening is still young."

She gurgled, and then cooed, "I can't wait."

"You said that aloud too." Larry grabbed his head. "You're a beast. The only time I remember you turning into this monster was when you were pregnant with the twins."

"That was all your fault, rubbing my belly and squeezing my huge breasts every chance you got."

"Yes, it was. It would help if you weren't so plump and cute." He tickled her side. "Don't worry, I'll fix your business later."

"You better." She giggled, hopping out of the car.

Larry hopped out too, a huge grin covering his face. "Come here, gorgeous." He encompassed her in his arms and delivered quick pecks against her lips.

"Hey! Hey! Not in the front yard," someone called out.

Smiles covered their faces as they walked towards Zane, Zadan, and Alexandria. They hugged Rozene before greeting their brother with shouts of, "Happy birthday!"

A few minutes later, inside the living room, Darlene, Alexandria's husband - Adam, their twin boys - Jayden and Jordan, and their daughter - Giselle, joined the happy gang for another mini celebration of Larry's birthday. Afterwards, when Larry and his brothers wandered off, Darlene asked Rozene to sit with her on the balcony, outside the living room.

Rozene had spoken to Darlene, but hadn't seen her in a while, so they chitchatted about everything.

"Let me know when your book is ready," Darlene said. "I'll place an order for the women's shelters."

"Thanks." Rozene smiled at her. "As usual, I appreciate your support."

"Are we still on for your presentation at the end of the month?"

"Of course. Wouldn't miss it for the world. Love those women."

They were both silent for a moment when Darlene broke the silence. "You are glowing. I wondered if you were -"

She paused as Rozene almost choked.

"Pregnant? Oh, no. I know you love your grandchildren. Hate to tell you, we're not planning to have any more children."

"Okayyy. Thanks for that bit of in-for-ma-tion." She smiled at Rozene. "I do love my grandkids. Mason and Madison called yesterday. They are settling in well."

"Yes, they are," Rozene agreed. "I hope I didn't come across too strong. Of course, if that happened, I wouldn't mind having another child. But no. No more children for us."

"That's okay."

Rozene smiled at her. "Truth is, menopause will be knocking on my front door any day now."

Darlene shook her head. "You have a way to go you know. So glad you and Larry are back together. Extremely happy. You'll both be able to talk about forgiveness and loving again, from a different standpoint."

"Forgiveness. You're right on that. I'm just grateful Larry took me back."

"Give yourself some credit too, dear. You're a forgiving woman."

"Forgiving?" Rozene eyed her, remorse etched in her gaze. "That was all Larry."

"God is good."

Rozene was sure she saw surprise flash in Darlene's eyes but it was gone in a second.

"I'm excited about you both renewing your vows," Darlene mentioned. "It's right around the corner - two weeks to be exact."

Rozene clasped her hands under her chin, smiling. "Yes. Our twentieth anniversary. I can't believe it. We'll have a big celebration later on in the year. Larry is doing most of the planning though."

"Wonderful. You know how I enjoy celebrations of all types, but this one is special."

Half an hour later, Larry and Rozene bid farewell to the rest of the Kanate clan and headed home. As the gray ribbon of road unfolded before them, each was submerged in their own thoughts.

You're a forgiving woman. Those words kept playing over and over in Rozene's mind. *What did she mean?*

She glanced across at Larry, and his mood had changed drastically. She saw him talking with his mother, and now she wondered what she had said to him that had so vexed his spirit.

Some twenty minutes later, they entered their bedroom without speaking. The silence was almost ominous. *Something is definitely wrong,* Rozene thought. *We should be celebrating right about now.*

Mentally, she asked the Lord for help as she removed her shoes, and then walked across to the dresser and began removing her jewelry. In the mirror, she saw Larry walking toward the lounge area in their bedroom. *Lord, help. Need to get to the bottom of this.* She was simply itching to question him about his mother's statement. She turned and watched as he plopped down on the daybed, legs spread wide.

She walked over and sat beside him, and it had to be her imagination that he pulled away from her, without looking at her.

"What's wrong?" she asked quietly.

Oh God. Guilt and fear sprinted through Larry's mind as he concocted a potential excuse. "Nothing," he told her, opening the top buttons of his shirt and letting the tie of his tux hang loose around his neck.

"It can't be nothing, Larry. Your whole mood has changed. Did your mother upset you?"

He tried to remember to breathe. "No, she just pointed out the obvious. I'm only upset with myself."

For the second time that evening, Rozene was puzzled. "Tell me."

He looked at her and swallowed. "I have been unfaithful to you."

Stunned, Rozene's jaw dropped but she snapped it shut. *Is he joking? Did he just?* "Wha-what?" A nervous chuckle ripped from her lips as she stifled the hammering in her heart.

Larry's lungs felt tight and unconsciously, he bit his lower lip, navigating the terrain. A bead of perspiration traveled down his back. His day of reckoning had arrived.

Rozene's body shivered. *Biting his lips.* Something he rarely did. But before she could gather her thoughts, he spoke again. Quietly. "I have not been faithful."

Her heart shuddered violently as his words slammed into her chest. She pulled away from him. Everything felt wrong. Everything.

Anxiety.

Shock.

Fear.

No, disbelief was the last emotion she suppressed before giving him her you-better-not-be-crazzzzy look that pinned him in place. "I don't understand," she said slowly. *No need for reckless emotion without a cause.*

Feeling at a disadvantage, Larry stood up as the fear emanating from both of them covered the room like a thick blanket.

The pain in his gaze said it all, and a chilling jolt shot through her body. She gazed at him, unaware that her mouth had hung open.

"Ple-please, Roz. I'm sorry. It only happened once."

Happened! Happened! Happened! Echoed everywhere. Rozene's breath was trapped in her now dry mouth. Head spinning, nothing Larry was saying was registering. *Did he? What? No, he didn't?* Her eyes began to widen as her outrage grew, and before she knew it, she flew off the daybed.

BAM!

The sound boomed everywhere as her hand connected with his face.

Larry grabbed her hands and she pushed him away. Jutting a finger in his face, she bellowed, "You're a liar, Larry. A cheater," before rushing past him towards the bed.

He followed closely on her heels. His voice filled with anguish, he pleaded with her for his life depended on it. "Roz, let me explain. Please."

Tears blurred her vision. "No. No." Then, she was up in his face, with her index finger pointing like a drill sergeant. "Don't. You. Speak to me. Don't you dare speak to me."

He touched her shoulder then BAM was the only sound that reverberated in the room as she backhanded him. The force of the slap turned his head in the opposite direction.

In the next breath, she collapsed on the bed as shockwaves of pain ripped through her. "Oh, God! Oh, my

God!" She wailed, over and over again, rocking back and forth.

Tears spilled from Larry's eyes as he sat beside her on the bed. "Roz, I-I'm sorry," he muttered. "Please stop crying."

He touched her shoulder and she sprang from the bed. "I hate you!" she screamed, throwing a fist out that landed on his shoulder.

As she winced in pain, he grabbed her, pinning her to the bed. "I love you," he told her emphatically.

"Get off me," she yelled at him, sobbing. "Get-Ge-Get away ..." She closed her eyes. *This cannot be real! This is not real!* "Oh, God," she cried loudly, "let it not be real."

He rolled off her, but held her in a spooned position as she cried her heart out. Even when she yelled, "Don't touch me!" he continued to hold her. He had to. The thought of losing her again made him hold her even tighter. Tears continued to stream out of his eyes as he buried his head in her hair.

Her entire body tingling, Rozene gasped for air as she pushed away images of Larry and some other woman.

Him and her!

Him and her!

Who's she?

He's sleeping with her!

Oh, God! Oh, God!

Don't think about it! Don't! Just stop! Stop thinking!

But as much as she tried, cruelly, her mind kept going there, over and over again. She stilled as she heard Larry apologizing again, realizing this wasn't some sort of joke, not a dream, but it was her life.

She pushed on his hands to release herself.

"Roz, I know you're hurting," he continued, through tears. "But we'll get through this."

Get through this. Man, please. She pushed against his hands, harder this time, but instead of letting her go, he tightened his arms around her.

"Let me go, Larry," she insisted.

Nerves trembled in the pit of his stomach as he released her. She quickly rolled off the bed.

"Roz ..." Larry clamped his mouth shut as she landed him an icy glare.

"Don't," she held up silencing hands. "Just don't."

He gulped down fear, and tears spewed from his eyes as he leaped off the bed and dropped to his knees before her. He dared not touch her. "Roz, please don't leave. PLEASE."

She shook her head violently, and then cocked her head to the side, regarding him.

"Roz, please, please don't ..." His words stumbled to a halt as she shot him a look that demanded his immediate silence. With every step she took away from him, his breath felt like it was exploding out of his lungs. He collapsed on the floor wailing and gasping for air. A few minutes later, panic and sorrows raged within when he heard heavy movements in the direction of her closet. She was leaving him.

CHAPTER 35

Submerged in the events of her chaotic life, Rozene got up from the bench in the park, and walked to the waterfall nearby. It was almost dawn. She had sat stoic for a while, replaying Larry's words over and over in her head. The soft light in the park enhanced the beautiful environment, but the beauty eluded her. She had to be dreaming, but would she ever wake up?

Larry's confession was so unexpected, it had crushed her soul. All she felt was pain; pain that was rapidly sucking the life out of her. Tears flowed down her face like a river. She didn't even bother to wipe them. What was the point? No matter how many times she blinked, they kept coming, insisting on remaining an endless stream. *Maybe one day they'll stop.*

Pulling the belt of her coat tighter around her waist, in a pointless attempt to ward off the bitter wind, she made her way back to her car.

After cruising around for hours, she had decided to sit for a while in the park and watch anything that would take her mind off the nightmare she was facing.

Despair knotted her insides.

Betrayal.

Breach of trust.

Lies.

A broken sob ripped from her lips. *I cannot go on like this.*

Betrayal.

Breach of trust.

Lies.

Cheating.

Deceit.

Lies. Too many lies.

She couldn't stop the string of endless dark thoughts that spewed out of her mind. She needed reprieve from the misery of thinking.

Wiping her eyes with her fingers, she inhaled then exhaled in an attempt to clear her heavy head. She had packed enough clothes that should last a week. At least, she hoped she did, because Larry and his sorry self, kept taking the clothes out of her case as soon as she dropped them in. No amount of "I'm sorry" that he'd pushed out of his lying lips was going to make her stay under the same roof with him.

What a sham? Had me fooled. He will be getting the divorce he wanted. Rozene blew her nose in a wad of tissue that was sitting on the passenger seat, and then began to rub her chest. She needed something, anything to relieve the terrible pain and the gnawing emptiness in her heart.

She grabbed her cell phone from the passenger seat. Forty missed calls, plus voicemails displayed. She cut her eyes at the phone. *No doubt trying to cover himself.* She dropped the phone in the cup holder, deciding it was too early to call her mom. She would just drive there.

An hour later, Rozene was lying under the bedcovers in her room at her parents' home.

"Mom, I'm broken. I can't even feel my heart, all I feel is pain," she lamented, using the bedcovers to wipe her eyes. "My whole life is falling apart again ... and I feel powerless to stop the downward spiral."

Her mother dabbed her own eyes. "Rozie, I know it's hard. But remember, God is still with you in this season. He is your present help in times of trouble. 'He will not allow your foot to be moved; He who keeps you will not slumber.' God will work this out for your good."

"Mom, who am I? What have I become? I slapped my husband. I wanted to fight him, Mom. I wanted to hurt him to make him feel the pain he was putting me through."

288

"Baby, I understand. It will get better. You've been through so much. Rest."

"You expect me to look away, Mom. I can't just look away. There is no reason for Larry to commit adultery. My heart is crushed, Mom. This breach of trust is killing me."

"Oh, baby, I know. Loving someone is never as simple as we want it to be. God will take care of you." Her mother pulled her into her arms, praying as Rozene wept uncontrollably.

CHAPTER 36

It had been three weeks since Rozene's earth-shattering discovery. Three weeks of agony. Three weeks of drifting and floating throughout various moments in her life. The good times. The not-so-good times. And, this terrifying time.

What happened to us?

Months ago, with the help of the Lord, she'd forgiven and released herself from her own dreadful sin and had gotten back into Larry's good graces. Back then, her life was so different from her now shadowy half existence. Back then, joy resounded in her heart.

Joy! It seemed so far away. She had already taken a long trek down the road of guilt and shame. Now, she was reliving that walk because of Larry's mirrored sin. And, she was tired. All her energy vaporized as she tried to fathom the events that had occurred in her life since she had committed adultery. She could no longer run. No longer hide. That was never her style. But everything had occurred in several short spurs, leaving her gasping for breath.

She needed a safe place. A place to breathe and get her thoughts together, so she could get back to the task of daily living.

Then, it hit her. *Move back home.*

And that she did, almost a week ago. It was Larry's turn to move out. But that was all in her mind ... hers alone. Confirmed, when Larry quietly told her he would not move out.

So, the war raged on.

Since then, she'd been sleeping in Madison's room and giving Larry mostly the silent treatment or responding to him in monosyllables, whenever he dared to speak. Not that that mattered to him. He was bent on communicating, and making himself available to get back in her good graces. Well, she had no intention of taking him up on any of his offers. However, it was getting tiring, trying to avoid him. Plus, too much energy to do all that bashing; and the task of landing him ugly looks was almost short-circuiting her brain. *Mercy! Didn't know it took so much work to be ugly.*

Nevertheless, she was keeping focused. She intended to keep all her appointments. All she needed to do was stay clear of Larry's puppy dog eyes, and his constant, 'I'm sorry. Please forgive me'.

Three days ago in one of their heated exchanges, he didn't miss a beat to remind her of her own words - "God Almighty, the Creator of the universe has forgiven me. I have forgiven myself and, I would have forgiven you, Larry. I'm not saying it would have been easy but I would have forgiven you."

He'd better be glad she was filled with the Holy Spirit. And call on the Holy Spirit was what she did that day, for backhanding him was the first thought that crossed her mind.

Truth be told though, that did hit a nerve, and it had caused her to pause. Forgiveness was something she had always encouraged. Something she believed in. But it was so much easier to say, when her heart, mind, soul, and body were not involved. Now, it was weighing heavily on her conscience. For after all, she did commit the same sin as he did. Albeit, stupidly so. To this day, she wondered how she found herself in that position with Chandler. 'The Chandler', according to Larry.

Nevertheless, today her hopes were up. She had to trust the Lord to work out her situation. Don had been anxious to meet with her, no doubt concerned about the ministry, even though she'd reassured him all was well.

She took a last glance in the mirror, grabbed her portfolio from the bed, and then exited the room. *I am*

291

called to serve a higher purpose, she declared as she descended the staircase. *The Spirit of the Lord is with me.*

Rozene smiled at Armela at the bottom of the stairs. "Good morning!"

"Good morning, Mrs. Kanate." She smiled warmly at Rozene. "I have set up breakfast with your favorites in the library as instructed by Mr. Kanate. Mr. Don is waiting outside the library."

Larry. Larry. There you go again. Anyway, with her stomach feeling a little queasy, she didn't know how much she could eat. She forced a smile. "Thanks, Armela. All is going well?"

"Yes, ma'am! All is well."

"How is your beautiful granddaughter doing?"

A brilliant smile popped on Armela's face. "Aisha is doing well. Back in college, and loving it. I miss her though."

"Totally understand. When Mason and Madison left for college, I didn't know how I would have managed. But I did, leaning on Jesus."

"Oh, yes. Leaning on Jesus." Armela agreed smiling. "Please let me know if you need anything else."

"I will. Thanks, Armela."

"You're welcome, ma'am," Armela said, before walking away.

A few minutes later, Don exclaimed, "Wow!" when he laid eyes on her yellow sleeveless blouse and flirty, white, knee-length skirt. "Happy Monday! You look like the sunshine. I'm about to do my victory dance right now."

He had come to the meeting with a bit of trepidation in his heart. Last week, she'd told him what had happened between her and Larry. Since then, he'd been praying almost nonstop for them, while hoping that her ministry wouldn't crumble.

She hugged him, grinning. "This is what God's strength looks like. I'm surprised I can even smile."

"Thank you, Jesus!" Don couldn't help exclaiming, and if time permitted, he would have danced around.

"Yes, only God." Rozene motioned with her hand towards the library and they walked in, and immediately moved towards the table spread with breakfast goodies. They piled wedges of French toast, scrambled eggs, and strips of bacon on their plates.

"How have you been?" Don asked, after blessing the food.

Rozene finished chewing on her bacon. "Much, much better, mentally that is. I was hoping I wouldn't have to go back to such a low place, but life happens."

Don shook his head with understanding. "God will keep you as you go through this situation. I'm praying for both of you." He encouraged. "You are stronger than you think. Your roots are strong in the Lord so I know you will get beyond this. I have that confidence in God." He swallowed a forkful of scrambled eggs.

"Thanks, Don." Rozene nursed her mug of cocoa. "To be honest, if I operate based on my feelings, I would have filed for a divorce." She eyed Don as he watched her carefully. "Seriously, I would."

"You and I know it is never good to operate based on feelings." He sipped orange juice, watching her over the rim of the glass, before telling her, "Please, don't call the undertakers."

Rozene couldn't help but chuckle. "Oh, Don! You're the best. I won't. I'm still declaring my best days are ahead of me. Hoping that my creativity will flourish in the midst of this crisis."

"Amen. Our God is a way maker."

"Amen," Rozene agreed, biting into her toast.

They were both quiet for a moment, before Rozene spoke. "What do you have for me?"

Don took his time opening his portfolio that was resting on the chair beside him. "Rozene, there's ..." His countenance pensive, Don tapped his pen several times on the table top.

Rozene eyed him curiously. "What is it?"

"I'm sorry about, Chandler," he said quietly. "I feel partly to be blamed for what happened. Felt I didn't protect you enough."

Rozene opened her mouth, and then paused. It was the first time Don had ever mentioned Chandler. Even though she knew he was aware of their past affair.

"I had no idea that he had deliberately set out to seduce you. I bragged about you and he discovered your TV program. Then, one day he heard me say that you should be writing more about the hard stuff so he set out to seduce you."

"Don, please don't blame yourself. It had nothing to do with you. Trust me, no matter what Chandler set out to do, I still had to say yes. Right?"

"I'm sorry nonetheless."

She sighed. "That's all over Don. Thank God."

"We completed the marriage series. You can view the video whenever -"

"How is he, Don?"

"He took it hard, you know. Real hard," he emphasized. "He's now working in Chicago. Our relationship is strained but I still try to keep in touch."

"Sorry about that, we'll continue to pray for him."

"Yes, let's do that." Don smiled at her. "Okay, let's go over your major appointments."

Almost two hours later, Rozene waved goodbye to Don, and then hopped into her car and drove away. Shortly thereafter, her cell phone rang and she glanced at the screen. A frown curved her lips. It was Larry. She deliberated whether or not to answer, and then decided not to. *Why bother to upset myself?* But it began to ring again.

"Yes," she answered.

A long sigh of relief escaped Larry. "Babes, you had me worried," he said in a doting voice.

"Do you need something, Larry?" She couldn't keep the annoyance out of her voice.

"Babes, can we talk, later?"

"Honestly, Larry, I'm all talked out. If that's it -"

"At least give me a chance to explain, please."

She remained silent. *A chance to explain. What would that fix?*

"Please. I know I lied to you and I'm sorry. I -"

"Larry, I need time."

"I understand, Roz. Just give me a chance to talk with you. Please."

Still nothing from her, she was busy shutting down her mother's voice in her head - 'You are doing the same thing that you had begged for him not to do to you. It took some time, but he extended forgiveness to you. You should do the same to him.'

"Please," Larry begged.

She sighed deeply, acknowledging her mother's words. "I'll let you know."

"Thanks. Are you home? Do you want to do lunch?"

"Not today. I'm driving. Meeting Mom for lunch."

"Babes, you know, I don't like when you're driving and using the phone."

"I know. I'm hanging up then."

"Okay."

She had just disconnected the call, when suddenly a sharp pain hit her abdomen. "Ohhh!" she puffed out, but the pain would not go away. "Ohhh!" Her body swayed, nausea creeping up her throat. She pulled off the road, and rested her head against the steering wheel. She reached for her cell phone in the cup holder, and called her mom. "Mom, I'm not feeling well. Not sure I'll make lunch."

CHAPTER 37

Anxiety drove Larry hard these days. This Saturday morning was no different. His gut ached as he watched Rozene from the kitchen window. She was reading in the gazebo. He observed her and her slight baby bump, every opportunity he got. His only desire - to touch her heart, again.

Nothing had prepared him for the news of her pregnancy when he'd come home from work that day. Clearly, she was unprepared too, for tears kept springing from her eyes. Thankfully, she seemed more contented now, and he'd tried his best not to add to her stress level.

Her pregnancy was welcomed news all around. Their parents and siblings were overjoyed, and no one seemed surprised except him and Rozene. The children, especially Madison, could not stop screaming with joy. Of course, Mason had to be himself, "Mom, I told you not to bring more babies in here."

The only drawback was that Rozene was still treating him like an outcast. She was 'raking him over the coals' but he refused to give up. Maybe … maybe today would be the day for his breakthrough.

It had been almost four weeks since they had learned of her pregnancy. He'd been praying almost nonstop, asking the Lord for a breakthrough to talk with her. She continued to put up resistance where he was concerned. Being in his presence was a chore for her, so talking was not even near the table.

He wanted to be a part of his child's life, and he surmised he'd already missed over three months. "Lord, I feel so desperate," he prayed aloud. "Help me not to do anything foolish to stress her out. But, Lord, please provide an open door for me to reach her."

A frustrated sigh escaped his lips as she stopped reading for a moment to rub her belly. His fingers curled with longing. That was his job, had been his job in the past and he wanted in. If only she would allow him. He was sure she'd heard him when he'd asked the gender of the baby. But, no, she would rather pretend to be deaf, telling him she was going to lie down.

He peered at her again and it took all of his strength not to call out to her. He closed his eyes and prayed silently for wisdom. When he opened his eyes again, he heard the door leading to the patio slam shut, and then he caught a glimpse of Rozene moving towards the kitchen nook.

"Babes," he called out.

No response.

He followed her. *Mercy, she is moving fast.* She was not in sight.

"Babes," he called out again, when he saw her.

"Morning," she murmured, but kept on moving.

He ignored the don't-speak-to-me sign on her back. "You doing all right?"

"I'm fine." She spoke while ascending the stairs, way too quickly in his mind.

"Careful. How's the baby?"

She shoved behind her ears, strands of her hair that had gotten loose during her flight. "Baby is fine."

"Roz, can you slow down for a minute?"

She didn't answer but kept walking along the circular landing.

Oh, boy, the resistance is strong. He raced up the stairs, and caught up with her as she entered the passageway to access the bedrooms. "Roz, I'm just making sure you're okay. And the baby."

She didn't speak but she stopped and faced him, her guard up. "We're okay. Okay." She gave him her I'm-not-in-the-mood look but he refused to be deterred.

He attempted a smile, one she didn't return. "You don't seem particularly happy to see me."

"I'm happy to see you," she responded drily, irritation etched in her voice.

"That's good." He touched her shoulder and she jerked away from him.

Tears burned his eyes and before he could stop them, they ran down his face as his heart shifted.

She watched as he pulled himself together.

"Roz, I was wrong for not telling you about my infidelity. I tried to tell you several times while we were at Abella but you kept shutting me down."

Her eyes were angry and determined. "You should have tried harder. Send a letter. A text. An email. Write it on your forehead." She turned to walk away and he held on to her arm. She landed him a scorching look, causing him to release her arm quickly.

Still, that was not off-putting. He dropped to his knees, hugged her legs, and then rested his head on her belly. "I want to be a part of my child's life," he agonized. "Please don't shut me out."

She squirmed a bit before becoming still when he wouldn't let her go.

"I'm sorry," he murmured, dotting kisses all over her belly, his voice filled with love.

"Hmmm," escaped her lips before she could stop it. Startled, she grabbed his shoulder to steady herself as his light kisses sent heat through her belly.

"I love you both," he murmured, rubbing his face gently on her belly.

Oh, that feels so good. She drew in a deep gulp of air, blood thundering in her ears.

His warm brown eyes gazed at her, his fingers now caressing her belly. "Can we talk?"

She looked blankly at him, and he continued to rub her belly, kissing it ever so often. She felt barely coherent. All she could think of was the warmth of his breath flowing through the thin fabric of her blouse and straight to her heart.

He stood up, his hands circling her waist. "Can we talk?" he asked softly.

She looked up at him and he was sure he shuddered, while drowning in her eyes. Heat passed between them, and in sync, they both inhaled.

Hearts thundering.

Mouths gaping.

Panting … heavy panting, they gazed at each other, everything else disappearing.

Rozene's body blazed with heat, like someone had lit a fire in it, and before she could stop herself, she was on the tips of her toes, straining her neck to taste his lips. "Thirsty," echoed in the air, and she wondered if she said it or he did.

He searched her eyes and instead of kissing her, his lips explored the length of her neck, and then along her quivering jawline, before his lips claimed hers with a raw need they both understood.

Helpless moans erupted from her lips, and she wrapped her arms around his neck, kissing him without restraint. His heart was super glad, for he'd wondered if her libido had again increased with this pregnancy. *Check!* And if his prayers were answered, he would be a very happy man.

Gentle groans escaped her lips as he attempted to release his mouth.

"Stay," she murmured breathlessly, hanging on to his lips with her own.

His breathing went shallow, desire taking a front seat. He lightly nipped her pouty lips, causing her to purr in anticipation. Delightful energy flowed between them, when he captured her soft mouth again in a deep, lingering kiss.

Murmurs of incomprehensible approval erupted from their lips, and he knew he had to slow his thoughts ... and he needed to slow her down too.

Threading his fingers through her hair, he lifted his lips from hers, and held her against him. She whimpered, protesting, and for a second time, he slowed his thoughts.

Slowed his breathing.

Slowed everything.

He had to keep focus.

He looked into the depths of her yearning eyes. "Can we talk?" His voice a hoarse whisper.

She pressed her damp palms against his chest, savoring the heat of his skin. Her breathing uneven and edgy, she nodded weakly.

Lord, help me, he pleaded. The last thing on his mind was talking. He lifted her and she clung to him, her lips nipping his neck with each stride he took. He reminded himself, first things first.

"Larry." She murmured his name in anticipation, clutching his shoulder as he closed their bedroom door.

"Later," he told her huskily, dropping a light kiss on her forehead. *Ten, nine, eight, seven, six ...* He counted backward to distract himself. The temptation was overwhelming but he managed to walk through the bedroom and enter the balcony. He placed her on the sofa and made sure she was comfortable, and then sat beside her.

She gazed at nothing in particular, slightly exasperated that her treacherous body wanted him. She tilted her head and considered him for a few seconds. The look on his face was an intense one ... and one of remorse.

Larry watched her too. Her expression was somewhere between adoration and annoyance.

Nevertheless, the adoration in her eyes spurred him on. He needed to speak frankly with her, but the only thought on his mind was to wrap his arms around her and comfort her. *Help me, Lord.* He closed his eyes briefly then opened them to find her still watching him.

"Roz, I love you with all my heart. I'm so sorry for what I did to you, and-and our marriage." Then, he was on his knees before her, holding her hands. "You keep me sane and when I am not in sync with you, I feel off balance, dreadfully so. I don't want to live my life without you."

His words touched her and annoyed her at the same time. Her eyes welled up with tears, for she remembered what he had done. She pulled her hands out of his. "You've, you've ..." Tears ran down her cheeks. "You've crushed my soul, Larry." She gulped. "I don't know if I'll ever recover."

"I'm sorry. I'm so sorry, babes. Please," he grabbed her hands again, his voice a desperate whisper, "forgive me. I'll do anything to win back your love. Please, please don't -"

She dragged her hands out of his, but it was the hard weight of her glare that halted him in mid-sentence.

"The way you treated me was cruel," she accused him. "It just doesn't make any sense. You committed the same sin."

"I know, babes. I know. I had gone crazy; jealous rage took a hold of me. I couldn't handle that you found someone else attractive ... that you had given yourself to someone else ... when I was literally dying to make love with you. Somehow, I blamed my infidelity on you. I know it sounds crazy, and it is.

Eventually, the Holy Spirit convicted my heart and I decided to tell you. I wanted to tell you at Abella but every time I tried, you shut me down. After that, you were so happy I couldn't risk destroying your happiness. So I kept quiet about it." He looked at her hoping for some kind of response, but nothing. He tensed. *Say something, please. Anything.* "Babes, say something, please."

She slumped against the chair and wrapped her arms around her chest, her countenance fallen. "Larry, I thought about this and I get it that we have both sinned. Thankfully, I also know that God has forgiven us. So for me, at this point, it is not about the sin because I have been there. What I still don't understand is why I had to grovel for months to get back into your good graces, when you did the same thing. Is it okay for you to do it but not me?"

He winced. "Babes, no. Not at all. It is not right for any of us to have sexual relationships outside of our marriage. I was shocked by my own action, but instead of dealing with it, I kept pushing it under the carpet, and focusing on what you had done. I still can't believe I took advantage of her."

She studied his features watching his body tensed before her eyes. She didn't want to know the rest of that story, but felt a pressing need to inquire. "Who have you been sleeping with?"

Astounded, he sat back on his heels, his eyes widening. "Roz, don't put it like that. It only happened once with Gabrielle."

"Gabrielle? Oh, my God!" She flew off the sofa and leaned against the railing on the balcony.

Larry followed and stood nearby. He attempted to speak but she lifted her hand, halting his speech. "How long has this been going on?" she croaked out.

"Babes," he pleaded, "It only happened once - The Wednesday before that Monday when I found out I had Chlamydia."

She turned to look at him, holding her hands tightly around her waist. "ONCE! So that makes it okay?"

Shame burned deep in his heart, and he looked away. "No. It doesn't."

The silence stretched on forever as her eyes pierced him.

"Babes," he edged nearer to her and held on to the railing. "I'm sorry. That was the furthest thing on my mind when I went to work that day. I wanted you. I wanted things between us to be back the way they were after the children left for MIT. Still, that doesn't excuse my behavior. I'm sorry. Please forgive me."

She eyeballed him, with barely-held contempt. "So you're the office lothario? How did you manage to seduce Gabrielle?"

Surprise shot through him and he looked away again, embarrassed.

"How did it happen?" She thrust out her chin. "Tell me!"

His face, raw with emotion, he begged, "Babes, please don't -"

She shot a glare in his direction. "I want to know."

His eyes hit the floor this time. "We-we were working, and we stopped to have a snack from her refrigerator." He paused to plead with her. "Babes, please don't make -"

"I want to know." Her eyes fixed themselves upon him. His usual confident demeanor weakened with uncertainty.

He swallowed hard. "I think we were both having marital issues, even though we didn't discuss it."

She jerked upright. "How did you know -"

"Her husband was scheduled to leave on another business trip, so I asked her if he'd left. Usually at the mention of his name, she would become a light bulb, but she wasn't like that. And, she is usually very chipper, but she wasn't that day. While we were snacking, I felt the

304

overwhelming need to comfort her so I gave her a massage. She didn't want me to at first, but-but I convinced her to relax and think about her husband." He let out a long sigh. "One thing led to another and even though she didn't want to, I-I … I coerced her to satisfy my own need." He gulped. "I am still horrified by what I did to her. She still refuses to take my calls, and when I did make contact months ago, she was still angry. She even threatened to call the police."

Rozene spat out a laugh. "Can you blame her?"

Larry gritted his teeth in embarrassment and his hands tightened on the railing but he didn't respond.

"What's happening with you and Pastor Fotola?"

"He was disappointed that I didn't tell you about my infidelity before you moved back home." He hung his head and avoided looking at her. "I was just trying to avoid any conversation with him so I wouldn't see the disappointment in his eyes."

Rozene didn't say anything else but walked away from him and sat on the sofa, clutching her hands close to her chest as if protecting herself.

He followed her, his steps slowing as he neared her. He quietly slipped on the sofa beside her.

They looked at each other in silence.

"Babes, please don't cry. Think of the baby too. You shouldn't be stressed." His eyes welled up with tears. "We'll get through this."

She glared at him. "That's easy for you to say."

"I'm sorry. Please … please, I need you. Please don't shut me out. I'll do whatever it takes to win back your love and -"

"Shut up! Just shut up!"

Shame constricted his breathing.

She walked away from him and stood at the railing again, tears spilling down her cheeks. Closing her eyes, she asked God to give her strength. She needed to keep calm, if for nothing else, than the baby's sake. She rubbed circles over her baby bump, in an effort to apologize to her unborn child, even though it didn't stop the excruciating pain that was in her heart.

She wiped her eyes and faced Larry who stood nearby. "You know what's the worst part of all of this?" She swallowed hard, her expression that of a lamb about to be slaughtered. "I don't know how to live without you." Her eyes speaking volumes, she swished past him, and kept moving until she disappeared into the bedroom.

Grief knotted Larry's throat as tears formed again in his red-rimmed eyes. His mouth opened, but no word came out. *God, help us,* was all that kept rolling through his mind.

CHAPTER 38

An eerie sense of loneliness washed over Rozene as she stood in Madison's room. Everything felt strange. As looming blackness threatened to overtake her, she sat on the bed, and reached for her devotional from the nightstand. Propping a pillow behind her head, she began reading. She had read only two lines when unhappy thoughts began swirling then dancing across her mind, and before long, she was curled up in a ball.

She hadn't spoken to Larry since their blow up last weekend. Not for lack of trying on his part. She scrunched up her face. *He's home way too often these days. But he might as well be if that's the woe-is-me countenance he's displaying at work.*

Tears stung her eyes. "Lord, I don't want to be mature. Why do I have to be mature in this situation? He took months to forgive me. You saw how he treated me. Had me running away from my own home. Running from what I had helped to build. This is my home too, and it took forever for me to move back here. I want to leave him hanging for at least the same amount of time I was out of this house."

However she knew that would not be enough.

She thought about calling her mother but immediately perished the thought. *This is a personal decision.*

The first tear fell, then another, and another.

"Lord, help me to pass this test," she whispered, mopping her eyes with a wad of tissue from the nightstand. "I want to, Lord, but every fiber in my body rejects doing the right thing. I don't want to forgive him."

The weight of the decision rested heavily on her and before long she fell asleep, an inner voice telling her, *You are responsible for your response.*

Some ten minutes later, Larry knocked on Madison's room door. When Rozene didn't respond, he quietly opened the door, and saw her curled up sleeping. A spasm of worry tightened his stomach when he observed the pieces of tissue on the floor beside the bed. Clearly, she'd been crying.

He closed the door, and leaned against it. "Lord, please take care of her," he muttered, tears burning his eyes.

Remorse swept through him as he made his way to the study and sat behind the desk. What could he do now but pray? "I surrender all to You," he choked out. "Everything ... withholding nothing. Withholding nothing. Lord, You are the cog that holds my life together."

He was about to rest his head on the desk and succumb to his tears, when a thought hit him. He sat back on the chair. It dawned on him that the same pain he'd felt about Rozene's infidelity, was the same pain she was feeling about his mirrored behavior. That gave him a new perspective and he began praying for her.

A few minutes later, he pulled out the desk drawer to retrieve the envelope with the divorce documents, only to discover that he had hidden her gift there. He opened the gold box to display the beautiful heart-shaped emerald jewelry set he had custom-made for her to celebrate their twentieth wedding anniversary.

He had been planning the events for their anniversary. It would have been a blast - a quiet, elegant ceremony for the renewal of their vows, and then a celebration like no other, towards the end of the year. But, suffice to say, everything was now on hold. Hopefully, not for forever.

He placed the jewelry box back in the drawer, and walked to the shredder in the corner of the study with the envelope in hand. "Make us one, Lord," he murmured over and over again as he shredded the divorce papers. Then, in a desperate move, he stretched out on the ground by the shredder.

> *"Make us one, Lord. Make us one in the Spirit. Wrap us and cover us in your glory, so that your nature flows from us; so that we are in agreement with You. Thank you, Lord. Amen."*

With that, Larry was quiet before the Lord of all creation.

An hour later, Rozene woke with a start. She had dreamed that Larry was moving out ... in a hurry too. *Really?* She gritted her teeth, and rolled on her back. *In a hurry, huh?* She didn't know why that annoyed her.

She massaged her belly thinking she needed to find food, but she was feeling too lazy to move. She thought of calling Armela to make her a sandwich, but remembered she had given her the weekend off.

Sitting up, she rubbed the sleep from her eyes and then swung her legs off the bed only to hit something below. She gasped, quickly pulling up her legs, and peeping over the edge of the bed.

It was Larry ... lying at the side of the bed.

He pulled himself into a sitting position on the floor, offering an apologetic smile.

Awkward silence stretched between them.

Larry couldn't bear to see the pain in her eyes. Once again, his heart was crushed over the anguish and suffering his infidelity was causing her. As the pain shifted in his heart, he continued to gaze at her, unsure what to say.

She swung her legs over the side of the bed, gazing at him through watery eyes, hoping for something, some kind of reassurance.

He shifted and knelt at her feet. "Babes, I love you. Please give our marriage a chance. We have weathered many storms by the grace of God. I want our marriage and I know you want it too. The presence of God is with us, has always been with us, so let us allow Him to guide our decisions."

She let the information sink in.

"My faith is stronger," he continued. "Going forward, I'll make sure my choices are based on the Word of God, and I will be honest in our marriage. Truthfully, I have learned that people with understanding keep the commandments of God. I have decided to do so with my whole heart."

Her heart warmed somewhat, but she did not speak.

"I love you. You are still the best part of my mornings and my nights," he told her softly, "And the best part of my days."

A slight smile creased her lips, for she remembered he'd told her the same thing on their honeymoon.

That smile was the ray of hope he needed. He pulled forward, and placed his head on her lap, circling her waist with his hands.

She let out a long sigh, and as his tears damped her clothes, she recalled her mother's advice, 'You are doing the same thing you had begged for him not to do to you. It took some time, but he extended forgiveness to you. You should do the same to him.'

She cradled his head with her arms, and he began to weep uncontrollably.

She wept too.

Soon, his weeping subsided, and he pulled away from her, studying the floor.

"Larry, come here," she said quietly.

His bloodshot eyes watched her guardedly as she patted the bed, and then he eagerly moved to sit beside her.

"Look at me," she told him softly.

And he did. But the insecurity in his eyes almost did her in. While uncertainty filled her heart, Godly determination pushed her forward. She exhaled, and touched his hand.

"I forgive you," she told him, hoping that whatever was ahead of them would be far better than their current situation.

"Tha-Thank you." Tears flowed from his eyes, and this time, he cradled her in his arms, gratitude flowing from his heart. "Thank -" His voice broke and tears ran down his face on to her cheeks. He shifted and dotted her forehead with kisses. "I love you," he whispered fiercely. "Thank you."

Sliding off the bed on to his knees, he dropped kisses on her belly. "I love you both."

Heat oozed from her belly, and spread like wildfire through her veins. She purred.

Larry gazed up at her, his hands on either side of her. "I want you to know that I love you. No. I need you to know that I love you. I choose you. It has always been you."

She nodded, not looking at him.

"Babes, please. Please look at me."

She looked at him, and then looked away, petrified by the love and tenderness in his eyes.

He waited, knowing she needed time.

A few seconds later, she shifted her head to look at him. *God, what am I to do with this man who won't let me go?* Her gaze soft, she touched his cheek with her hand. "I'm embarrassed. I'm sorry I slapped you. I shouldn't have done that."

He pushed away from her. "I deserved it," he lamented, sitting back with his knees up.

"No matter. It's against everything I believe in. It won't happen again."

He nodded, and then his eyebrows climbed his forehead. "You almost slapped the Holy Spirit out of me."

"Beat you up pretty bad, huh?" She gave him a wry smile, and his chest bubbled with hope.

"Pretty bad," he joked, even though it didn't reach his eyes. "I don't know if I'll ever recover, especially my pride."

She watched the brokenness in his eyes, for he'd realized she had not committed to giving their marriage a second chance.

Silence stretched between them as she stared blankly at him, not making a sound.

Larry's nerves almost reached snapping point.

But he didn't have to wait long, for she seemed to have found whatever she was seeking. In the next second, she leaped from the bed.

He reeled back, almost losing his balance when she landed on his chest, her arms tangling around his neck. Murmurs of "Thank you" erupted from his lips as he caught her and wrapped his arms around her.

With a contented sigh, she snuggled closer to him. She wanted to pass the test - *Can I still model the principles of godliness when my back is against the wall?*

Perhaps for the first time since their soul crushing take down of each other, she was filled with renewed hope, and something ignited in her heart. He was still the man of her dreams, the man to whom she had pledged until death do we part. And he was hers to keep.

He stroked her hair gently, before reaching down and rubbing his hand lightly over her belly. She gasped and whimpered softly, before sighing in pure bliss, her face wearing an expression of sheer pleasure.

When he wanted to kiss her lips, she allowed him. And she kissed him back too, encouraging his tempo … zealously. For she remembered, *"Love suffers long and is kind; love does not envy; love does not parade itself, is not puffed up; does not behave rudely, does not seek its own, is not provoked, thinks no evil; does not rejoice in iniquity, but rejoices in the truth; bears all things, believes all things, hopes all things, endures all things. Love never fails."*

He paused for a moment to smile at her, ignoring her breathless murmurings. He no longer felt fearful, instead he felt never-ending hope. The pain had diminished somewhat in her eyes, and there was a spark of hope there. He had much work to do to regain her love and trust but he was confident that because they were trusting in God, all would be well.

He hovered even closer, their breaths mingling and every nerve in his body came alive. *I could never get tired of this view.* The air crackled with expectation as he eased her into a sitting position, got to his feet, and then bent to lift her in his arms.

She clung to him with bated breath as he placed her on the soft, rumpled sheets.

He fell in bed beside her, only to hear her muttering, "Trying to be patient here." Smiling, he leaned back against the pillows and opened his arms to grant her access to all parts of him.

She grinned down at him. "I love you, my husband."

Tears filled his eyes and his breathing was labored. "I love you too, my wife." His heart warmed as he looked into her eyes. *Thank you, Lord, for my bold, brilliant, beautiful, and blessed wife.* He was grateful for they were on the edge of tomorrow and it was good.

He reversed their positions, careful not to rest on her belly. Then, he remembered a pressing question that was on his heart. "Are we having a boy or girl?"

"Talk later," she replied, anticipation making her breathless. Right now, they had unfinished business. This was no time to discuss having twins, and worse to fight again over not knowing their genders.

His senses attuned to hers, he ran a finger down her cheek. "You better be glad I love you."

"You do?" She lost a breath and giggled.

"Yes, I do. I love you so much." His voice was a soft timbre caressing her ears. Pushing away strands of her hair from her cheeks, he smiled tenderly at her. "I have never loved you more." Then, unable to help himself, he rained gentle kisses all over her face, while delighting in the quick intake of her breath. When he knew she could take no more, he pulled back and gazed at her, a slight smile touching the corners of his lips.

She laced her arms around his neck, bringing his face closer to hers. *Good Lord, I love this view.* Far deeper than that, she sensed that Larry loved her. And in that moment, her husband was everything she remembered, and so much more.

Her finger traced his lips, and it was almost his undoing.

"Play nice," he groaned out hoarsely, shuddering, before allowing his lips to dance over hers.

Her hands seemed to be everywhere on his powerful frame as a rush of heat enveloped her, then another, and another …

When he lifted his lips from hers, she reached for him causing his heart to pound at full throttle. Without hesitation, he captured her lips once more, kissing her slowly - tasting and teasing - and without restraint. They groaned in sync as delicious jolts of pleasure ricocheted through them.

They would definitely be making new, precious memories. And, yes, they would be driving each other to the brink, for this was no ordinary love. They had gained a deeper love for each other. A love that was heaven sent and perfected by the Holy Spirit. For their mirrored hearts were now reflecting the heart of God, and forever sealed by the fire of the Holy Spirit.

READING GROUP GUIDE

01. Which character can you relate to most, and why?

02. Do you believe in love at first sight?

03. Why do you think it was so difficult for Larry to forgive Rozene?

04. Discuss the strategies that Larry used to win back Rozene's affection.

05. Can you identify with how Rozene felt when she found out about Larry's deception?

06. Why do you think Rozene ended up in an affair with Chandler?

07. Why did Larry's father want him to be head of the family business?

08. Larry told his mother about his infidelity. Was that a good idea?

09. How is it possible that two people who love each other committed adultery?

10. When we don't deal with past issues they become giants in our lives. Can you see where this occurred in Larry's life?

11. Do you agree that the grass is never greener on the other side?

12. Can you recall a time in your life when you needed someone's forgiveness?

13. What role did Pastor Fotola play in helping to restore Larry and Rozene's marriage?

14. Why is it important to guard our hearts? (Proverbs 4:23)

15. How well are you guarding your heart?

A NOTE FROM THE AUTHOR

Thank you for taking the time to read *Mirrored Hearts: Sealed by Fire,* and for your continued support. As always, I am excited to share what God has placed on my heart. He continues to do amazing things on my writing journey, and I am simply happy to do my Father's will.

Mirrored Hearts: Sealed by Fire is Book 2 in the *Encounters of the Heart* series. This series is based on Proverbs 4:23 –"Keep your heart with all diligence, for out of it spring the issues of life." Book 1 - *Shades of the Heart* is a novel about the courage to love in the midst of broken promises, and ultimately about the healing power of forgiveness. Although the books are in a series, they are also stand-alone novels.

I pray that the story of Larry and Rozene touched your heart in a meaningful way, and that you experienced the amazing grace of God as you read. Remember, "Love suffers long and is kind; love does not envy; love does not parade itself, is not puffed up; does not behave rudely, does not seek its own, is not provoked, thinks no evil; does not rejoice in iniquity, but rejoices in the truth;" (1 Corinthians 13:4-6)

Don't you ever forget, you are Victorious By Design. Happy reading!

With love,
Ann Marie

CONNECT WITH THE AUTHOR

I would love to hear from you. Tell me how *Mirrored Hearts: Sealed by Fire* may have spoken to you. As always, I would like to hear your testimony about God's faithfulness.

Please connect with me at:

Email: abryan@victoriousbydesign.com
Website: www.victoriousbydesign.com
Facebook: victoriousbydes
Twitter: victoriousbydes
Pinterest: victoriousbydes

Stay victorious.
Ann Marie

VICTORIOUS BY DESIGN

Lighting the path to your next level

You are one of a kind.

You are fearfully and wonderfully made.

Embrace your uniqueness, talents and abilities.

You are designed for your purpose.

You are perfect for your purpose.

You are Victorious By Design.

Visit www.victoriousbydesign.com for more information

www.ingramcontent.com/pod-product-compliance
Lightning Source LLC
Chambersburg PA
CBHW062110170626
46813CB00002B/396